Ridin' with the Pack

Also by the Authors

McCain Chronicles

B.N. Rundell

Matt Bannister Series

Ken Pratt

The Woman Who Series

C.K. Crigger

Dunbar Series

John D. Nesbitt

Rowdy Series

Chris Mullen

This New Country

Harlan Hague

Yellow Hair Series

Ron Briggs

Bullets Trilogy

Nicholas Osborn

Praise for the Authors

Ridin' with the Pack

Volume Two

B.N. Rundell   Ken Pratt   C.K. Crigger

John D. Nesbitt   Chris Mullen   Harlan Hague

Ron Briggs   Nicholas Osborn

WOLFPACK
PUBLISHING
— EST 2013 —

Ridin' with the Pack: Volume Two
Paperback Edition
Copyright © 2024 by the Individual Authors:
B.N. Rundell; Ken Pratt; C.K. Crigger; John D. Nesbitt; Chris Mullen;
Harlan Hague; Ron Briggs; Nicholas Osborn

Wolfpack Publishing
1707 E. Diana Street
Tampa, FL 33610

www.wolfpackpublishing.com

Ebook ISBN 979-8-89567-009-5
Paperback ISBN 979-8-89567-010-1
LCCN 2024948964

Contents

Foreword

Dear Reader,

Welcome to our anthology of short Western fiction, *Ridin' with the Pack: Volume Two*. This collection is a testament to the enduring appeal of Western narratives, featuring stories from some of the most talented authors in the genre. It's my pleasure to present these tales, which blend the rugged spirit of the Old West with contemporary storytelling, showcasing the skills of both established and emerging writers.

Western fiction has always held a special place in our hearts. It captures the essence of adventure, the complexity of human nature, and the raw beauty of the American landscape. This anthology is a celebration of that tradition, bringing together stories that resonate with authenticity, grit, and an unwavering sense of justice.

Within these pages, you'll encounter a diverse cast of characters and settings. From Wilson Brand's quest for redemption in John D. Nesbitt's tense and threatening tale to the mysterious and haunting journey of Chris Mullen's protagonist in a contemporary Western thriller, each story offers a unique perspective on the Western experience. You'll find narratives that explore classic themes of courage and honor, as well as those that push the boundaries of the genre, delving into psychological depths and moral complexities.

At Wolfpack Publishing, we're dedicated to preserving the rich heritage of Western fiction while also nurturing its evolution. This anthology represents that commitment, interweaving the voices of seasoned veterans with the fresh insights of new talents. Each author contributes not just a story but a piece of the larger tapestry that defines our understanding of the Western spirit.

I extend my heartfelt gratitude to our authors, whose creativity and dedication have made this collection possible. Their stories remind us why we fell in love with Western fiction in the first place, carrying forward the legacy of great Western writers while blazing new trails for future generations.

I invite you to immerse yourself in this anthology and embark on a journey through the heart and soul of the American West. These stories are a tribute to the enduring legacy of the Western spirit, a spirit that continues to captivate and inspire us. So, saddle up and join us on this literary adventure. The frontier awaits!

Warm regards,

Jake Bray
Editor
President, Wolfpack Publishing

Ridin' with the Pack

Mark 'em Out!

A Short Story

By B.N. Rundell

National

HE TOOK A DEEP BREATH, PUT HIS HANDS ON THE TOP RAILS and stretched out his long legs, putting his spurs on either side of the big bay's mane. The horse, officially known as #86, and some called *Blood 'n Guts*, trembled in the narrow chute, his head down as he tensed under the touch of the cowboy. Cody grabbed the bareback rigging, pushing his gloved fingers through the handhold, and tucking the ends of the glove fingers back to his palm, the resin sticking to the palm and the handhold. Cody gripped it tight, his right hand on the top back rail of the chute, the toes of his boots up near the neck of the big animal and he slowly lowered his weight down on the back of the nervous horse, feeling the heat of his body beneath him. Cody settled down, pulled himself up to his hand that gripped the handhold in the rigging, lowered his spurs to the sides of the horse's neck, just below the mane. Took another deep breath, nodded to the gate handler, and the gate swung open to the shout, "Mark him out!"

The crowd roared as the announcer proclaimed, "Chute number three, Cody Baker from Gunnison,

Colorado! This is his first ride with the PRCA. Make him welcome!" and the crowd roared. But Cody did not hear the crowd, he felt the big bronc try to climb the invisible stairway to Heaven and Cody saw nothing but blue sky between the toes of his boots. Then the head of the bronc disappeared as Cody lay back. He felt the monster under him bend his back and twist like a tornado, his head going right, his hind legs going left and his back arching. Cody saw the ground coming up, and he leaned as far back as he could, his spurs clawing at the upper neck of the big bay, his bright blue and white fringed chaps waving in the wind, and then the freight train beneath him stabbed his front feet at the dirt and Cody felt like he hit a brick wall, his middle driving against his hand as he raked his spurs back toward the rigging. The bronc twisted in the middle, stabbing his front feet into the dirt again, kicking at the top row of the bleachers with his hind feet and snorting with every dive.

The front feet came off the ground as the hind feet dug into the dirt, the bay lifting his head and shoulders high, stretching upward on his hind legs, squealing and twisting around to try to bite the nuisance on his back, and stumbled forward. All the while, Cody was raking the bay's shoulders with his spurs as he lay back, feeling the rise and kick of his rear end. The smell of sweat, dust, and manure filled his nostrils as he gasped for air. His heart was trying to beat itself out of his chest, and his eyes saw nothing but black mane waving in the air before him, the crowd was screaming and cheering and in that instant Cody was transported to the jungles of Viet Nam and the blood-curdling scream of the attacking hordes of Viet Cong guerrillas and the staccato blasts of their weapons.

Cody squeezed his eyes shut, rode by the feel of the horse, and looked at the head and ears of the beast, driving and diving as he stabbed the dirt and sought to rid himself of this thing on his back. The eight seconds seemed to last a lifetime, but the buzzer sounded and the pick-up men were quickly at his side, one snatching off the flanker strap, the other leaning close for Cody to grab at his waist and pull himself off. Cody took a deep breath as the man slowed his horse and lowered Cody to his feet. Cody's boots hit the dirt and he stopped, dropped his hands to his knees and sucked air, then came upright to the shouts and cheers of the crowd. He shook his head, walked slowly back to the chutes and climbed the fence to disappear from the crowd. He reached behind his legs to unhook the straps of his chaps, let them flop loosely as he walked to the parking area behind the chutes and went to his truck, the rusty looking '56 Ford pickup that was his home away from home.

The crowd was still raucous, the announcer irritating, the dust plenteous, and the smells constant, but Cody loved it all. This was his first rodeo since he came home and he had dreamed about it, looked forward to it, all the while he was in uniform and serving his country in the First Air Cavalry in Vietnam. He climbed in the truck, settled back in the seat and took off his resin thick gloves, rolled them up tight and sat them on the seat beside him. He looked around at the scene. This was the outdoor arena where the slack, the excess numbers of qualified riders, had their chance to make the final go-round. There were too many registered riders for the regular events for the main arena and the performances under the lights, but all had the opportunity to prove themselves and if they scored well, could be part of the final go-round and the big money. This was Cody's first time with the PRCA, he held a permit that allowed him to compete, and when he qualified with a thousand dollars in winnings, he could get his regular card with no restrictions as to shows or events. But he was not concerned about that as much as he was about the problems at home, and those problems came back as he leaned his head back and tried to relax, close his eyes, and get some rest.

———

It was the day after high school graduation and Cody was stepping up to board the Trailways bus, another glance around and he saw no familiar faces. He dropped his head and stepped aboard, looked for an empty seat and saw one by the window near the back and he trudged down the long aisle and tossed his pack in the overhead and plopped down on the seat to look out the window.

He remembered telling his dad about his decision to sign up with the Army recruiter and that he would leave right after graduation. His dad just looked at him, frowned, dropped his eyes and walked out the back door, slamming it as he left. And his father had not talked to him since, and it was only at his mother's insistence that he even went to the graduation, after grumbling, "Don' know what the big deal is—he's leavin' home an' we prob'ly won't see him again!" But those words were spoken to his mother and Cody never heard them, nor any others since. When he came home, still in uniform, his dad turned his back and went to the barn until Cody told his mother goodbye, went to his pickup and pulled out of the driveway.

His mother had tried to explain, "Cody, he was counting on you working here at the ranch, helping him with the cattle and such, and I really think he was afraid of losing you. You remember he lost his brother in the war over in France, and, well..." she shrugged her shoulders. "There's something else you need to know, Cody.

He's worried about losing the ranch. The last few years have not been good, the drought ruined our hay crop, the prices were down on cattle, and..." she shrugged again. "He's just worried. Got a lot on his shoulders, you know."

Cody shook his head, looked at his mother, "Mom, you're always making excuses for him. But I was dodgin' bullets, killing men, trying to save the lives of my friends, trying to keep from getting killed, not about some payment to a bank!" He shook his head, "And all that time, all I could think about was what did I do to make him so upset with me. There were so many times I was in tight scrapes and all I could thing about then was that I was going to die and not make things right with Dad." He huffed, turned away, turned back and hugged his mother, "I'm leaving. I'll call you."

He had thought about it for some time, considered his plan to fulfill his dream and compete in the PRCA, maybe make a name for himself and get enough prize money to begin to build a new life, but after finding out about his folks possibly losing the ranch, the only way he could think of helping was to get some prize money to help pay the mortgage. If he did well, he could earn more money in a year competing, than what he could make in five years working at some factory job or something. He never went to college, although he wanted to, and had no particular skills other than with an M16 or an XM177 he used as a Ranger attached to the First Air Cavalry. He had been a part of the 101st Airborne when he became a Ranger, and went to Nam as a Ranger. And there weren't too many jobs in private industry for those skills. But even if there were, he wanted to put that part of his life behind him. He had too many sleepless nights reliving those days, and he knew he could pretty well keep his mind on other things when he was astraddle a bareback bronc in a rodeo.

A banging on the front fender of his truck brought him wide awake as he jerked upright to see a familiar smiling face of Laurie Cutler, a face from the past. He grinned, opened the door as she moved close and reached out to touch his face. "Nobody told me you were home! When'd you get back?" she asked, holding his face between her hands and stepping close between his knees. He reached his hands around her waist and chuckled, "Couple days ago. Didn't tell anybody I was coming, you ridin' today?"

She boldly kissed him, pulled back smiling, and said, "Welcome home, cowboy. And yes, I am riding, or rather rode. I did a 16.8 and I'm sittin' second in the go-round!" she declared proudly. "And you! Did'ju hear? You're sittin' on top with an 86! I knew you would do it! You always were the best in all those high school rodeos!"

Cody chuckled, pulled her close, "Well, that deserves another kiss!" and gave her what she deserved. They pulled apart, laughing, and she shook her head, "I have missed you! And I'm so glad you're back!"

"You gonna be at the dance tonight?" asked Cody, keeping his hands at her waist as she looked up at him. He had a rugged face, a nose that had been broken and showed it, dark wavy hair, broad shoulders, and a strong chin.

She was not used to seeing him with whiskers and his were just a couple days old, but she rubbed her hands against the rough dark face and said, "Only if you shave!"

"Hey now! First day back and you're already givin' orders? What am I gonna do with you?"

"Nothin'," she smiled and wiggled in his arms. He pushed her back and stood beside the truck. He stood head and shoulders above her, but slouched a little to have her hug his chest. He remembered the many times they sat by the lake, dreaming of a future together, enjoying picnics and time with friends. They had talked about getting married, but when he surprised her with his enlistment, she drew back, worry showing on her face, but leaned against him, "I can't lose you!"

"You won't! But I hafta do this," he pleaded, "It's just something I've got to do. You know I've thought about it before."

"Promise you'll come back to me?"

Cody chuckled, "Wild horses couldn't keep me from you!"

———

IT WAS as if they both were remembering the same times together as she looked up at him, standing beside the same pickup, and said, "You once told me wild horses could not keep you from me, and now what do you do? First thing, you climb on a wild horse and show your stuff!"

She shook her head, letting a slow smile split her face. She pulled back and said, "If we're goin' to the dance, I need to go home and get ready! Meet me there?" she called as she started away, skipping and starting to run. She waved at him and turned away before he could answer, but he just chuckled and shook his head, and climbed back in his truck. He could go to the truck stop and wash up, shave, change clothes, and still have plenty of time for something to eat and make it to the dance on time.

———

THE NATIONAL WESTERN Stock Show and Rodeo was usually the earliest rodeo on the docket, leaving the rest of the year open for many of the lesser shows. He stretched out in his pickup, needing a bit of a snooze before the dance and lay with hands clasped behind his head, staring at the headliner and pondered. With the winnings from the National, he would qualify for his ticket with the PRCA. With a second overall and prize money totaling close to five thousand dollars, he was well on his way. And as he thought of Laurie, a grin split his face and he knew she had turned his head, and brought up a lot of memories, so much so, *I think I'll head to Gunnison, I've got some time to spare and who knows...*he shrugged as he decided to make the home town rodeo, Cattlemen's Days in Gunnison. It was usually a well-attended show and with a lot of riders, the pot should be sizable and could make for a good kitty to provide enough for entry fees and to see him on his way for the season.

Working

THE TALL LANKY COWBOY WAS USUALLY A LONER, AND BY most standards, a quiet man. He avoided most crowds and kept to himself, especially after his time in the service. But Laurie had smiled and looked over her shoulder as if tempting him when she invited him to the dance for the cowboys and girls that were the competitors in the National Western. Begrudgingly, Cody Baker agreed to meet her there, but the place was packed and raucous, the music blaring and the alcohol flowing. Not his kind of place, but he pushed his way into the crowd, looking around for the long-legged beauty that had hung on his arm through most of their high school years. Her long red hair framed a beautiful face that was worthy of gracing the cover of any fashion magazine and her green eyes showed a hint of mischief and trouble whenever she flashed them your way.

She was easy to spot, low-cut blouse that was filled out and tight bell-bottom stretch pants that were laced with silver, and as she moved on the dance floor, few of the men were looking at anyone else. Cody hung back in the shadows, watching her move on the dance floor, flirting with all the men, dancing with a well-known cowboy that had been atop the PRCA rankings for the last couple years, and she was very friendly with the man. Cody watched for a while, shook his head, and turned away. Maybe one time he might have been tempted to cut in and show a devil-may-care attitude to the crowd, but those days were long past. He pushed his way through the crowd and left the building.

As he walked back to his truck, he turned a little pensive, remembering the many friends he had served with and had fallen in combat. One man, who had been at his side from the first day, was Dutch Dishong. He was a joker and always fun to be around, never took life too serious, until he received a letter and picture from his girlfriend. It showed a smiling pert blonde holding a tiny little baby girl with a pink pacifier in her mouth. The letter said, "Congratulations Daddy! Can't wait for you to get home!" But Dutch didn't come home and Cody had promised his friend that he would look in on Darlene, his intended and the little girl. They lived here in Denver and he thought about her, *maybe after I pick up my winnings, I'll stop by and see how she's doing.* Just the thought brought a smile to his face and gave him a new purpose.

He climbed into the cab of his pickup, grabbed his warbag off the floor and stuffed it in the corner to use as a pillow. He had a horse blanket over the seat and used it as a cover as he settled down for the night. His truck was his home and with one bedroom, it was a little cramped. As he was drifting off to sleep he was thinking about maybe getting a topper for his truck to give a little more room and comfort, but he would have to wait until he had a little more money to spare.

Sunday was the last day of the National Western and Cody went to the paymaster to collect his winnings. His score was the second highest for the entire show and netted him a good check that would see him through the downtime until more rodeos started up in the spring. Now with money in his pocket, he was thinking of Dutch Dishong and his new daughter rather than giving any more thought to the redhead Laurie. When he woke, he sat up, looked around at the different rigs pulling out, and dug in his warbag for the notebook that had Darlene's address. It was a house on the south end of town and it would take him a little bit to get there, but he would make a stop at a gas station to freshen up, knock down some whiskers, and try to look a little more presentable.

Darlene was sitting on the porch with the baby in a playpen, and she was rocking and humming to the little one. She saw the rusty looking pickup pull up, frowned, but when the long-legged cowboy walked around the pickup and paused with a broad grin, she instantly recognized him from the many pictures she had inside on the buffet that showed Dutch and his friends. She stood up, waved and called out, "Well, don't be such a stranger! I know who you are! C'mon up here!" she directed, smiling broadly, glancing from the baby to Cody.

The day passed quickly, the time for getting acquainted, sharing memories and more came to a close. Darlene said, "I thought you knew? Dutch and I were married. We were married the week before he left, and thankfully, there was the insurance that has made things easier. I'll still have to work, but at least we have our home and the baby will be fine."

"I'm surprised Dutch didn't say anything about it. He bragged about you often, said he wanted to have a family, but the way he talked, you two were just sweethearts," shared Cody.

"Oh, we were sweethearts alright. He was quite the romantic and I miss him terribly."

"Well, he had also stuffed a little away out of his pay, and I've got that for you. I'll stay in touch, and if there's ever anything I can do, you let me know. Promise?"

She smiled, accepted the five one hundred-dollar bills from Cody, tears coming into her eyes. "This will help, especially right now. It's a godsend."

Cody smiled, gave her a big hug, and turned to go to his pickup. Dutch had not given him any money for her, but...if he knew what was going to happen, Cody was certain he would have. Besides, God had blessed him with the winnings and it was the least he could do.

The National Western was one of the first pro-sanctioned rodeos of the year, while most waited until warmer weather because of having outdoor arenas. It was this slack time that sent Cody back to his hometown of Gunnison, Colorado. He had returned home when he was discharged, but was not welcomed by his dad and he left. But he still had longtime friends in the area, and maybe he could see his mother. As the trusty truck rattled down the highway he was thinking of the Valentine Ranch. It was one of the biggest in the valley and they always needed extra hands for the spring branding and they had a bunkhouse. *I'll give 'em a call when I hit town, maybe try Mom too,* he mused as he enjoyed the scenery over Monarch Pass. It was easy for him to lose himself in the mountains, looking at all the towering peaks, catching a view of the *Devil's Landslide* in his rearview as he rounded the last bend before the crest. From here it was less than an hour on to Gunnison and he grinned at the thought of his hometown.

"Why shore, Cody, we'd definitely put you to work! We'll be startin' roundup here in a couple days, and then the brandin'. How long you reckon on stayin'?" asked Homer Valentine, the old man of the ranch, one of the more respected and successful ranchers in the valley.

"Oh, prob'ly till Cattlemen's Days. That'll kick off the season, then I'll be on the road hittin' the different shows, tryin' to qualify for the NFR."

"The NFR? Boy, you set your sights mighty high din'tchu? I din't even know you turned pro!"

"Got my permit when I came home, qualified after the National Western, tryin' to make some money to get a start on things."

"Wal, if'n you placed in the National, you got a good start. Will we see you later today?"

"Yessir. I've got some things to do in town, then I'll be out later, and thanks!"

"Oh, don't go thankin' me yet! After we get done with the brandin', you might be wishin' you never heard of the Valentine!" Chuckled the old man, hanging up the phone.

Cody grinned, hung up the phone and stepped away from the pay phone that hung on the side of the drugstore. He looked around, stretched, and decided to take a walk down Main Street, see what had changed. He passed the different businesses, some catering to the college crowd, others to the locals, the usual hardware store, couple restaurants, several taverns, a western wear store, cobbler, and more. He saw the familiar Alamo, a popular watering hole owned by Otto and Charlie Metrose, two brothers that had been sort of mentors in Cody's early rodeo days. He stepped into the dim interior, looked around but saw no familiar faces, and left.

He crossed the street, found another pay phone, and called his home, ready to hang up if his father answered, but he heard the familiar voice of his mother and he asked, "Mom, can you talk?"

"Oh, Cody. It's so good to hear your voice. Where are you, son?"

"I'm here in Gunnison. I'm going to work for the

Valentines, stay in their bunkhouse. I'd like to see you, Mom."

"Yes, Mabel, I'll be at church like usual. I'll see you before and we can sit together, Mabel."

Cody grinned, knowing his mother was telling him his father came in and was listening. But he got the message and answered, "Alright, I'll see you Sunday. Thanks, Mom," and hung up the phone.

———

THE ROUND-UP KEPT thirty cowboys busy for more than a week. The Valentines had over five thousand mother cows with calves alongside. Cody knew most of the men, had worked with them before and the two Valentine sons, both older and married with families, were the ramrods. As they brought the herd into the lower pasture and the corrals, they separated the cows and calves and began the branding. With ten men on the branding irons and cutting, ten roping and dragging, and the other ten working the gates and running the bigger calves and yearlings through the chutes for doctoring.

Cody volunteered for the roping and was given the big palomino gelding called Golddigger for his roping horse. He was a big plow-horse-looking animal but his size was deceptive for he was lightning quick on his feet and Cody had all he could do to keep his rump in the saddle. When he dragged a bigger-than-usual calf to the fire, one of the men commented, "We were expectin' to see a rodeo with you on Golddigger! Not many men can stick with that big boy!"

"Oh, me'n him are old friends, but not too good 'o friends. That's why I'm stayin' aboard. I'm afraid if he bucked me off, he'd stomp me to death!"

The branding crew laughed, remembering many

times when other cowboys had to take to the fence after Golddigger had unseated them. They were about half finished when Homer called, "We'll be takin' tomorrow off so all you honyoks can go to church! We'll get back at it hot'n heavy come Monday!"

The men were all tired, dirty, and eager for the day off and Cody grinned, thinking of meeting up with his mother again. They had been meeting at church the last couple Sundays and time was getting short for him to start back on the rodeo circuit, but he enjoyed the time with his mother.

Cattlemen's

THE COMMUNITY CHURCH WAS CROWDED, THE MOST popular church and one of the oldest in the community, and most families had roots and memories in this church. The pastor stood before the crowd. "My message this morning is from I Corinthians 6:20 *For ye are bought with a price: therefore glorify God in your body, and in your spirit, which are God's.* Many people wonder, some even ask me, 'Why am I here, what am I supposed to do with my life.' And your answer is right here, you are to *glorify God.* And of course many ask, 'How can I glorify God?' It's simple, to glorify God is to turn the spotlight of your life on Him. When the spotlight is on Him, all else falls in darkness and everyone focuses their attention on God. He gets all the credit, all the glory, all the accolades, and more.

"But we, you and me, we want to make our mark in life. We want people to know who we are, what we've done, what great accomplishments we claim. We want to be considered successful and that's usually with big bank accounts, big houses, fancy cars, and more. In other words, we want to be in the spotlight. But…" He paused, looking around the crowd and coming from behind the pulpit, "The sole purpose for your life is to turn the spotlight on God. Glorify Him! We do that when we give God all the credit for those things in our life that the world equates with honor and success. But we could achieve nothing without God. So...let's commit ourselves to turn the spotlight of our lives upon God, give Him the glory, to glorify God!"

The message rang true and personal with Cody, he slowly shook his head and dropped his eyes thinking about what he wanted to accomplish with his life this year, and now he had something more to think about. He walked out with his mother, shook hands with the pastor, and walked to his mother's car with her. He leaned against the fender, "Mom, my work with the Valentines will be over in about another week. Then I'll be hitting the road for the rodeo circuit, of course the first one comes up next week here in Gunnison, so..." he shrugged.

His mother nodded, stepped closer and leaned on him, hugging him tight. She stepped back, looked thoughtful and explained, "You know your dad blames you for just about everything bad at home. Sometimes, I believe he thinks even the drought is your fault. When I had my heart attack after you left, he blamed you for that. But Cody, your dad's problems all go back to the ranch. You know that was my family's place, and I inherited it after my folks passed. And your dad just, well, he couldn't get past it and I think some of his drinking buddies won't let him forget that he married the ranch, he didn't buy it or earn it. He resents that and it's just that it's easier to blame you, but he knows the truth, and I'm hopeful that one day he'll face up to it." She paused, stepped away, and leaned on the car beside Cody. "I went to the banker the other day, added your name to the papers so you can have access to it anytime. You said you wanted to help and you already have, but any time you have any questions, you can talk to Byron Totten at the bank."

"Thanks, Mom. I was wonderin' about that. How far behind are you?"

"Almost three months. But he set things up for quarterly payments and the next one will be due the end of the month."

"Can you make it?"

"I dunno, your dad doesn't like me looking at the checkbook. I have to sneak around to do it. But I don't think we can make the full payment."

"Maybe I can help. After I get a check from Valentine's and if I finish in the money here at Cattlemen's Days, I'll do all I can. I'll send it direct to the bank, so be sure to tell Byron to keep it to himself. I'd rather Pa think he's under the gun. Maybe it'll keep him at work instead of at the club."

His mother sighed heavily, turned and hugged Cody again, and without any more than an "I love you," climbed in her car and with a wave and a smile, turned to go home.

―――――

THE PRESSURE WAS on the cowboys as the weatherman predicted heavy rainstorms by the end of the week and they wanted to get all the branding and cutting done before the bad weather hit. When they roped and dragged the calves to the branding and cutting crew, they could do more and faster than crowding them into the corrals and branding chute. Each ground crew had one man cutting, two stretching with one on the back legs, one on the head and front legs, and one on the iron, they could drop, stretch, cut, and brand a calf in just a few minutes and let the bawling and bouncing calf run back to its mother. With everyone on the ground crews and a dozen men roping, they were filling the pails with *Rocky Mountain Oysters* and filling the sky with dust and smoke.

The ropers, competitors all, worked fast, each one determined to show the others who was the top cowboy. By the end of the day, the horses were lathered, the cowboys sweating and dirty, and everyone was worn to a frazzle. The line to the showers in the bunkhouse stretched the length of the bunkhouse, and the drains were fighting to keep from clogging. Cody dropped to his bunk, willing to stretch out and try to relax and wait his turn.

"Hey Cody! You sent in your entry fees for Cattlemen's Days?" asked the roper known as Tex Monihan. He was an experienced cowboy and one of the top hands at roping, both calf roping and team roping, and he would also be traveling the circuit during the summer months.

"Yeah! I dropped 'em off yesterday. Went to the office at the fairgrounds. You?"

"Yeah, now I'm broke! You gotta any extry?"

"Not to spare, I don't. I've already sent in the rest of my spare money for entries in the next three rodeos, Cheyenne, Pikes Peak, Casper."

"Ooooeee, if you got that kinda money for entry fees, you're walkin' in tall cotton!"

"Don't have it now, sent it in."

"All the big names'll be at those," added Monihan, plopping down on the bunk across from Cody.

"Well we both know, it ain't the names of the cowboys, it's the luck of the draw, and the names of the stock. I'm just hopin' for some good luck on the draws."

Tex grew serious, looked at the floor and back to Cody. "Cody, you're a good man, and I'm glad to see you got your ticket with the PRCA. I always thought you had the stuff to do it, and I know you've come through some pretty bad things, the war an' all, and I want you to know, I'm pullin' for you!" He chuckled, "At least as long as you don't take up ropin' and you stay with the rough stock!"

And Cody's luck held—he drew #55 in the bareback, a horse that was called *Twister* a well-earned name given him by the riders that could not believe a horse could twist like a tornado but this one did, each and every time he came from the chute. Cody drew the second performance, the night rodeo, and would be riding under the lights. The crowd was usually larger at night, and Cody hoped to see his mom and maybe even his dad there, but he didn't really believe they would be there.

He focused his attention on the details—his rigging, his gear, spurs, chaps, gloves, the resin, and more. When he walked to the chutes, he handed off his rigging to the men at the chutes that would place the rigging and the flanker strap on *Twister* when he was brought to the chutes, and Cody would be called. The crowd was cheering one of the earlier riders, and the bareback riding was usually in the middle of the events, with the rough stock, saddle bronc, and bulls, coming near the end of the rodeo. The calf roping, team roping, barrel racing, bull-dogging, were usually in the early parts and between the other events. Cody had sat on the fence watching the barrel racing and cheered on Laurie, but she did not see him, nor did he make it a point of being seen.

Five riders took the first five broncs and Cody's #55 was in the second group of five, driven into chute three. The riggers quickly put the rigging and flank strap on, tightened down on the rigging and nodded to Cody. Cody slapped his gloves together to rid them of the excess resin, pulled them on tight and stretched across the chute to put his left boot on the top rail, and with his left hand on the outside top rail, his right on the inside, he slipped his right boot down below the mane, lowered himself on the back of the horse and felt the bronc jerk, try to move forward, and fought the chute enough for Cody to rise back up, and when he settled down again, lowered himself. He slipped his left hand into the hand-hold, which resembled the handle on a suitcase, and tightened his grip, pulling the fingertips of the gloves to tuck them into his palm. He slid forward on the rigging, his crotch against his left hand, put both feet high on the horse's neck, spurs just shy of touching hair, and with his right hand loosely on the top rail, he nodded to the gate handler.

As the gate swept open, one of the men that handled the rigging, pulled tight on the flanking strap and hollered, "Mark 'em out!" Every bareback rider knew he had to have his spurs above the front shoulders and high on the neck of the horse when the first dive hit the dirt. When the bronc put his head between his feet and stabbed his front hooves into the dirt, the impact was like a head-on collision and the cowboys spurs had to be high when that happened. If he failed at marking him out, he would be disqualified and get what they called a goose egg for a score.

Cody's spurs dug into the calloused hide of Twister as the bronc stabbed his hooves into the dirt and kicked his hind legs at the announcer sitting high above the chutes behind him. The announcer called, "And outta chute number three, a local boy, Cody Baker, on Twister!" and the crowd roared, not because many knew Cody, but because of the high kicking twisting bronc that was deter-mined to put on a show and rid himself of this man on his back. Like most crowds, people want to see the most spectacular wreck possible and at every buck, they expected a wreck or at least a crash where the cowboy would lose his grip and try flying through the air, only to come to a crashing stop in the loose dirt of the arena. But Cody was not concerned about what the crowd shouted for, his only concern was to stay astraddle of this twisting tornado that was blacker than the darkest corner of Hades itself and was snorting and farting with every buck, kicking and screaming, tossing his head, twisting in the middle, rearing as high and kicking higher with each successive buck. And all the while, Cody's chaps were flopping and flying as his spurs dug deep, dragging back along the neck and shoulders of Twister, and Cody lay back, the brim of his straw hat buckling as his head hit the rump of the horse, and the horse did his best to be true to his name.

Cody's focus never wavered, he was in his own world, and he moved with every muscle of the bucking horse, feeling every movement as it was begun, and going with the gyrations and twists of the big beast. The eight seconds were filled with every possible contortion by both bronc and cowboy and the buzzer sounded and the pick-up men were alongside, shouting for Cody to "get off! Grab hold!" and he waited until the man on his right came close and Cody stretched out to grab hold of the man's chaps belt, and dragged himself off. When Twister moved away, Cody dropped to the ground, fell to one knee, said a quick thank you to the Lord, and stood to trot off the arena to the fence. The crowd cheered, whistled, and many stood as the applause filled the stands and more. Cody was exhausted and it took everything he had to lift a hand to wave, and even more to climb the fence.

He twisted around to sit down on the top rail so he could see if they posted his score and to watch the rest of the bareback riders, and to catch his breath. Seven more came from the chutes, four making qualified rides, two very good rides. He did not know what the earlier riders scored, but his 85 put him on top of the last two and maybe even better than the others. But there was another two performances and he would not know how he finished until it was all over.

When he climbed into his pickup after Sunday night's show, the last performance of the rodeo, Cody was smiling and sitting high. He had finished first and had the check in his pocket to prove it. He was happy, relieved, a little sore, but anxious to make it to Cheyenne and the next rodeo. If only his luck would hold and he could stay in the money, this could be a good year.

Cheyenne

On the way through Denver, Cody stopped to visit with Darlene and the little one, Debbie, who was approaching two years old and toddling around the house. She was a cutie with blonde curls that bounced with every step, and she liked Cody, always anxious for him to pick her up and to sit on his lap. She was bouncing on a knee when Cody asked, "So, have you had to get a job yet?" looking to Darlene.

"Oh, I can't leave her, she's just too little and needs her mother. I'd rather do without than leave her with anybody. My folks, well, there's only my mother and she's not well. And Dutch's folks are down in Pueblo and they just don't seem interested. They saw the baby right after she was born, but since Dutch was killed, the only time I've seen them was at his memorial." She shrugged as she watched Cody bounce Debbie on his knee, giggling all the while.

Cody was enjoying the time but looked at Darlene, "I've got to get moving. I need to make Cheyenne 'fore dark so I can find the entry office and get my draw and number." He looked at Darlene. "I'll be coming back through after Cheyenne on my way to the Pikes Peak rodeo in Colorado Springs. Is it alright if I stop by?"

"Of course! We're always glad to see you. You're our best friend and you're the only man she gets to see and its good for her, but…" She paused, dropping her eyes to the little one, "if you're not careful, she might get to thinking of you like a father."

Cody did not miss a bounce, laughing with Debbie as she rode his knee, "That'd be fine with me, I'd consider it an honor to fill those boots!" he chuckled, stopped the bouncing and sat her down to toddle to her mother. He stood, picked up his hat and said, "Now, I need to hit the road." Darlene walked him to the truck, Debbie on her hip, and as he started to open the door, she stepped close, stood on tiptoes, and pulled his head down for a lingering kiss. When they pulled apart, she giggled, "I've been wanting to do that for some time now. So, don't take too long 'fore you come back now, y'hear?"

Cody chuckled, "I'll be back in a couple two, three days, dependin'. And I'll make it just as soon as I can!"

Cody had a good draw, a horse known as Chief Cloud Walker, "That's the one that always rears up and acts like he's climbin' a ladder to get to the clouds. Several riders have made money on him, but…" paused the man beside him, "he's known to be a killer too. One man down in Fort Worth got stomped on and almost got kilt, but he came out of it. And that's what we know, but there's been rumors of others that didn't." The speaker was a bronc rider from the panhandle of Oklahoma and was well respected, often finishing in the money and had made the NFR twice, Charlie Semple, a descendant of the chiefs of the Choctaw nation. He looked at Cody, "You're that new rider that took the money in the National, aren't you?"

"Took? I didn't take anything, I won it!" declared

Cody, grinning, "and yeah, I'm Cody Baker," he extended his hand to shake with Charlie.

Charlie chuckled, shook Cody's hand, "With that horse, after you mark him out, he'll start climbin' the ladder, so be careful with him, that's when he usually rids himself of the unsuspecting rider."

Cody appreciated the advice, asked Charlie, "What'd you draw?"

"Blood and Guts!" He chuckled.

Cody responded, "He can be a moneymaker. He's the one I had at the National. He's a climber and a twister, but he'll make you money if you stick with him!"

The men shook hands and parted company, each anxious to get ready for their rides as both had drawn their rides for the first day of the three day and night rodeo. The bareback would follow the team roping that would follow the chuckwagon races, a highlight of the Cheyenne Frontier Days.

When Cody left Cheyenne, he had 3rd place money in his pocket, a little over twenty-five hundred dollars, and he was on his way to see Darlene and Debbie in Denver, but it would be a short stop as he was headed on to Colorado Springs and the Pikes Peak or Bust roundup. But this time it was harder to leave Darlene and Debbie behind, but he had commitments to keep and miles to go.

The Pikes Peak rodeo is always a big draw and attracts those what would not otherwise attend a rodeo, and the added prize money attracts all the big names among the cowboys. A different stock contractor and different horses gave Cody a draw of a horse that he did not know, nor did any of those nearby. Number 77 was called *Thunderbolt* and the clerks could tell Cody nothing about the horse. After the draw, Cody did like many other competitors and walked to the holding corrals to look over the stock. He spotted a big black with the yellow tag hanging from his mane with #77 and the horse showed a blaze face, one white stocking on the front, and a white streak that fell from his withers on one side. Cody shook his head, looking at the horse, *That must be where he gets his name, better that than the way he bucks!* He didn't realize he was talking out loud until a voice from behind him said, "If he was named for his buck, he'd prob'ly be called Undertaker!" Cody turned to see an older man, pot bellied with suspenders holding up his britches and a broad grin splitting his face. He extended his hand to Cody, "I'm Walt Atkins, the contractor, and that horse has been in the family since a colt, an' he ain't never been rode!"

"Never?" asked Cody, surprised.

"Never had a qualifying ride yet! You draw him?"

"I did, first round tomorrow."

"You any good?"

"Won some, placed, bucked off, you know."

"Ummhmm, this'ns tricky, he'll stumble around, make you think he ain't gonna do nuthin' then he'll explode!" He paused, looked Cody up and down, "but you might do it, dunno."

―――――

WHEN THE GATE swung wide and the chute rigger shouted, "Mark 'em out!" Cody lay back and had his spurs high and dug in. The big horse exploded out of the gate, gave a big long hop, dropped his head and stumbled and went down on his neck, qualifying Cody for a re-ride, but before Cody could kick free and get off, the big black came up and exploded! Cody was certain the monster had come apart at the seams and was tearing Cody limb from limb and all he saw was blue sky and dust clouds, but he kept spurring and riding, and suddenly the buzzer sounded and the crowd roared and the announcer said, "He done it! He done it! That's the first time that horse has ever been ridden! Cody Baker done it!" and Cody was looking for the pick-up man but he was nowhere to be seen. Cody reached down, peeled his resin-covered glove from the rigging, the horse still bucking, and once free, Cody caught the hind end coming up and he lifted his legs and took flight, landing on his rear in a dust cloud and the big black bucking and snorting past him.

But he left Colorado Springs with a paycheck in his pocket and a smile on his face, and news that he was sitting twelfth in the overall standings and he knew he had a long way to go but the top fifteen riders would qualify for the National Finals Rodeo, and he was excited about that. His stop in Denver was just for a day, then he headed to Casper and then on to Sheridan. Both were good shows with added purses and he was hopeful.

He got a goose egg in Casper for failing to mark out, but he finished on top in Sheridan, pocketing over five thousand and helping his standings. There was still a few months before the NFR and he had to make as many shows as possible. When he was headed to his pickup at Sheridan, getting ready to pull out, he heard someone holler from behind him and turned to see three men stomping their way toward him. The man in the lead was the same man that had been dancing with Laurie in Denver, and he looked to have a mad on.

He strutted up to Cody, standing a little too close and glared at him, "Just who do you think you are, dude! You come in here and start puttin' on a show, takin' our prize money with drug store cowboy rides and makin' the judges think you're somethin' just cuz you were in the Army? I'm tired of it and this is your warning," he started, sticking his finger in Cody's chest, stepping close and snarling at him. "You hit the trail and get off our rounds, this is our country an' you ain't welcome!" He stepped back and started a roundhouse swing, but Cody gave a short step to the side, leaned back away from the swing and caught the blowhard's wrist as it passed and dropped his arm down, twisted it behind his back and bent it up behind him, shoving him onto the hood of his pickup. The other two stepped back, wide-eyed and watching.

Cody leaned against the man, growled in his ear, "Now—you listen, punk! You ever come near me again or so much as look my way I'm going to break your arm in so many places you'll never grip a bareback rigging again! You hear me?"

The man whined, mumbled something, and Cody repeated, "You want me to break it now, get it over with? Is that what you said?" and shoved his arm higher to emphasize what he said. He looked back at the other two who stepped back further, fear showing in their eyes.

"No, nooo, noo…" whined the frightened man that had jeans and boots on but had lost the right to call himself a cowboy. Cody had recognized him as a nephew of one of the all-time great all around cowboys of the PRCA, but it takes more than a name to make a man.

Cody pulled him away from the truck, used his foot to sweep the man's feet from under him and let him fall to the ground, his arm bent behind his back. The blowhard twisted and squirmed, whining as he moved and turned to look at Cody who stood over him, waiting for him to do anything, but the sniveler crawled away and jumped to his feet to run away. Cody watched the three go, shaking his head, *It's their kind that give cowboys a bad name.*

Finals

DARLENE WAS ALL SMILES AND GIGGLES WHEN SHE OPENED the envelope and pulled out the tickets. She frowned as she looked at them, looked up at Cody, "Las Vegas?"

"Ummhmm, and those other tickets are for the Finals rodeo, all shows. You have reservations at the Sands hotel, a rental car in your name, and if you'll dig deeper, you'll see there's money in there too!"

"But..." she started to question, not understanding until she looked at Cody and he continued, "Now what do they do in Las Vegas?"

"Uh, get quickie divorces, lose money, I dunno."

"They also get married." He smiled at her, still standing near the door and held out his arms.

She looked up at him, wide-eyed, "You mean..."

"Ummhmm."

She ran to his arms and squealed with delight. He pushed her back, "I also sent tickets and such to my mother. I don't know if she'll come, but she has two tickets for everything so she could bring Dad or a friend. And her seats are right next to yours."

"Oh Cody, that'll be wonderful! I can't wait!" she squealed, hugging him tight.

———

CODY HAD FINISHED out the circuit with a 9th place standing which qualified him for the finals, and he was anxious to be there and be a part, but he also wanted to share it with those that meant so much to him. He was hopeful his dad would come and they would have a chance to settle things. Cody had paid off the note that was against the ranch and it was free and clear now, like it was before his dad and mom took it over and maybe they would do better this time around. But now, he had to prepare for the Finals.

He had a good draw, was to ride in the second day show, and readied himself for one of the top horses on the circuit, *Crackerjack*, a dapple grey gelding that had only one qualified ride in the past two seasons, bucking off all the big name old timers. While Cody looked over the stock, the same man, Walt Atkins, stepped up on the fence beside him, glanced at Cody and said, "Hey, I remember you! You're the one what rode Thunderbolt!"

Cody chuckled, "If you wanna call hanging on for dear life a ride, then yeah, that was me."

"Don't tell me you drawed *Crackerjack!*"

Cody just nodded, looking at the horse that seemed to push the others aside as they milled around in the corral. He took a deep breath, "You gonna tell me what to do and what not to do?"

The older man chuckled and looked at Cody, "Young man, there ain't nuthin' this ol' man can tell *you.*"

And it was a spectacular ride, and many of the spectators would say later that they seldom saw that horse's feet on the ground, it was like he was always in the air, as if he had wings, but Cody had his pilot's license and he landed that dapple grey like the professional he had become. When he hit the ground, he dropped to one knee, lowered his head and said a quick prayer of thanks, pointed heavenward to give God the glory, and stood with hat in hand and hands high to the roar of the crowd.

In the stands, all the ticketed seats were full and sitting beside Cody's mom, was his dad. When some loud mouth behind them spat, "Look at that guy! Who's he think he is, some kinda preacher prayin' or sumpin'. He ain't no cowboy, cowboys don't do that!"

Cody's dad, Buddy Baker, came to his feet and turned to face the complainer and said, "I'll have you know that man's a Christian first and a cowboy second. And not only that, he's my son and I am *proud* of him! You wanna say somethin' else, punk?" he growled, stepping closer to the loudmouth.

The young man stepped back, wide-eyed, stammered, "Uh, no, no."

"You ever tried to ride a bronc like that, sonny boy?"

"No, unuh, never," he whined.

Buddy shook his head, "Figgers!" he said and sat back down beside a very happy woman and a young lady on the far side, both of whom were quite proud of the cowboy who just scored an 89 and would go on to finish second in the finals, making his mark in the record books and being careful to give God all the glory.

When they stood together at the altar in the wedding chapel, Cody looked back at his mom and dad, standing behind them and pride showing, and he smiled, turned back to look at his bride and the toddler that squirmed as she held the pillow with the ring, and he knew his life could not get much better.

And he even bought a new truck, a Chevy!

The Treasure of Henry Bass

A Short Story

By Ken Pratt

1

DOMINICK WEBSTER WAS EXCITED. IT WAS SATURDAY morning, and the Oregon Coast weather couldn't be better. The sky was clear and blue with the warmth of the sun shining down instead of the usual cold breeze, light rain, or gray haze of the marine layer covering the coastline. It was the perfect weather for such an exciting day. Dominick saddled two horses and picked up his beloved Helen before riding up Severson Mountain.

They hitched their horses to a wind-blown shore pine tree's limbs. They carried a bucket up a narrow and rough trail along the edge of a cliff that was three hundred feet above the ocean's crashing waves. A thick patch of native rhododendrons blooming with pink flowers pressed against the trail, making it a tighter squeeze between the branches and the cliff's edge.

Helen stopped, unsure about taking another step on the uneven ground. The sound of the waves crashing against the rocks so far below her and the pressure of the branches of the rhododendron bushes pushing her closer to the edge made her uneasy.

"Dom, I want to go back."

Dominick looked back at her and held a hand out for her to take. "We're almost there. I can see the clearing. Take my hand. Trust me."

"I do trust you, but this is dumb. One misstep and I could fall. My dress is getting snagged on these branches, and I don't appreciate you risking my life to pick berries. We can pick blackberries in much safer places."

"It's a beautiful day, Helen. Trust me. Take my hand. We're almost there."

"Fine! But if I fall, I'm taking you with me. If I die at twenty years old from this foolishness, I'll kill you when we get to heaven. The Lord will have to keep you on the far side of heaven because I'll never stop being mad at you," she said as she climbed up the last five feet of a steep incline and entered a wide meadow of grass littered beautifully with bright wildflowers. All around the isolated meadow was a thick wall of blackberry bushes filled with berries.

Helen gasped at the beauty of the meadow's flowers and soft fragrance. "Wow. It's beautiful."

Dominick set the bucket down and took hold of her hand to lead her to the edge of the cliff, where the light blue sky appeared endless over the dark blue Pacific Ocean. "Helen." He kneeled on one knee.

"What are you doing?" she asked with a growing grin that refused to be hidden as her excitement rose.

He pulled a wedding ring out of his pocket and held it out to her. His eyes were moist, and his voice trembled. "Helen, you are the most beautiful woman in the world to me. I love you more than I can express. I'd be the luckiest man in the world if you would be my wife. Will you marry me?"

She gasped. "Yes. Yes! Yes, I will."

Dominick stood and lifted her off the ground in a

tight embrace with a roar of laughter as he twirled her around. He kissed her in a long embrace.

Helen could hardly contain her excitement. "I love you, Dom. Of course, I'll marry you."

"Helen. I'm going to make you the happiest wife on the whole coast and beyond. Nothing is going to stop me from giving you the world. You just made me the happiest man south of heaven. I swear it!"

———

THE BLACKBERRIES WERE PLUMP, sweet and juicy as the newly engaged couple picked a bucket full of berries. The weather was wonderful, and the moment could not have gone more perfectly for Dominick. They had a bucket of fresh berries, and there was no doubt that the pie Helen had promised to make would be the best she'd ever made.

"Ouch," Helen said lightly. She had pricked her fingertip on a blackberry thorn.

Dominick affectionately tossed a berry at her. "Are you okay?"

"I'm fine. It's not the first time a thorn got me." She asked anxiously, "We don't have to go down the same way we came up, do we? That cliff scares me."

Dominick smiled. "No. We'll circle around back to the horses."

"Good. Think fast!" Helen warned and threw a berry at him, much harder than the one he tossed. It splattered his shirt.

"You dirty scoundrel." He chuckled. He picked four berries off a vine and stepped toward her, threatening to mash them into her hair. She playfully screamed and began to run through the grass. Dominick chased her.

"Don't you dare!" She laughed and turned quickly to

face him with her playful smile and spirited blue eyes. Part of her long light-brown bangs had broken free of a hair comb and dangled over one eye. She brushed it aside. "Don't..." she warned.

Dominick lowered his arm and drew in close to feed her a berry. "I would never do that to you."

She tasted the berry and closed her eyes. "That tastes good. Let me have one." She took a berry from his hand and, unexpectedly, smashed it in his face. She laughed heartedly and turned around to run. A terrified expression took the place of her laughter.

Dominick's hand touched the top of her shoulder. His voice was soft. "Back up, slowly. Just back up behind me. Keep backing up. Don't run," he said as he stepped in front of Helen.

In front of them was a large sow black bear that had come out of a trail through the blackberries, followed by two small spring cubs. The large bear was sniffing the air and lumbering slowly toward them.

"Let's just back away," Dominick said, taking a defensive pose in front of her while guiding her back toward an opening in the briar patch thirty yards away. "We'll just take it nice and slow. Stay calm." He had brought a rifle but left it in his scabbard on his saddle a hundred yards or so away. Glancing down, Domnick used his outspread arms to guide Helen toward their full bucket and picked it up.

The bear lumbered toward them, smelling the berries freshly picked in the convenience of the bucket. The two cubs playfully followed their mother while one attacked the other repeatedly. Dominick had directed Helen back into a cove of thick blackberries and realized there wasn't an exit. They were trapped in a semi-circle of blackberry bushes fifteen feet tall and dense with intertwined vines, thick with berries and thorns.

The large sow slowly came toward them, followed by the two cubs. It didn't appear to be threatening, even with the cubs, but a bear's calm demeanor can change in the blink of an eye. Dominick knew the worst predicament to be in was between a mother bear and her cubs.

"Here you go, mother bear," he said quietly, tossing the bucket out into the open away from them. The bucket landed on the ground, spilling their picked harvest. The large sow sniffed the air and changed her direction toward the bucket.

Dominick held Helen's hand as he slowly skirted the briars out of the alcove to pass by the bear. They had almost made their way when one of the cubs ran toward them curiously. The large sow turned from the bucket and charged toward them.

"Run!" Dominick shouted.

He allowed Helen to run ahead of him as they quickly ran across the grass-covered meadow, terrified that the bear was just behind them. Suddenly, Helen tripped over a stone hidden in the tall grass and fell to the ground, hurting her forearm. Dominick turned toward the charging bear, preparing to be mauled in an effort to protect Helen. He had no plan except to fight and sacrifice himself while Helen ran to safety. To his relief, the large sow had stopped charging and was eating their bucket of berries.

Dominick nearly collapsed, growing faint from the exhilaration of the moment. Breathing heavily, he turned around to see Helen on the ground, wiping the dead grass and a layer of dirt off the rock she tripped over. "Are you okay?" he asked.

"I hurt my arm a little bit, but I'm fine. Are you?"

"We need to go before she comes back, or the cubs come running this way. Come on, let's get back to the horses." He exhaled with relief. "I should have brought my rifle."

"Dom, what is this? Look, it has sketches of something."

Dominick glanced back to see the bear contently eating berries. He kneeled to help clear the layers of dead grass from the stone. He furrowed his brow curiously. "I have no idea." The stone was shaped into an obelisk that lay horizontally embedded in the ground. Chisel marks had cut a double X at the top, the initials C.T. and an arrow pointing down at the base.

"Maybe it's a grave," Dominick suggested.

"There are no dates. And what would the two X's mean?" Helen questioned.

"I don't know. It could be a man's initials; I'm guessing. Let's go before the bear wants more berries. I'd rather not be mauled before our wedding."

"CONGRATULATIONS, SWEETHEART," Franz Johnson said while hugging his daughter. "I know when Dom asked me for your hand, giving my blessing was the right thing to do. Your mother, God bless her memory, would be so proud of you. She'd be so happy to know you are marrying well. And you," he said to Dominick. "You better be good to my baby girl. This young lady is my world and I spent my lifetime raising her, so you treat her like a queen."

"I will, sir. You got my word on that."

"Father," Helen said, "we found the strangest thing on the mountain. It was an obelisk-shaped rock with writing carved into it. It had two Xs, an arrow pointing down, and the letters C. T. Was someone buried up there?"

"Not that I know of," Franz said. "But you should ask that old hermit, Henry Bass, who lives out of town on the river. Supposedly, Henry's been looking for a treasure on that mountain for thirty or forty years."

Dominick chuckled. "Henry works for us when he needs money. He's a bit eccentric, but I've never heard him talk about a treasure."

"You might have found it before old Henry," Franz said.

Dominick waved the thought away. "What kind of a treasure could possibly be up there? This is Oregon, not the Caribbean or somewhere the pirates roamed. There is nothing here now, so there was absolutely nothing here back then. A treasure load of furs, maybe. That tombstone is probably some old fur trapper's grave."

"I'm sure it is," Franz Johnson said. "I say we let the dead guy rest and discuss my only daughter's wedding plans."

———

"Oh, come on, let's ask him," Helen pressed him with a nudge of her shoulder. "What if there is a treasure, and we found it? You know, those pirate stories, X marks the spot? What if, Dom?"

Dominick chuckled. "No. Henry doesn't say much as it is, and I don't want to bother him about it. He's just an old, lonely fur trapper who lived past his prime with nothing to show for it. That's what my father said, anyway."

"Come on, it might be fun. Maybe the old man knows whose grave it is. Or he could tell us about the treasure."

"There is no treasure. We're better off just leaving Henry alone. He doesn't like to be bothered. Besides, we have a wedding to plan. So, let's sit here on the dock and watch the sunset." Dominick held Helen's hand while sitting on the edge of the dock over the bay. Her bare feet dangled a foot above the water while his arm rested over her shoulder.

The sunset cast an orange, yellow, and reddish glow over the bay's calm water, reflecting the colors beautifully. The light sound of calm waves crashing against the sandy beach on the other side of the bay filled the quiet last rays of a fading day.

Dominick gazed into her eyes. "I love you, Helen. We are going to have a very blessed life together, you and me. I know we will."

"Of course we will. How could we not?" They kissed in the final moments of the colorful rays of the setting sun.

2

"JUNE, I DON'T UNDERSTAND. I JUST NEED MORE TIME. I AM right on the verge of finding it. I know I am."

"It's been three years, Henry. That mountain has spent more time with you in one day than I get in three weeks. I love you, and I've waited patiently for you to get this treasure nonsense out of your system, but it's only become a stronger obsession. I'm done waiting."

"June, you know I love you. You know you mean more to me than anything else, right? All I'm asking for is a little more time. I am on the verge of discovering the Crescent Tonalee treasure. I know I am. And then, we'll be rich. Richer than you can imagine."

June Wynn closed her eyes with a heavy sigh. "Henry, while you were out looking for invisible dreams and imaginary dragons, I…" She hesitated.

"It's real!" Henry snapped. "It's not imaginary. Why can't you support me? As my future wife, you are supposed to support me, June!"

"What?" she gasped incredulously. "You're the man. You're supposed to support me! Are you expecting me to go to work at my father's store to support you while you go off searching for fairy dust?" She took a deep breath to calm her voice. "I came here tonight to end our engagement."

"What? Why?" he shouted. "What do you think I'm doing? I am working to support you! Trust me, I just need a little more time. June, I am this close to finding it," he said, holding his thumb and finger barely apart. "How many times do I have to ask you to grant me that? That's all I ask. Please. Just give me a little more time. I beg you."

June closed her eyes and then looked at Henry with moistened eyes. She admitted quietly, "Henry, I fell in love with somebody else."

"June, no," he gasped. The air that filled his lungs was siphoned out by the painful words he heard her say. An excruciating grimace twisted his expression with the sudden realization that he may have lost the love of his life. "June, we are meant to be together. You know that. Everyone says we're good together."

"No, Henry. They ask where you are." A tear slipped quietly down her cheek.

"I'll do anything you want, just please, don't leave me, June. I love you!"

June's head lifted with a touch of hope. "Will you stop looking for that stupid treasure? That's the only thing I'm asking you to do."

His anguished expression slowly hardened like a touch of mud on a hot day. His fist tightened as a scowl formed on his lips. He turned and hit the plank wall of his small one-room shack with a loud bang. The rough sawn plank ripped the skin from his knuckles, leaving two of them bloody.

He shouted, "Why can't you believe in me? I'm not out there messing with other women, drinking or gambling. Damn it, June, I'm trying to find a fortune so we can live like kings! I'm working as hard as I can, and I am so close. Please, just believe in me."

June had never seen him become so violent and stepped back toward the door. "I have to go."

"Wait." He forced himself to calm his composure. "I'm sorry. June, you know I would never hurt you. Please, wait a minute. How could you fall in love with someone else when you know I'm in love with you? How could you do that to me?"

Her brow furrowed as her chin twitched with emotion. "You were gone all the time. Even when you did come back, all you talked about was that treasure. He listened to me, and we could have conversations that mattered to me. He was here for me and with me when I needed someone. He cheered me up, made me laugh, and cared. The same things you used to do before you learned about that treasure. He's employed and makes a good living. Henry, he asked me to go away with him." She paused. "I told him yes. I've decided to marry him, Henry."

The strength left Henry's legs, and he sat heavily on a dining table chair. His eyes filled with burning tears as he tried to grasp the weight that was suddenly upon him. "It's Steven from the store, isn't it? I've seen him looking at you before."

"I brought you a gift." She opened the door, reached down and picked up a green bottle of wine, and held it close to her breasts with both hands. "It's better for both of us this way. You'll see. I wish you good luck in finding your treasure. I can't believe in it or you, but just in case, I got this bottle of wine for you. Promise me you won't open it until the day you do find that treasure. Will you promise me that?"

He nodded sorrowfully.

"Goodbye, Henry."

———

HENRY BASS PULLED his thoughts to the present and shifted his bitter blue eyes to the green bottle of wine on the top shelf layered with years of dust. He wore a scowl on his aging face that was as permanent as the basalt rock that made up Severson Mountain's cliff face. The waves could crash against the rock with all the fury that the winter storms could create, and the cliffs remained unscathed by the power of the sea. The frown on the man's face never lifted; if anyone had ever witnessed Henry Bass smile, it was doubtful they were still alive to say so.

Henry had found his way to the coastal mountains as a young man to try his hand at trapping furs. However, he arrived toward the end of the trade and found work in Astoria as a store clerk. The store owner's daughter, June Wynn, was a shining jewel among broken crab shells, and it didn't take long for Henry to fall in love with the most impressive young lady he had ever met. As destiny would have it, June took a shining to him, and they began courting. They hiked the mountains to catch the prettiest sunset, walked barefoot through the mudflats, laughed, and talked for hours. She was made for him like Eve was created for Adam. When the woman that a man loves is his best friend, there is nothing in the world that can hold him back with her by his side. Henry asked June to be his bride, and the happiest moment of his life, without a doubt, was the moment June accepted his wedding invitation. His life was beautiful. Then, one day, Henry met a new friend named Johann, who told him about the rumor of a buried treasure on Severson Mountain.

Henry wanted to open that bottle of wine countless times over the years, but a promise was a promise, even if it was forty-five years ago. If nothing else, he could say until his dying day that June had held that bottle in her arms. It was the closest he'd ever get to her again. The lingering thoughts of what might have been with June were a plague that affected him day after day. He loved her. It was a harsh thing to accept that he had spent all these years living the life of a fool chasing imaginary dragons, fairy dust and invisible dreams instead of investing his life in making sure June knew she was loved, appreciated, and just how important she was to him.

———

"MAYBE THIS IS A BAD IDEA. I've heard a lot of bad rumors about him," Helen Johnson said as she and Dominick walked up the St. Joseph River toward Henry's isolated cabin.

"This was your idea, Helen." Dominick chuckled. "Henry's not a bad man. He's just a little different and likes his privacy. He may look as unfriendly as a poked crab, but if you can get him talking, he's an interesting man."

"The rumors about him are interesting, too. Have you ever realized they're all bad? That's the one thing they all have in common. I mean, why would anyone want to be alone all the time unless at least one of the rumors were true?"

"It's just gossip, Helen. He's an old man who likes to be alone. Some people are just like that."

Henry was the town's most eccentric citizen and as such, rumors followed him from the absurd, like being a cannibal who devoured his wife and kids during a winter freeze. To the more suspicious, like a mad fur trapper who murdered lone travelers along the lonely roads. The rumors varied but were always for the worst. The years of gossip had made most people wary of the man.

Dominick's family owned an oyster farm on the mudflats of Shamrock Bay, and Henry occasionally worked there when he needed money. Dominick knew Henry wasn't the vicious war criminal or cannibal that the gossip had made him out to be. The simple truth was that gossip always dragged people through the mud; no one ever gossiped about the favorable deeds or hearts of good people. There was a deep-seated pleasure in gossiping about others that made one feel superior in some small way. If there was anything a person could count on, it was knowing that no one is immune to another person's taking pleasure in gossiping about them. Like every other small town, Shelton had a full share of town gossip seven days a week. Dominick had heard almost all of the rumors about Henry over the years and the ones about himself as well.

Helen spoke with a quieter voice as they got closer to Henry's residence. "I still think this is a bad idea. It just doesn't feel right." Henry's small windowless one-room log cabin was set back among the thick forest along the river. His barn was set near a narrow meadow that had become the pasture for his two donkeys.

"Relax. He's a good man once you get to know him." Dominick's attention went to where Henry was pulling in a drift net he had set across the river. There were a few salmon, a steelhead and three trout caught in it. One of the ways Henry made extra money was by selling smoked fish to the local market.

"Nice catch," Dominick said as they approached.

Henry was surprised to hear him and looked at the couple with annoyance. He nodded in agreement. "What are you two doing out here?" he asked without a hint of a smile.

"We thought we'd go for a walk."

Henry pointed back toward town. "The beach is that way. There's nothing out here except ticks, bears, and mountain lion tracks. Fresh ones, I saw just up the trail. You kids might want to go back the way you came." He tossed a large salmon from the net into a wicker basket.

"Actually, Henry, we came out here to talk to you."

"I plan on working for your father in a couple of days, but not until then. I have other things to do. You can tell him that."

"I will. Helen's father suggested we might ask you about a tombstone we found on Severson Mountain."

Henry stopped what he was doing and turned his attention to them. "Fairytales and invisible dragons. Don't waste your time on it."

Dominick furrowed his brow. "On what?"

Henry sighed. "The treasure stones. They're not real. So do yourself a favor and forget about it. Go home."

Dominick said, "I have heard something about a treasure being up there, but as you said, it's a fairy tale. There were never any swash-buckling pirates that came to Oregon. There is nothing worth pillaging here now, so there was absolutely nothing here a hundred or two hundred years ago."

"You're right," Henry said and turned his attention back to the salmon in the net. "Forget about the treasure rock you found. It's all a lie."

Dominick said, "I don't know anything about treasure rocks, but we found a tombstone, I'm pretty sure."

Helen spoke for the first time as she asked, "Was someone buried up there that you're aware of?"

Henry hesitated to answer and rubbed the side of his nose. "Did your tombstone say Johann Barker?"

Helen shook her head. "No. It looked more like a tombstone for two people to me. Didn't it to you, Dom?"

He nodded and asked, "Do the initials X.X. and C.T. sound familiar to you?"

Henry's attention was aroused. His head lifted, dropped his net and took a step closer to them. "What did you say? What kind of a stone was it?"

Dominick answered. "It was an obelisk stone about a foot and a half long. Maybe two feet, it was lying down and buried by grass, so it's hard to say what kind of stone it was. It was gray."

"No. What did it say?" Henry asked abruptly.

"It had two Xs and C.T. It looked like it had fallen over, but it had an arrow pointing down."

"Where did you find that?" Henry asked, stepping even closer. "Will you show me where you found it? Will you take me there?"

"We could, but we'll need to do it tomorrow and bring guns. We were almost attacked by a bear with two cubs yesterday."

"There's still time today," Henry said, looking at the sun. His enthusiasm had lifted with a hint of a smile tugging at the corners of his lips.

Dominick shook his head. "Henry, it's getting a little late in the day for us to go up there today. Why do you want us to show you that?"

Henry hesitated and looked at the ground as he moved a pine comb around with his toe. He inhaled deeply before saying, "That would be where they buried my wife."

"I didn't know you were ever married," Dominick said.

Henry nodded slowly. "I don't talk about it. We were picnicking up there one summer day and a group of Indians attacked us. She was killed, and I was seriously injured. I barely made it back to get help and was too hurt to go back up there. You said the initials were C.T.?

Her name was Camille Tucker. We weren't married yet; we were engaged. That was the closest I've ever been to getting married. The search party buried what was left of her up there. It burns my soul, but they tossed an Indian I killed in the fight into her grave with her. I figure that must be the double X since they didn't know his name. I've been looking for that grave for all these years and never found it. Forgive my anxiousness to see it, but I would like to visit my lady."

"Of course," Helen said. "Tomorrow morning, we can take you up there. Couldn't we, Dom?"

"Yeah. We can go up there tomorrow. We'll come by in the morning."

"Excellent. Listen, I'd appreciate it if you two would keep this between us. I am sure you two are aware that there is enough gossip about me without the town knowing my personal business. I've never been able to grieve for June's." He paused. "I mean, Camille's leaving me the way she did. I'd appreciate being able to see her grave before anyone in town knows about it. I want that much privacy, at the very least. Not a word to anyone, please. I like to keep my life private and don't need more rumors being spread about me going to her grave before I even get there."

"Sure," Dominick agreed. "I won't tell a soul."

"Miss?" Henry asked, expecting her to keep it private as well.

"Of course," Helen agreed.

"Then tomorrow morning it is."

LIKE A SPLASH of kerosene and pitch-covered kindling can resurrect a flame, the fire inside Henry's broken spirit was renewed. The local Indians told the story of a ship that was damaged at sea and had anchored in what is now known as Shamrock Bay. The White men were the first the Indians had seen, and curious about the strange men, they watched from a distance as the men carried a large trunk filled with silver and gold from the boat to the mountain. The Indian legend claimed that the white men were aware the Indians were watching. In an effort to keep the natives from getting too curious, the tall leader of the White men shoved a sword through a black man in chains and tossed his dead body on top of the chest before burying it. A stone with writing carved into it was put in the ground to mark where the treasure was buried. Sometime later, the ship was repaired and sailed out of the bay. No ship had ever returned to collect the treasure.

The Indian legend had no historical value on its own, but the treasure stones proved it was true. Henry had found seven treasure stones with English letters, numbers, and strange symbols carved into them. There was an organization to the map that was brilliant yet overly frustrating as the English letters and numbers led Henry back to the beginning more times than he could count. The strange symbols on each rock, written one after another like a sentence, were a language that didn't exist and had to be made up from a man's imagination. Those symbols that no man could translate without a ciphering key had to be the authentic map to the treasure. The English letters and numbers didn't lead anywhere but back to the beginning. Somewhere on the mountain, Henry was sure there was a rock that had the answers to what the symbols meant. There had to be a cave, a cliff face, or a large enough stone to translate the symbols into English for them to be understood.

There were seven stones placed in a semi-circle around the mountain. Henry had mapped them out, paced the distance between them, and tried to use common sense and arithmetic to figure out the most practical places for a treasure to be buried. He had dug holes all over the mountain and yet had come up empty. He was missing something and that something might be the stone the two kids had found. Henry was hopeful and excited, and now, after all these years, he may have just found the treasure with the help of two ignorant kids who knew nothing about its history.

Henry had doubted the existence of a possible treasure until he had spoken to a sea captain in a saloon one night, who told him that it was far more feasible than he might imagine and to read up on an English pirate named Captain Thomas Swain.

3

CAPTAIN THOMAS SWAIN WAS NOT THE MOST FAMOUS OF pirates who roamed the seas in the early seventeenth century. He was an English Explorer who had a long career as a privateer and slave trader before turning to piracy. Captain Swain sailed with three other ships in his fleet as he led attacks on Spanish and Portuguese vessels throughout the Atlantic and Caribbean. Thomas Swain sailed along the shores of South America, raiding settlements and attacking merchant ships. A battle with a Spanish war fleet brought the end to one of his ships, but Thomas Swain's boat, the *Crescent Tonalee* and her sister ship, the *Viper's Eye,* escaped.

The captain of the *Viper's Eye* refused to take his vessel through the Strait of Magellan to enter the Pacific. He and his crew had no interest in circumnavigating the globe but were anxious to take their share of plunder and return to England. The two ships parted company, and Captain Swain entered the Pacific Ocean. He sailed up the shoreline, raiding unsuspecting small villages and merchant ships along the way. The exploring nature of Thomas Swain kept him sailing north to explore the west coast of the American Continent.

A severe winter storm, along with a strong king tide, forced the *Crescent Tonalee* near the shore and rammed her into some submerged rocks, damaging the boat. As the sun peeked over the coastal mountains, Shamrock Bay came into view, and Captain Swain sailed his ship into the bay.

The crew camped along the St. Joseph River, which emptied into Shamrock Bay for just over a month while careening the *Crescent Tonalee*. The local natives were curious about the strangers and proved to be friendly, and trading was helpful for meat and other foods. However, the good relations were strained when the ship's carpenter and another crewman got drunk and became aggressive with a couple native women. Hearing their frightened cries, several native men killed the ship's carpenter and the other crewman. Captain Swain stopped his crew from retaliating on the natives to keep a peaceful relationship or none of them would live to see England again.

The ship was repaired, but the work was done without the skill and vast knowledge of their carpenter. The boat was carrying a heavy cargo, and the captain knew the Pacific was a vast ocean. The storm they encountered was equal to the worst he had ever experienced. Considering their limited resources to make the proper repairs and it being winter, Thomas Swain thought it might be wise to lighten the cargo except for what they would need for their journey across the rough sea. It was decided that the heaviest trunk filled with gold and silver and some other heavy items would be left behind in the name of safety.

Captain Swain knew the natives would not bother a grave, so he murdered his slave and tossed him on top of the treasure before burying it. To mark the way to the treasure, he used stones to point the way.

The *Crescent Tonalee* made it back to England, but they never returned to collect the treasure. Captain Thomas Swain and the *Crescent Tonalee* found their end in the Atlantic Ocean when Thomas Swain surrendered to a fleet of French warships. Thomas Swain was hung at sea while his ship was burned.

All that Henry knew of the voyage was learned from an old book the sea captain in the saloon had told him about, titled *The Crescent Tonalee's Careening in the New Land*, written by B. L. Linehan. He wrote it many years later about his adventures while sailing around the world with Captain Thomas Swain. B. L. Linehan never sailed again once he got back to England.

Henry held the book in his hand and reread the chapter about the treasure in the lamp's light. He could already taste the gold and silver on his tongue. When Henry had finished reading, he set the book down on the table and stood. He stepped over to the shelf and reached up to grab the bottle of wine. He wiped the dust off the bottle and smiled victoriously. "I have a feeling I'll be opening you tomorrow." He pulled the bottle to his chest and held it with both arms as June had done. It was as close to her memory as he could get.

4

A THICK FOG HAD SETTLED OVER THE COASTLINE OVERNIGHT, which happened often enough during the summer months as the marine layer rolled onto shore. "Morning," Henry called to Dominick and Helen as they rode two horses along the road.

"Good morning. Are you ready?" Dominick asked.

Henry nodded. "You two ride ahead and lead the way. I like riding alone, especially today, as I think about her. If you don't mind, I'll follow your tracks up and meet you at the grave."

"Okay. We can do that." Dominick couldn't wait to share the news. "We're getting married," he said with a grin.

"Yep," Helen agreed with a pleasant smile. "I'm going to make him an honest man."

Helen's horse was beside his, and they grabbed hands and leaned over their saddles to kiss.

"I already am," Dominick said to his bride-to-be.

Henry nodded. "Congratulations," he said without any emotion. "Go on and lead the way. I'll meet you up there."

THE MOUNTAIN WAS BURIED in thick fog that limited the vision to twenty yards in the cool of the morning. Dominick carried his rifle with him as he and Helen hitched their horses to a tree and walked through a small opening through the briars of berries into the meadow to stand by the grave marker. The forest was deadly quiet as the gentle waves far below were the only sound, faint as it was. The fog rolled by with a phantom breeze that did not touch their skin.

Before long, the sound of a small bell was heard as Henry rode his donkey through the narrow trail. He was leading a second donkey as a pack animal with a shovel and pick attached to it. It pulled a travois behind it as well.

"He brought a shovel?" Helen asked Dominick curiously. "Is he going to dig her up?"

"Glad you made it, Henry. What's all that for?"

Henry stepped down and grinned. "Oh, I always bring it. Never know. I might shoot an elk." He kneeled to hobble the front legs of his lead donkey. He did the same with the pack animal. "You said you saw a bear here. I can't have my critters running back home and leaving me here. They spook easy."

"I don't think they could have picked a prettier spot to bury your fiancée," Helen said as Henry stepped past her to the grave. "The wildflowers were beautiful the other day."

Henry ignored the comment and dropped to his knees next to the stone. His finger traced the letters. He began to weep.

Helen watched Henry compassionately. She nudged Dominick and mouthed the words, *say something.*

"You must have loved her," he said awkwardly. He gave Helen a slight shrug, not knowing what she wanted him to say.

Henry began to chuckle through his weeping. "Yeah." He looked up at Dominick with a wide grin on his face. "After all these years. Thank you."

"You're welcome," he answered.

Henry stood with a lopsided grin. "I brought a shovel. We have to dig."

"What?" Helen gasped. "No! You can't dig her up. She's nothing but bones, Mr. Bass. We won't help you do that. Will we, Dom?"

"No! I'm sorry, Henry, but I'm not digging up a grave."

Henry laughed for the first time. It seemed to reverberate through the forest. "No!" Henry laughed. "I lied about the woman."

"You were never engaged?" Helen asked.

"Oh, I was. Her name was June, but she left me. Do you know why she left me?"

"No," Helen answered. She was confused about why he would lie about such a horrible thing.

His blue eyes and odd laugh gave her an uneasy feeling stirring in her stomach. Maybe it was the eerie fog and silence that motivated it, but she wanted to leave.

Henry pointed his finger at the stone. "Because of that rock right there! I searched this mountain up and down for most of my life for the treasure, and you two found it! We'll split it fifty-fifty, but you have to help me dig it up. We found the treasure!" he yelled enthusiastically in celebration. "I never imagined they'd carry it all the way up the mountain. It figures! Those treasure rocks were just a ploy to keep everyone guessing. Brilliant! Come on, let's get the shovel and pick."

"I thought the treasure was a fairy tale?" Dominick asked, perplexed.

"No!" Henry paused with a grin. "I'll tell you the story later. But we are rich! Richer than you can imagine. Come on, let's dig!"

5

DOMINICK SWUNG THE PICK TO BREAK UP THE DIRT WHILE Henry shoveled out the soil. They worked for half an hour digging a four-foot square hole under where the marker was set. Dominick's pick sank into the hardened ground. It made the hollow sound of metal hitting rock several times, and each time, Henry's face lit up with expected enthusiasm, only to anxiously pull the rock out of the hole. Another swing of the pick and the telltale sound of the sweet clang of metal striking metal brought an end to Dominick's swinging of the pick.

"Let me in there," Henry said and stepped into the hole with his shovel to begin the work of revealing what Dom had hit. The old man's energy level increased as he uncovered the iron corner bracket of an old wooden chest wrapped in oiled canvas. He hollered with excitement as he quickly dug around the large chest. He pulled a knife from his belt and cut the canvas to expose an oak chest three feet long and two feet high. The aged oak boards were encased by several iron straps that were rusting but held the tongue-in-groove boards together. Henry's excitement could hardly be contained as he instructed Dominick to help him lift the chest out of the hole.

The two men grabbed the iron handles and strained to lift the heavy chest as it dripped water that had found its way inside the wooden barrier. Just as the chest was lifted out of the hole, Dominick's handle broke loose, dropping his end onto the ground. Henry dropped the chest and stretched the strained muscles in his back. His grin beamed with excitement.

Henry paused, he spoke through heavy breaths. "I have spent my life searching for this treasure. People thought I was crazy, but here it is. This chest is filled with silver pieces of eight and gold bullion. Jewels and diamonds, possibly. I don't know, but I do know we are richer than you've ever imagined."

"Well, open it!" Helen exclaimed, filled with excitement to see what was inside. The riches they had found would allow her father to live in ease wherever he wanted to live and allow Dom and her to do the same.

Henry held up a finger. "I've waited a long time for this. I brought a bottle of wine that I was given by my fiancée, June, to open when I found the treasure. She gave it to me as a bitter parting gift when she left me. She never thought I'd find it. My friend Johann Barker told me about this treasure, and he even helped me look for it for a while, but then he gave up. I didn't. I knew it was real. I never opened this bottle, but I will now. And I will gladly say to hell with her. I'll spend the entire fortune to find her and say, I told you so. Forgive me for rambling. I'll go get the wine and then we'll open it."

As Henry walked away toward his mule, Helen said, "I can't wait. Open it, Dom."

Dominick grinned as he took Helen in his arms. "We may be rich, but opening that chest will mean more to

Henry than all the worth of the treasure, no matter how much it is."

Helen wrinkled her nose and bounced on her toes like an excited child to open a present. "How much do you think we'll get? We did find it, after all."

"I don't know. But we'd think it was a tombstone if not for Henry."

"That's true."

Dominick kissed his lady while holding her close in his embrace. The explosion of a gunshot startled him at the same time that Helen's body jerked into his, and Dominick gasped as the bullet went through Helen's back and into his upper abdomen just below his sternum. Helen's eyes looked into Dom's with confusion before she collapsed to the ground through his arms, groaning in agony. Dominick stared in shock at Henry, who aimed a smoking revolver with an animalistic expression, twisting his face while he held a green bottle of wine in his other hand.

Dominick's lips moved, but no words came out.

Henry aimed his revolver at Dominick's head. "The treasure is mine! That's why." He squeezed the trigger, placing a bullet between Dominick's eyes. He watched as Helen struggled to breathe and reached her slender hand outward to take Dominick's in hers. One final shot echoing through the silent forest ended her life.

Henry let the revolver fall to the ground and opened the bottle of wine. He took a long drink. "Thank you, June!" he yelled and laughed before taking another long drink. He grabbed the shovel and began striking the rusted padlock. It broke open and he dropped to his knees to get the first look at the treasure as he lifted the lid. His mouth dropped open while his eyes narrowed. To his horror, the chest was filled with plain river rocks. He tossed the rocks out one after the other, only to reveal more rocks.

"No!" he screamed. He stood, bewildered. He turned his head to look at the two dead bodies and knew he had made a grave mistake. His upper lip lifted into a snarl as moisture wet his eyes from pure outrage. He kicked the chest and cursed loudly. He sat on the edge of the hole, grabbed the bottle of wine, and had a long drink and then another.

He grabbed the shovel, stepped into the hole with his stiff knees, and began digging it deeper. He had a lot of work to do to bury the two young lovers and try to think of a reasonable explanation for what might have happened to Dominick Webster and Helen Johnson. Their disappearance would immediately cause alarm, and a search party would be immediate and thorough. Henry hoped the two kids had not told a soul that they would be with him. But if either one had, he knew he would be suspected of treachery if he did not have a believable explanation of why he returned and they had not. He pulled the two bodies into the hole and buried them.

He needed to get rid of the two horses that the young lovers rode up the mountain. He led the first horse to the edge of a high cliff overlooking the sea and stood it broadside to the edge. Holding the reins with his left hand, he put the revolver to the horse's head and fired while giving it a shove. The horse fell over the cliff's edge down three hundred feet to the crashing waves and rocks below.

He led the second horse to the same cliff and arranged it broadside to the edge, held the reins and placed the revolver near its head, but as he pulled the trigger, the horse jerked its head upward, wounding its jaw. The horse reared, yanking the reins from Henry's hand and ran away. Henry aimed his revolver to shoot as the horse galloped across the meadow but discovered the cylinder was filled with spent cartridges when he pulled the trigger.

Henry cursed with a rage-filled scream. He knew the horse would not stop running until it reached the Webster family's barn.

6

HOWARD WEBSTER WAS IMMEDIATELY CONCERNED TO SEE Dominick's horse return without him. The horse had a deep wound under its jaw from what looked to be a bullet. He immediately got hold of the town marshal and rounded up a search party to find his son and Helen. The town marshal, Gary Rickshaw, led the search party as he followed the horse's blood trail along the road until they came to the cabin belonging to Henry Bass. Henry was waiting beside the road for them.

"Henry, where are Dominick and Helen?" Howard Webster questioned with concern.

Henry had hoped that Dominick and Helen had kept their promise, not to mention they were taking him up on the mountain. It was clear now that Dominick had broken that promise. To lie in an effort to buy time was pointless. The treasure didn't exist, and he would not be able to deny his actions once the fresh ground was dug up.

Henry wiped his palms on his pants nervously, lowered his head, and held his wrists outward. "You just as well save yourself the trouble and arrest me now. They came at me with a pick and shovel when we found the treasure. I had no choice; I had to defend myself. I buried them up there."

———

HENRY BASS WAS ARRESTED, pleaded innocent and faced a jury in a case that had become state-wide news known as *The Crescent Tonalee Treasure Murders*. Henry insisted it was an act of self-defense despite the bullet in Helen's back and the bodies having been shot twice and the attempt to hide the horses. Henry's best defense did not line up with the evidence, leading to the jury finding Henry guilty of murdering Dominick Webster and Helen Johnson. Henry was sentenced to death.

The date of his execution was nearing. He was isolated in the state prison in a cell that offered no comforts to an old man except time to reflect on his upcoming appointment with the hangman. He had no family, friends, or visitors. He spent his time trying to solve the mystery of the treasure chest of rocks. Why would the pirate Thomas Swain bury a chest filled with stones under the post that marked the treasure? It was a ploy, he figured. It took some time, but he was figuring it out. He had never believed the pirates would carry a heavy chest from the bay all the way up to the top of Severson Mountain, but they had. The treasure rocks were there to mislead him or anyone else to run in circles all the way around the true location of the treasure. It was brilliant, and now he understood. He appreciated Captain Thomas Swain's wisdom now that he had time to do nothing except think about it. If he could escape prison, even if for one day to be on that mountaintop, he knew he could find it. The stones inside the chest were the key. They were to be counted and stepped off from the marker in the direction that the arrow on the marker pointed. That was where the treasure truly was buried. The marker was an obelisk intentionally laid on its side to point the way to the treasure. Everything Thomas Swain did was a ruse to hide his treasure, but Henry had figured it out.

Unexpectedly, one of the guards put a key in his door and unlocked it. "You have a visitor, Henry. Come with me."

Henry was taken to another cell that faced a wall and a wooden bench. He sat in a chair with a small bench table in front of the bars that separated him from visitors.

A side door opened, and a guard led an old man inside the room. The old man wore a gray suit and walked with a silver wolf head cane. He was a clean-shaven man who was bald on top with short gray hair on the sides and wore gold-rimmed spectacles. He sat on the bench and looked at Henry with a friendly smile. "Hello, Henry."

"Who are you?" Henry asked curiously.

"My name is David Dubois. We met many years ago."

"We did? I don't remember you."

"You don't? Look closely."

Henry shook his head. "What do you want? Are you an attorney or something?"

"No. So you found the treasure?"

"I found rocks. But now I know how to find it. The rocks are the key."

"How so?" David asked.

"I'm not telling you! I don't know who you are or what you want. Did you just come here to gawk at me?"

David Dubois grinned. "I told you my name. I thought you might know where the treasure is, and I think I'm right. What did you mean the rocks are the key?"

Henry shook his head with a sigh. "I suppose it

doesn't matter. They brought the stone down for the trial, so you'll never find it. If I had counted the rocks and taken that many steps from the arrow on the stone. That's where the treasure is buried. I just didn't think about it at the time. But the stone is gone and the grass has grown over the hole by now. You'll never find it," he said victoriously.

David Dubois chuckled. "Oh, I wish I could play this game all day with you and see what your crazy mind is up to now. I put the rocks in there. I moved the stone and placed it where you should have found it easily. I'm surprised it took you this long."

"What are you talking about?"

"It's me, Johann Barker."

"Johann?" Henry gasped. He did not recognize his old friend without the long hair and beard. "I watched you die."

"Your bullet grazed me, and I fell off that ravine's bank into fifteen feet of blackberry bushes and mud. I was hurt and cut to shreds from the thorns, but not dead. I wanted to kill you for betraying me, but then I crawled under all those briars right into the treasure." He grinned. "Because of your greed, I found the treasure." He chuckled. "The only day I've labored since then was the day I lugged that stone and chest up the mountain where you found it. Thank you, Henry. You changed my life."

Henry could feel the moisture clouding his eyes. "You kept it?"

"Did you expect me to share it with you?" He laughed. "You tried to kill me. I thought about getting even, but I figured my best revenge was to let you keep searching for it. I'm glad you did. You persevered and kept searching. I knew you'd never give up."

"You're lying," Henry said, not wanting to believe his old friend had found it.

David Dubois reached into his jacket pocket and pulled out a silver Spanish piece of eight coin. "I wouldn't lie to you about that. It meant too much to both of us. Of course, the better man found it, thanks to you. And I do thank you, Henry. I wouldn't have found it without you."

Henry grit his teeth. "You let me keep searching for all these years?"

He nodded. "You tried to kill me for what? We thought we were getting close, and that was too much for you. We were close; we just didn't think it would be in that gully, but it was. I knew if you heard I found it, you'd kill me and take it. So, I left the area and changed my name. Yes, I hoped you'd spend your life searching for rocks." He put the silver coin back in his pocket. "Well, at least you got to see a part of it. The rest bought me a few businesses and a large farm. My wife and I have had a blessed life and have many children. Would you like to meet her?"

"No," Henry said, hating his old friend. "I should have put a dozen bullets into you."

"Like you did those two kids? Well, before I go, let me introduce you to my wife."

"I don't want to meet your wife!" Henry shouted.

"Sure, you do." He opened the side door. "My lady." He held the door open as an old woman wearing a purple dress and a wide-brimmed white hat came into the small room. She stood back, refusing to sit down.

"Hello, Henry," she said. "I wish I could say it's nice to see you, but knowing you murdered two young people in love sickens my stomach. I told you that night that the treasure was an invisible dream, a fairy tale. I was wrong; David had already found it."

"June," Henry gasped. The hardened heart that had grown cold and unfeeling over the years suddenly stirred like a donkey engine frozen in ice trying to start. His breathing was hard to catch as his throat went dry.

David put his arm around June's waist. "While you were looking for treasure, I was doing some hunting myself. I need to thank you for June, too. You see, she told me she wanted to give you an ultimatum before she could answer my marriage proposal. She loved you, Henry, and wanted to give you one last chance to keep her. But you chose the treasure. I knew you would, so I suggested the wine as a parting gift. I knew you couldn't stop searching for that treasure."

Henry's eyes filled with thick tears. "You married him?"

"I gave you a chance, Henry. I stated it plainly. I have no regrets. David and I have a beautiful family and a wonderful life. I did what was best for me."

Henry wiped his eyes and sniffled. "You knew he had the treasure and didn't tell me? You let me spend my life searching that mountain for a treasure that you were living on? It's your fault I wasted my life for nothing! You should be behind these bars, not me! I would never have done that to you. Love doesn't do that!" he shouted.

"You didn't love me, Henry. If you did, you'd want to be with me instead of weeks apart, looking for something that you couldn't find. Well, I'm going to go. I'm sorry things turned out the way they did for you, but it was your choice." She paused to peer at her old fiancé. "I don't know what got into you, Henry, but the obsession with that treasure changed you into a cold-blooded killer. You were not my Henry anymore when I left you. I hope the wine was good. It was the cheapest on the shelf. Goodbye."

"It was bland and boring, just like you!" Henry shouted as the door closed behind her. He sighed heavily with an emotional gasp. "June," he said softly, regretting what he had just yelled. He turned his head to face his old friend. "You ruined my life. If you never told me about the treasure, she'd still be mine."

"We both know you shot me because you're greedy, but you should have shot me because I had my eye on her. I wanted your girl. You knew that from the beginning, though. She didn't know I had the treasure until after we were married, just so you know. Nonetheless, I won't be here to watch you hang on Saturday, so I'd better tell you now. Thank you for the bullet, the treasure, and the life June has given me. I owe it all to you, old friend."

"All these years, you knew I was still looking, didn't you?"

"No. I didn't think about you at all until I read about you in the paper. I thought you'd have given up, found a wife, and raised a family by now."

"I wish I had. I lived my whole life for nothing. Absolutely nothing."

David peered at his old friend. "That's not true. We are all driven by what we treasure most in life. Thanks to you, I've treasured June and my family for all these years. Henry Bass, my old friend, when you're standing on the gallows with that rope around your neck and about to meet your maker, remember what you willingly sacrificed for your life's treasure."

Redemption

A Short Story
By C.K. Crigger

Redemption

"Shoot 'im, you cowards. Kill 'im." Herbert Truett howled loud as wind in a Louisiana hurricane, reining his horse round and round, growing more strident by the second. He was the only one doing any shooting. Any howling, either, for that matter.

The other five men present hung back. If their faces hadn't had burlap sacks over their heads cutting down their vision, Liggin Browne figured he would've seen every single one with his mouth hanging open, words of denial on his lips. Himself included.

Well, maybe not Jimmy Truett, Herb's son. A kid with fat fingers and a perpetual scowl, he did what his pa told him. Most of the time.

Neither Liggin nor his three neighbors had come here for this. A few mild threats, sure. Wave their guns around, shoot a bullet or two into the ground if necessary, although he hadn't even done that. Make a strong suggestion to this young farmer that he'd be better off heading for greener pastures. That's why Liggin had reluctantly agreed to Truett's steamrolling him to come along. That's what they'd all signed up for.

Not this. Not Truett's uncontrolled urge to cause pain.

They'd been running their horses, circling the farmer and his hovel of a house, yowling like wild Indians. Easy to see the farmer was spooked. Trouble is, he had an old revolver and, in trying to be brave, he shot at Herb. Hit Herb's horse Barney, as it happened, drawing a little blood and making the horse buck. Dumped Herb onto the ground like a sack of...well, something wet and stinking.

"He shot Barney," Herb yelped when he'd gotten up and settled back in his saddle. "I want him dead."

Liggin didn't figure the rage was because of his horse.

Only Jimmy obeyed. Why this time, Liggin never knew. Excitement, probably.

"No!" Liggin yelled, but it was already too late.

One of the bullets from Jimmy's .44 caught the farmer dead center in the chest, a splash of red spreading over his dirty work shirt as his heart beat a few more times after he went down.

The circling and shooting stopped cold.

Then, from inside the house—truly no more than a refurbished old line shack—a high-pitched scream pierced the still silence.

A woman, hardly more than a girl, burst from the doorway lugging a shotgun. She ran to the dead man, screaming out words a lady shouldn't know and saying she was gonna kill the killer. Could be it was her raw fury that made Herb do what he did when she pointed her shotgun at Jimmy. A noted marksman, his shot took her right in the middle of her forehead.

Liggin kind of thought she should've shot Herb first and done her screamin' after.

He'd suspected joining up with Herb Truett had been the wrong thing to do from the start. He didn't like the man. Didn't trust him. But he didn't like these durn sodbusters coming in and tearing up the prairie with their plows, either. This Montana dirt didn't run deep enough to support wheat farming. He blamed the government for giving the land to the railroads. He blamed the railroads for selling it cheap to homesteaders and making millions. As for the sodbusters, they'd make a crop or two, and that would be it. The tilth gone and moisture used up, the dry dirt blew away in the wind. Native grasses that'd grown here and fed first the buffalo, then the cattle, would be gone, never to return.

The little man, as always, was the loser. This killing simply proved Liggin's point. What's more, he wasn't just putting the sodbuster and his woman in this loser category. He and these three neighbors were barely a notch better what with Herbert Truett and his boy making them all guilty of murder.

"See if this farmer has a shovel," Truett said into the frozen silence. "We'll bury them so deep nobody'll ever find them."

"Guess who's going to do the digging," Bill Arkwright muttered to Liggin.

Gerald Powell had a different idea, he being a man of considerable rectitude. "We can't do that. We have to report this…this accident to the sheriff."

Herb shot down Powell's words before they were fully out of his mouth. "I ain't talking to nobody. Ain't anybody gonna care about some ignorant sodbuster. Folks around here who count are gonna say, 'good riddance.'"

Liggin guessed that might just be true.

"We don't have to say who did it," Powell conceded. "We can say we found them like this. Or it was self-defense." He finagled the burlap bag off his head, revealing cheeks wet with either sweat or tears. "But it isn't right to have them disappear. They are—they were

—young. They must have kinfolk somewhere who'll wonder about them."

The men muttered agreement but Truett waved away the argument as if swatting a fly.

"Let 'em wonder," he said hardly, and so it was settled. "Now find that shovel."

The place he chose for the burial was a mile from the house. Nothing about the site differentiated it from the hundreds of square miles surrounding it.

They all took turns digging, even, to Liggin's surprise, Jimmy and Herb. And though the ground was hard as concrete, they did eventually manage a deep hole. Deep enough, anyhow. The man got thrown to the bottom, a cushion to his wife when Jimmy threw her on top of him. Covered up, the soil tamped down, in a matter of hours the couple was erased as if they'd never been.

The five of them rode away and after a while, Liggin looked back. The grave was invisible, lost on the rise and fall of the prairie.

"I doubt I could find it again," he said.

Bill agreed. "Nobody could."

"Can we burn the shack, Pa?" Jimmy, already suspected of causing more than one fire for the homesteaders to contend with, looked hopeful.

Head bobbing as if about to agree, Truett changed his mind. "Not this time, Jimmy. If anybody ever did come looking, their suspicions might get raised if they see a burned house."

Along the banks of some little no-name creek, the men separated, going off in different directions. Liggin headed west, bypassing the town. When he answered Truett's call to action this morning, he'd thought to stop in at the saloon for a drink when done and maybe play a friendly game of faro with whoever was there.

Not now. What he and the rest of them had done this

day must be writ on his face, painted there in the murdered couple's blood. Guilt made him sick. Twice, after he separated from the others, he had to leap from his horse and vomit until nothing was left inside him but regret.

———

AS THE CROW FLIES, Liggin's ranch, the #LB, didn't lay so awful far from the murdered sodbuster's place. It occurred to him he didn't even know their names. In the weeks that followed, he took to riding over that way now and again. Once he rode right up to the house and found it undisturbed. Spilled blood had been rained into the ground, the mud dried, turned to dust and blown away. The house door stood open just as they had left it. While he didn't dismount, he peered into the interior.

There wasn't much to see. A steamer trunk. A mighty few kitchen implements. A rough table and two stools. A rope bed, the blankets apparently now home to rodents and maybe rattlers.

If Truett figured to convince anyone—should questions ever be asked—that the couple had simply gone on to parts unknown, anybody with a brain would wonder why those things were still there. Jimmy might should've had his way and burned it after all.

No way was Liggin about to touch any of it. The place, to his mind, was haunted.

In the fall, a man came around asking questions. Liggin heard about him, a fancy, trumped-up sort of fellow according to Bill who'd met him. Seems he'd been sent out from some attorney's office back in Cleveland, Ohio. He was making inquiries about the sodbuster and his wife. They had family looking for them.

Bill, in town on a Saturday to pick up supplies, leaned

down from his wagon seat to speak quietly to Liggin, also in town and bent on the same chore.

"Turns out," Bill said, his pale eyes squinting and worry lines wrinkling his face, "they wasn't as inconsequential as Truett told us. He had no business killing them. None." His voice broke on the last word.

Liggin shook his head. "No, he didn't. And we had no business letting him get by with it. Him and that trouble-making son of his. When you come right down to brass tacks, Bill, there ain't none of them folks who want to farm any different than those of us who want to run cattle. We all just want to make a living."

"True." Bill nodded. "But Truett says they ruin the country, tearing up the grass and building fences."

Being younger and maybe a touch more progressive than Truett—or even Bill—still Liggin had to agree with them. "Don't do it any good, to my mind. But everyone one of us left where we were when times got too hard and came here to build a better life. There's a lot of folks, maybe most folks, say a place is better off with more people. They build towns, community. Think of it this-away, whether they're miners or bankers, loggers or saloonkeepers, cattlemen or farmers, they eat, they buy, they bring prosperity and spread it around. They grow the country, the whole US of A. It's just the way it is."

"Say there, Liggin," Bill said, appearing a little thunderstruck. "You're getting downright philosophical. Are you meaning to say the farmers got as much right to land as ranchers?"

"Maybe." He didn't want to discuss the subject anymore, figuring word might get around and he'd be the one with his masked neighbors circling him on their horses, shooting off their six-shooters. He'd be lucky not to reach the same fate as the sodbusters if Truett got word of it. "But I'm thinking days of the open range are done."

Bill, a thoughtful expression on his face, nodded.

Stepping back, Liggin raised his hand in farewell. "Well," he said, "there ain't nothing to be done about it now. A guilty conscience doesn't take away the wrong we done."

"No, it don't," Bill said. His face drew down again and snapping the whip over his horses' backs, he drove off at a right smart pace.

The mantra served Liggin during the winter. Sometimes the memory faded, if only a little, and sometimes it rushed in with the regret and horror as strong as ever. But mostly he recalled his own words. *There was nothing to be done about it now.*

And so the winter passed. Spring came again, the snow melted and rains washed the old year away.

Along about the first week of May, Liggin set out to chase down any strays escaped from the first wave of branding. As it chanced, riding hot on the trail of a couple cows and their babies, he passed near the sodbuster shack. Near enough to spot smoke rising from the rickety chimney and spy a freshly dug plot of ground apparently set aside for a kitchen garden. Startled, he hoped he'd be forgiven for the first thought flooding his mind. The one where he was grateful they'd buried the young couple a mile or so away from the house and that they'd buried them deep. Deeper than a plow would dig, at least.

But then he was ashamed, especially as his second thought worried about Truett and his son hearing someone had moved onto the place. About whether history would, as the saying went, repeat itself.

Well, not if he could help it. The least he could do is give warning.

"C'mon, Shad," he told his horse, and they headed down off the rise overlooking the shack. There'd been some improvements to the place since last fall. The door fixed, porch with a couple new boards, the shed out back with its roof patched, and wonder of wonders, a functional corral. There was even a chicken coop with a bunch of squawking hens. Beyond that, closer to the shed than the house, and under the shade of the only tree in sight, somebody was down in the old hand-dug well flinging out mud and debris.

Whoever it was evidently didn't hear him coming as he rode right up to the well head. Or if he was heard, the feller wasn't curious enough to stop work and say howdy.

"Hey there," Liggin called out. "You in the well. Hello."

The digging stopped. A head popped into sight. Then the double barrels of a shotgun.

"State your business." The person—a woman, much to Liggin's surprise—rested the shotgun on the edge of the stone collar encircling the well. The barrels were aimed dead center at Liggin's chest, steady as a fossil in a rock, and the gun at full cock.

Liggin became aware of his mouth hanging open. He closed it with a snap.

A blob of mud plastered a section of the woman's curly mop of brown hair against her forehead. A streak down her cheek showed where she'd scrubbed at another blob. What he could see of her shirt was a disgrace. For any other woman he'd ever heard of, at least. Only her hands were clean, showing she'd been wearing gloves until he arrived and only removed them to handle the gun.

"You should get a dog," he told her. "A dog would let you know somebody is coming. Keep you from getting snuck up on."

She stared at him out of intense gray eyes. "Do tell." The eyes narrowed. "Is that important?"

Liggin flinched. If she only knew. "Maybe," he said, and added, "So's you don't get taken by surprise."

They stared at each other a minute or two longer, Liggin growing a bit nervous.

"And that's important," she said. It wasn't a question this time.

He gave a little tilt of his head, not quite a nod, not quite a denial. "Do you know how to use that shotgun?"

"I do." She waved the gun barrel, drawing his attention from her face. "Do I need to prove it right now?"

"No, ma'am. Not on my behalf."

She must've believed him because she uncocked the gun and set it aside. Even then, she didn't climb out of the well but simply leaned over the stone collar and studied him.

"I suppose introductions are in order," she said. "I'm Miss Portia Simchuck. I bought this homestead from the Thomas Forth estate and moved here last month. You are?"

Miss Portia Simchuck?

"Miss?" Liggin said, startled. "*You* bought the place? You mean you ain't got a husband?"

"That's what I mean." One eyebrow, and fine eyebrow it was, arched upward.

"But...what are you going to do with the place? It's a hundred and sixty acres, ain't it? You ain't planning on farming, are you?" *Please, God, no,* Liggin thought. "Farming ain't a real profitable venture in this part of the country."

"So I've heard," the woman, Portia Simchuck, said. "But it's mine. I can do as I like." Her mouth twisted. "I can dig holes. I can scream if I want. I can cry if I want. I can search for any bodies that might be buried on this land." She made a gesture. An angry gesture. "Take this well, for instance. I'm making sure no bodies have been dumped in it before I take one sip of water."

Liggin froze. Then, "Bodies?"

"Yes. The bodies of the previous owners, Thomas and Adelia Forth. They disappeared, as I'm sure you know. Gone without a trace, but leaving all their possessions behind. Which leads me to believe they're still here, somewhere. Or their bones are. So if you want to know what I'm doing here, that's it. I'm looking for them and for whoever killed them."

She'd just declared war.

His mouth so dry Liggin could hardly talk, he swallowed and said, "Maybe they just moved on."

"They didn't 'just move on.' I know they were murdered. Now," she stood up straight and, reaching into her curly hair, brushed at the mud drying there, "if you don't intend on killing me in the next couple minutes, I'd be interested in learning your name and what your business is here."

"Killing you? Why, no ma'am. Why would I do that?"

She shrugged, a graceful lifting of one shoulder.

Wishing his curiosity had never led him down the hill, Liggin figured after that he had no choice but to answer her question. "Browne. My name is Liggin Browne. Reckon I'm your nearest neighbor. I have a ranch over south of here about five miles." He cocked a thumb in the general direction.

"Five miles? So what are you doing over this way?"

He read distrust in her question and was glad he had a truthful answer to give.

"Lookin' for some runaway cows," he told her. "I had a couple cows with their calves wander in this direction and come to chase them home. Then I saw smoke from your chimney and thought to see what's what."

Miss Portia Simchuck waved a hand. "Ah. Then be my guest and feel free to round up your cattle, Mr. Browne." The corner of her mouth turned up. "A good fence would keep them where they belong."

Liggin about fell off his horse. Didn't she know those were fighting words in open range? If she'd said that to say, Herbert or Jimmy Truett, the good Lord only knows what they'd do to her. It didn't bear thinking about.

He cleared his throat. "That might be true, but fences aren't kindly looked on by some folks." He hesitated. "There's some who will do anything to keep fences off the open land. They'll stop those who'd build them by any means at hand. *Any means,* if you get my meaning."

"Will do?" she said. "Or have done?"

He couldn't bring himself to answer directly. "Take my advice, Miss Simchuck. You keep your eyes peeled and that shotgun close. I mean all the time. Don't leave your house without it."

Something moved in those gray eyes of hers, and he thought, *Yeah. She ain't completely unaware.*

An hour later he'd found his stock and turned them toward their home range. As he passed her place, he paused Shad and surveyed her progress at the well. Evidently she'd satisfied herself as to its purity, since he spotted a big old plowhorse nosing water as a trough filled.

"Huh," he told Shad. "A woman of mystery. How many women do we know can put together a running water system from scratch?" He scratched his head. "I'll tell you. None." Didn't know any women looking to find a killer, either. But then, it occurred to him later, he didn't actually know very many women. Single women, he meant, other than some who were either babies or old grandmas.

Such thoughts didn't belong in his head anyway. He'd

been on hand when the Truetts shot the young couple down like they were no more than prairie dog vermin. Worse, he hadn't done a thing to stop them. Hadn't told a soul about what happened, either. So while he hadn't pulled the trigger, he was guilty all the same.

————

ON SATURDAY, when Liggin went to town to stock up on salt for his livestock and some foodstuffs for himself, he found a group of men huddled around the pot-bellied stove in Mickelson's store. A fire blazed in the stove, a sign that although the calendar might say May, spring was only intermittent.

He started to join them, the ride into town having been on the chilly side. That's until he saw one of the men was Herbert Truett, along with his son, Jimmy. Truett was holding forth like king of the county, his demeanor showing he expected the others to hear and obey his every word. He was complaining about a couple new homesteaders moving in, and about how they needed run out. "No more homesteaders," he said. "You'd think they'd have learned their lesson by now. Who's with me?"

No one volunteered, which Liggin could see didn't set well with Truett. The few low mutters could've meant anything. Agreement or protest, Liggin figured he knew which.

"Mickelson!" Undeterred, Truett turned to call out to the storekeeper. "What do you hear about the woman that took over the sodbuster's place? You know, the one who disappeared last summer?"

Wasn't anybody could miss the know-it-all smirk on Jimmy Truett's face. Head bobbing, another of the men nodded along as if in the know. And maybe he was,

Liggin reflected. Hard telling who the Truetts had bragged to about what happened. Another two men present were Bill Arkwright and Thomas Parsons. Both had been there along with Liggin. Their eyes were fixed on the floor, their expressions indicating maybe they'd rather crawl under the boards than stay where they were.

Gerald Powell had left the country after what happened. Gathered up his family and his livestock and headed out for Idaho. Liggin figured he knew why. If he hadn't been so stubborn, he might've done the same. But he'd built a house and increased his herd and started to make something of his land. He didn't want to leave.

"Mickelson," Truett bellowed again when the storekeeper, busy giving a female customer's needs a little more attention than they might have warranted, ignored his first summons.

Apparently, Truett didn't see the glare Mickelson sent his way. Liggin did.

"Coming," Mickelson said but he didn't bother to hurry.

Liggin grinned. He didn't blame the storekeeper. It was well known that Truett ran a tab at the store and took his time about paying it off.

"What do you want?" Mickelson said, dusting down his semi-white apron.

Truett sat with his boots cocked up on a railing installed around the stove to keep folks from getting too close and being burned. Mud hung from his heels, dropping to the floor as it dried. "I asked what you know about the woman who moved into the abandoned sodbuster cabin." He shot a glance at Liggin who, it must be said, still hadn't joined the group, and added, "The one over the line from Browne's land."

"I don't know anything about her." Mickelson

scowled at Truett. "Just her name is Miz Simchuck and *she* pays cash for what she buys at the time *she buys it.*"

Whoo, Liggin thought, amazed at the storekeeper's temerity and pure nerve at what was a blatant poke in the rancher's belly.

But Truett only grinned and said, "Do tell. Where do you suppose she gets the cash? She got visitors out at her shack at night, does she? Maybe I ought to send Jimmy over to check into her activities."

Jimmy laughed. "Yeah, Pa. Maybe I will, if she ain't too ugly."

They all knew what he was implying, and though Liggin could tell it didn't sit well with the others, nobody said anything. Until, that is, he discovered words coming out of his own mouth. Words he hadn't intended to say.

"You should think twice before you go spreading rumors about a decent woman, Truett. Most folks don't much respect a man who talks dirty about a woman. They get to wondering what led him to say such a thing, and like as not, it don't reflect well on him." His little speech meant a whole lot more than just the words, and there were at least four men who knew it. At least three of them who nodded in agreement.

Truett's boots clomped to the floor, dropping more mud. But it was Jimmy, bent on punishing the man challenging his pa, who, being an idiot in more ways than one, snagged his gun getting it out of the holster. The .45 fired, grazing the young man's leg and boring a hole through the floor.

Jimmy screamed like a child.

Liggin clicked his tongue. "Well, well. Look at that. Appears all blood runs red, no matter who spills it. Serves you right for trying to shoot down an unarmed man." He knew he sounded cool, but he sure in hell didn't feel it.

"Somebody go get the doctor," Truett roared, and then to his son, only a little more quietly, "Hush your caterwaulin'. You ain't hurt bad."

Not one single person in the store moved to obey.

Next, Truett's glare settled on Liggin. "This is your fault, Browne. You and that woman both."

The storekeeper stared at Truett. "What are you talking about? Why blame Browne? Or Miss Simchuck? You and your boy are in the wrong and you know it. We all know it." He made a gesture encompassing the group. "Shame on you."

Truett's face turned almost purple, color fed by his rising anger. "You'll be sorry for that, Mickelson. You, too, Browne. As for that woman, well, we'll see."

With that, he hauled Jimmy to his feet and got him moving toward the entry. Dead silence reigned for several moments, until one female witnessing the altercation said to another, "So rude." And the other replied, "Who does he think he is?"

Liggin could've told them. Could've said Truett was a bad man, a murderer, a thief, a no-account big mouth. The fact he was ruthless, wealthy, and the big man in this territory just made matters worse.

And he might've added that he'd no doubt made a big mistake by calling Truett out. But he couldn't be sorry he'd done it. Maybe it made up in some small way for not preventing the deaths of those young homesteaders.

———

THE NEXT MORNING, he rode over to Miss Simchuck's homestead, bound to warn the lady trouble was ahead and that it was, in part, due to him. Would he confess what he knew to her? His innards shrank into a hard ball thinking about it. Would it do anyone any good if he did?

As far as reporting to the sheriff, well, Truett had backed him in the recent election, which was apt to mean Truett owned him. The basis of Truett's support is what had made Liggin vote for the other guy.

A rattle of gunfire reached him as he approached the rise above the homestead. Shad, not being a horse that appreciated a lot of racket, shook his head in protest, forcing Liggin into using his spurs to keep him moving. At the top, Liggin dismounted and found a stick to poke in the ground to hitch Shad to. Drawing his rifle from the saddle scabbard, he edged forward until the the ranch yard spread before him.

Heart beating fast, he was relieved to hear the thump of Miss Simchuck's shotgun rise above the lighter crack of six-guns and at least one carbine. Halfway down the slope, four horses had been tethered to sturdy clumps of brush growing out of the rock-strewn mouth of a gully. One of the horses was Barney, Truett's favorite mount. The riders had all taken positions wherever they could find cover several yards below the horses.

To him, it looked like they'd gotten themselves in trouble, as the invaders were laying out in the open, more or less. Meanwhile, Portia Simchuck had taken refuge, her and her shotgun, behind the stones protecting the well. Every now and then she popped up like a prairie dog out of its burrow, let off a blast or two from her 12-gauge, and ducked down again before anyone could draw a bead on her.

Not, Liggin believed, a safe long-term strategy. To his mind, it was only a matter of time before they got her. Her shotgun hadn't the range to do more than keep them at a distance. Sooner or later, one of them would get in a perfectly timed shot with their more powerful weapons.

He'd have to take a hand. First thing, he decided, was to create a distraction.

The Truett men's horses flinched as he came up behind them. He'd watched where he put his feet and was almost silent in his approach. In a matter of seconds, he'd untied the horses and begun shooing them away. They were eager enough to go, disliking the noise, the confusion, and maybe the smell of a stranger. Barney, perhaps remembering last time he was here having came out of it with a graze across his rump, was first to trot away.

Liggin waved his arms to hurry the others and, as the last horse crested, let out a shrill whistle that caused Jimmy to look behind him. Liggin had ducked down by then, but Jimmy spied the last of the horses sprinting over the top of the hill.

"Son of a…" Jimmy bellowed. "The horses! Pa!"

Distracted, Herb fired another shot and turned around. His face, visible even at Liggin's distance, turned an alarming red. "Pete," he yelled. "You catch up them horses. And make sure they don't get away this time."

Pete, his expression showing he was more than happy to be delivered from shooting at a woman hiding in a well, said, "Yessir," and scrambled to his feet.

Judging this his best opportunity to narrow the odds of surviving the fight, Liggin jumped from behind his rock and conked Pete behind the ear with the butt of his rifle as he ran past.

Pete went down like a pole-axed steer and lay still. Liggin confiscated his weapons and a rope Pete had dangling from his belt, thinking it might come in handy. Then he started wriggling on his belly toward the next nearest man, Jimmy.

Oblivious to everything going on around him, and no doubt considering himself safely out of reach of the buckshot loaded in Portia Simchuck's shotgun, Jimmy was emptying his .44 in her general direction as if he owned an ammunition store.

Liggin figured the kid spent as much time reloading the pistol as he did shooting it. Which, when thinking the situation over, suited him fine as it gave him precious seconds in which to move up behind the young ruffian.

He jammed the barrel of his .38 in Jimmy's ear and whispered, "Enough. Move a muscle and I'll blow your head off."

Apparently, Jimmy believed him since, eyes opening wide, he held still as petrified wood.

In seconds, Liggin had trussed the kid up like a calf to be dragged to the branding fire, with his own dirty bandana stuffed in his mouth. Leaving Jimmy lying in the dirt whimpering in a muffled kind of way, he moved forward again.

A few yards below, Herb and the last one of his men, Buck by name, were still shooting, whooping like wild men every once in a while when a loose stone fell from the well's collar.

Liggin, beginning to be afraid the whole durn shebang might fall down any second now, figured he'd better finish this up as soon as possible.

He might've gotten a little careless, become too confident considering his luck so far as he broke from the scant cover and headed for Herb, who was the closest man to him. Might've hurried, while he was at it, aware that Portia Simchuck must've seen him seeing the blasts of her shotgun were timed to his movements now. Either that or she was running low on ammunition.

For whatever reason, when a stone rolled under his boot and he went down on one knee, Truett heard his involuntary grunt.

"I told you to stay behind me, son," the rancher said. "I don't want you getting in reach of the damn woman's shotgun." But then he turned around, maybe, since Jimmy wasn't good at obeying orders, to emphasize the point and saw Liggin. "You! What the..."

Truett's ranch hand heard the change of his boss's tone and spun around. A grin split his face with a show of snaggle teeth in a bearded jaw. He and Liggin had traded blows more than once. Liggin had won both times, but now the other man had the advantage. Before Liggin could pick himself up and get set, a bullet ripped along his hip, ruining a fairly decent pair of britches and drawing blood.

Knocked him askew, too, which might've saved his life as Truett fanned his handgun. One, two, three. The .45 ran dry, but Truett pounced on him like a cat on a mouse. Thing is, Liggin was no mouse even if Truett did consider him prey. The rancher fell on top of him and started in pummeling with fists and feet. Buck, ignoring Portia and her shotgun as no account, ran to help his boss. Fortunately for Liggin, Buck was thwarted by Truett being on top and therefore prevented from doing anything worse than dancing around the pair rolling on the ground.

"C'mon, boss, you got 'em," Buck kept yelling in-between yips like an excited coyote. He didn't see Portia leaping from the cover of the well's stone walls and running to help. Liggin did though, fear for her giving him new strength.

Clenching Truett's shirt in both fists to hold the older man too close to get in a good swing, Liggin let go with one hand and came up with a strong roundhouse blow to the side of Truett's head.

The rancher went sprawling. Stayed down, too.

Buck, sure now of a kill shot, lifted his revolver, only to have a shotgun poked between his shoulder blades.

"You just drop that gun, shut your mouth, and sit

down, buster. Right now, provided you don't want a load of buckshot in your spine." The level voice marked the order with a sharp poke.

Buck briefly considered his boss sprawled in the dirt and out of the fight. Wisely, he dropped, shut, and sat as ordered.

Portia, standing behind her captive's back, grinned at Liggin and winked.

They'd won the round.

Next, Liggin figured, came the hard part. The confession. His confession.

But that would have to wait, as Portia said, "Who's that?" She was looking over his shoulder to where two riders sat horses at the crest of the hill. One, Liggin saw was Bill Arkwright. The other, judging by the sunlight flashing off the badge pinned to the man's chest, was the sheriff. And even from a good many yards off, his posture made him look mad as a half-drowned cat.

The sheriff, Thompson being his name, rode off the hill in a hurry having taken in the scene in Portia Simchuck's yard. He sat his horse, looking down at them from a kingly height, his horse being a tall one.

"What's going on? We heard shooting from a mile away."

Behind him, Bill nodded, his eyes questioning Liggin. Liggin shrugged.

Struggling to his feet, Truett started talking, self-important as always.

The sheriff cut him off. "I'll hear from Miz Simchuck first, this being her property and the rest of you, from the looks of things, uninvited visitors." He glanced at Portia who still held her shotgun on Buck. "I believe you can let this man go, ma'am. He won't do anything now I'm here."

Ever so slowly, she lowered the shotgun a few inches.

"I'll just hang on to it if you don't mind, Sheriff," she said coolly.

Wasn't a man of them unaware of where the shotgun pointed now. Especially Buck.

Liggin grinned.

So did the sheriff, just the tightest of lip twitches. He cast a glance around at Jimmy hogtied on the ground, his face red. At Pete, just now sitting up. At Buck, whose face had drained of color at the thought of Portia's gun, and at Herb Truett, so full of his own importance and influence he was already gathering breath to give orders.

"See here," Truett started, but ignoring him, Sheriff Thompson invited Portia to tell him what happened.

"Keep an eye on them, Arkwright," he told Bill. "Give a holler if any one of them gets out of line."

Bill, setting hand to his holstered revolver, nodded brightly. "Yessir, Sheriff." He seemed pleased as Punch.

"Now, Miss Simchuck," Liggin, standing back, heard Thompson say to Portia, "start from when these yahoos showed up. What happened to get the shootin' started."

Portia laughed, a shaky little laugh. "What got it started? Me, I guess. Just by being alive and occupying this piece of ground. I told you my intentions when I arrived here, Sheriff Thompson, about researching the facts regarding the disappearance of Thomas and Adelia Forth, and that I'm writing a book about it. From the look of things, the news got around and a certain faction doesn't want those facts known. I'd say this opens up the story."

"I'd say you're right." Thompson cocked back his hat, resetting it at a lower angle. "You're lucky you saw Truett and his men coming."

"A neighbor came by a few days ago. He suggested I keep my shotgun with me at all times and that I stay alert." Her gaze flicked to Liggin and back again. "I'd already staked the well out as the best place to defend myself if I got caught in the open. I figured the rock surround provided the best protection. They couldn't burn it and, with the clear ground around me, they couldn't sneak up on me."

Thompson nodded. "What did Truett say to you?"

"Nothing. I spotted Mr. Truett and his men the moment they barreled on over the top of the hill. They weren't in the least stealthy, and when they saw me in the yard, they started shooting." She cast Truett a disparaging glance. "Fortunately for me, none of them bothered to take aim. I guess they figured to paralyze me with fear." She gave that little laugh again. "Their miscalculated rush gave me time to make it to the well, where I held them off."

The sheriff turned and studied the scene. Pete still sitting nursing his head where Liggin had left him. Jimmy, who nobody had thought to release from his bond. Possibly because not even his father wanted to listen to his lamentations. Buck sat on a rock keeping his mouth shut for a change, and watching his boss pace.

Liggin noted Truett's strut was not so confident as usual. Looks, he thought, like maybe the sheriff was not so bought and paid for as Truett had believed.

Or as Liggin himself had feared.

Meanwhile, Portia was finishing up her story. "I was never so relieved in my life as when Mr. Browne rode over the hill and took a hand. He disposed of those men lickety split. I'd come near to running out of ammunition."

The thought of that happening made Liggin break out in a sweat.

The sheriff tipped his hat back on his head and stared at Truett. "I'll arrest these men for assault and attempted murder."

"First-degree murder," Portia corrected in a firm voice.

"But you're not dead, and without witnesses or the bodies of the missing Forth couple, I don't know as I can accuse them of murder. Not and have it stand up in court."

Portia made a sound, a cross between disgust and despair.

Liggin drew in a deep, shuddering breath. This had to end somewhere. With him, he guessed. "You got your witness, Sheriff." His voice shook as he avoided Portia's eyes.

"Witness? You?" Thompson glared at him.

"Me," he said. He didn't name the others. Bill who stood staring at him, his short beard trembling in time with his wobbling jaw. Gerald Powell, who'd already moved on. Thomas Parsons, who'd turned into a remorseful hermit these last few months.

"Tell me," the sheriff said.

"I was there. We'd got together to sound a warning to the feller setting up to build a fence around the homestead. He, Forth, that is, fired off a warning shot and Jimmy shot him dead. The woman ran out of the house and Herb killed her. Shot her right in the middle of her forehead. The rest of us...me...I...I should've stopped them." Unable to meet Thompson's eyes, he looked down. "I should've stopped them."

Several heartbeats later, Thompson asked, "Where are the bodies?"

Liggin waved in the proper direction. "Out there about a mile. Buried. I reckon I can find the place again."

"That's a lie," Truett shouted. "An out 'n out lie. Sheriff, don't you believe a word he says."

Which is when Bill Arkwright, as woebegone as a man can be, spoke up. "Liggin's not lying. I was there, one of other men. It happened so fast we couldn't stop them. But Liggin's right. We should've. And we should've reported it right away."

"Both of you. Lily-livered chicken shit sons of bitches." Truett reached for his gun again, which Thompson put a stop to in a hurry. But Herb raved on, hanging himself with his own words. "I should've killed Browne too, right then and there. I could see he didn't like the solution to the problem. And you, Arkwright. All of you, standing there with your eyes bugged out so a feller could've wiped 'em off with a broomstick and fussing over a couple no-account sodbusters."

Liggin glanced only once at Portia. It was like she'd been struck dumb. After a while, without another word, she walked back to her house, entered, and closed the door.

SHERIFF THOMPSON SENT LIGGIN and Bill home, after which Liggin, too ashamed to show his face, kept to himself all through June and July. Finally, in dire need of coffee, salt, and flour, he ventured into town, entering the Mickleson store by the back door and staying out of sight. To his astonishment, Mickleson acted as if nothing had changed.

"Have you heard?" he said. "The Truett trial is on Judge Polanski's docket to start in two weeks. Got your summons yet?"

Liggin shook his head, but the very next day a deputy rode out to his place and personally handed him the paperwork.

"Sheriff says to show up in plenty of time and be prepared to tell the truth," the deputy said. "Says he and the prosecutor will do the rest."

It was the longest two weeks of Liggin's life. And, once inside the courtroom, the longest hour as he testified to his guilt of harassing the young farmer and of not saving the couples' lives.

"You're not on trial," the prosecutor said. "At least, not yet. Keep your testimony to the matter at hand, which is finding James Truett and his father, Herbert Truett, each guilty of murder."

Portia Simchuck sat right up front, watching and listening, her expression, when Liggin dared to glance at her, unreadable.

Bill Arkwright's testimony copied his own almost word for word. The Truetts were sentenced to prison, this being cattle country and the jury not prepared to hang two of their own.

As for Liggin, Bill, and Tom Parsons, charges were never filed, the authorities evidently figuring they were properly contrite without the state having to pay their way inside the prison system.

But that didn't mean Liggin was off the hook. Some time or another, he still had Portia Simchuck to face.

He didn't know it, but that face-off came about only a few days later. And she came to him, or as far as the gate leading to his property, upon which he happened to be brushing a coat of linseed oil to preserve the wood.

She sat in a buckboard drawn by that big old plowhorse of hers, one eyebrow arched, and staring first at the gate, then at him. "Why on earth do you have a gate? You have no fence on either side. You said fences aren't welcome around these parts."

He knew his face was turning red. He could feel the heat of it. "I know what I said. The gate, it just marks my property, that's all. I like the look of it."

She studied it a while longer, glancing over to where his small house stood on a knoll. The house had a single story now, but he'd thought it a simple matter to add a second if he ever had a family. "Hmmm," she said. "I think I do, too. Like the look of it, I mean."

"Miss Simchuck..." he started, but she held a finger to her lips to silence him.

"Less said, soonest mended, Mr. Browne. That's what I came to say. And call me Portia."

Liggin hoped he wasn't standing there with his mouth hanging open. Did she mean—? "I'm Liggin," he said.

"I know. And I know with the Truetts gone, what happened to the Forths will never be tolerated in this valley again. Not with the way you and Mr. Arkwright, and even, in the end, Mr. Larson spoke out."

"We were late to it," Liggin said. "For which I'm sorry, we're all sorry, as can be."

"I know you are. You proved that." Portia fell silent then, but she didn't stay that way. Her head cocked to the side. "I've been thinking about this gate of yours. Maybe you could give me some pointers on how to erect one on my property. Show me how it's done."

Liggin's heart gave a big leap. Nearly right out of his chest, he suspected. "Be glad to. Or better yet," and here he turned shy, "maybe I could help you with it."

"Maybe you could," she returned. "And maybe one of these days, a fence on either side of the gate will become acceptable as folks accustom themselves to change. Fences," she added soberly, "make good neighbors."

Liggin nodded soberly. "I read that somewhere. I'm guessing it's true."

"What do you say we give it a test?" Portia said and smiled at him.

So they did.

Hard to Kill

An El Despiadado Story

By Chris Mullen

Hard to Kill

BLACK WATER SPILLING OVER FACE AND INTO MOUTH AND nose; splinters stinging, gouging, beams pounding, drawing blood; lungs burning; shockwaves dissipating, fire spreading, rippling as the man, struggling in weight-lessness is dragged down, down, in the darkness down. He fights, aimlessly surging, eyes fluttering, forced open to the murk, but which way is up? Choking, drowning in the surrounding rush and flow, high-pitched ringing pierces ear and brain, everlasting and yet growing ever faint. The man is consumed, swallowed whole by dark-ness, an ending; then, splashing, bubbling, pulling, his body gives in, limp limbs settle, then drag and slosh.

———

AWAKENED IN A POOL OF SWEAT, the man screamed out, sat up and stretched his fingers before him as if reaching for something, or someone, who was not there.

"¡Ten piedad!"

His voice was hoarse. The room tamped its volume. A lone candle on a mantle near the man's bed slowly melted beneath its flaming hat. A cool draft sent shivers across his skin. A thin sheet draped over his waist was soaked. His legs trembled as did his lips. A knock, like iron on wood, clanged out.

"*Señor. ¿Señor?*"

The man lowered his arms as ambient light from the hall followed the tiny voice through the creaking crack between the door and its frame.

"*¿Está todo bien?*" Then in broken English, "You... okay?"

There was a gentleness carrying the words, a mother's worry with a hint of caution.

When the man did not reply, the door swung open further. Peering in and blocking only a fraction of light, was the face of a little old woman. Shadowed wrinkles trailed across her forehead following the landscape of concern from her gaze.

"Where am I?" the man asked.

Gripping the door, her fingers looked no more than flesh and bone in the dim light.

Who is this woman, the man thought.

Keeping her distance but swinging the door open half-way, the woman revealed her full form. Deep eyes looked on from sunken sockets. Black hair, streaked with strands of white and pulled back from her forehead, formed a tight knot atop her scalp. Her olive skin looked weathered, wise from years of sun and wind. She stood no more than five feet tall. Her frail frame was covered by layers of plain, saggy clothing. It was as if a child stood before the man, yet seasons of age and diminishing posture told a different story.

The man rubbed his eyes, then went to wipe the sweat from his brow, but instead of skin, his palm found satu-rated cloth wrapped around his head. Sliding his fingers along the torn fabric to the back of his head, he flinched where stinging and throbbing screamed out beneath his touch.

Shaken from the twilight of his night terror, the man felt, in his first conscious moments, a wave of nausea wash over him.

The woman walked to his bedside.

"Down, lie down. Ees better for you."

With coarse palms and a gentle touch, she cupped his left arm, coaxing him back on the bed.

"See? Ees better."

The man's head spun. His stomach churned. Flashes of warmth and swirling dizziness became too much for his body to endure. With a sudden jerk, the man rolled away from the woman and retched. A slow burn leaked into his throat as he had very little food in his stomach to mix with what he heaved.

Behind him, the old woman's hands supported him. She patted his back as he convulsed. "Shhh, shhh, shhh." Her voice was soothing, accepting of what was happening without disgust or revulsion.

The man retched again, but this time produced nothing. His empty stomach cramped. The muscles in his neck felt strained. As he found his breath, the suffocating feeling began to fade. Before rolling onto his back, the man licked his lips and spat. Fresh sweat beaded across his brow. The sting and burn from his head resurfaced, but the man withstood a second dive into darkness. He squeezed his eyes closed, trying to make sense of everything. It was not clarity he received behind his pressed lids, for in that moment of pure blackness, he heard the whispers of a new voice rumble from somewhere in the depths within him. One word. A name. Strange as the moment was, he did not recognize it, but he could not ignore what he had heard.

Opening his eyes, the man allowed the woman to help him lie back yet again.

When their eyes met, she smiled. She straightened, as much as her posture would allow, and walked to the lighted mantle across the room. At its base sat a basket woven made from sotol leaves, and from it she pulled a fresh cloth, large enough to replace the sweat-soaked sheet still covering the man.

She returned to the bed, draped the fresh sheet over the man, then reached beneath and removed the soiled one before he could object to her boldness. Without another word, the woman retreated to the half-open door and exited the room. Old hinges, acting like brittle bones, creaked with discomfort as she closed the door behind her.

The sharp flicker of flame cast a ring of dancing light from the mantle to the ceiling, falling into shadow before reaching the man on the bed.

Covered, dry, and left alone, the man focused on his breathing. He leaned left, ensuring his injury didn't press against the meager pillow.

Again, the voice returned, whispering from within. This time, the man held on to the word, the name, memorizing it as if it were the most important thing in the world. Before drifting off to sleep, the man stared at the cracks running along the ceiling like lightning streaking across a deserted sky and mouthed the word one last time. The name lingered, unfamiliar, yet it felt like it belonged to him in a way he could not explain.

"Mata."

———

STREAKS of golden sunlight poked their way through imperfections in a *serape* hung in front of the only window in the room. The colorful weave and blended patterns glowed with brilliance like the coat Jacob gifted to Joseph as it blocked the sun's rays. The man sat on the edge of the bed, bare feet on the floor, hands rubbing his knees, and mind grappling with how he came to be in this room, and most important, who he was.

"Mata." He spoke to the room like whispering secrets to an old friend. "If that is a part of who I am," he murmured, almost hoping it would unlock something within him, "let the name remain."

Sliding his hands from his knees, he braced himself on the mattress. Moving with the slow, creaking effort of an old man, he took a deep breath and discovered a new sting beneath his left arm as he stood. His muscles groaned in protest, not just stiff from time in bed, but from deeper wounds only now awakening. A cool rush met his skin as the sheet fell to the floor.

Do not come in now, old woman, Mata thought. *You will get more than you bargained for.*

Mata looked around the room. The candle on the mantel had burned down into a pool of wax. The door remained closed, triggering more questions for which he had no answers. The window covering exuded a warmth that felt inviting.

He took a first step, wobbling under a wave of dizziness that swept over him. His heart pounded, each beat growing heavier, more insistent. Steadying himself, Mata focused on breathing, each breath easing his dizziness. His heart still pounded in his chest, but gradually, the rapid thudding began to soften, matching the rhythm of his breath. He felt the tension in his limbs begin to ease, the weight of his own body become bearable again. The fog in his mind began to lift, and with it, his focus returned.

Each step was a victory, each movement toward the

window brought him closer to discovering more about where he was. On ginger feet, he stopped within arm's reach of the *serape*. Before pulling it aside, he listened. As he leaned closer still, the warm fabric brushed the side of his head, then pressed against the thin windowpane. Everything outside seemed still.

Twisting around, Mata used his right hand to pull the *serape* aside. Light poured through the window, flooding the room with a warm, golden glow. Tiny specks of dust hung in the air, sparkling like delicate snowflakes suspended in sunlight. He glanced out, first from the edge of the window, then stepped fully into its frame, taking in the view. Had he held any expectations, they would have crumbled into disappointment. Beyond the room, desolation stretched to the horizon, rolling from peak to valley, then across a vast expanse, which he could only assume was where water overtook the land.

"Where am I?"

The words fell from his lips, weighted with uncertainty. Mata stepped away from the window, letting the *serape* fall back into place. He turned and faced the door, then looked down at his naked body. His eyes drifted to the basket, from which the woman had pulled the cloth to cover him on the bed last night, and he saw a pair of old blue jeans and a plain white t-shirt folded in its center. Reaching down, he took the clothes to the bed and sat.

One leg at a time, he stepped into the pants, pulling them up to his thighs. With a careful bounce and a tug at the waistband, he pulled the jeans the rest of the way, fastening the button and zipping the fly. He reached for the shirt, then paused, letting it drop onto the bed beside him. Looking down at his body, he ran his fingers over his skin, tracing the tattoos that formed a somber mosaic across his chest and arms. Skulls with blades stabbing out from their eye sockets covered his right shoulder. A black scorpion, its claws shaped like daggers, coiled around his forearm, ending with a woman's torso emerging from the grotesque creature, and wielding a foreign-looking sword. Tiny crosses etched into the scales on the scorpion's belly, and a weeping Virgin Mary carved into his chest over his heart, added a religious undertone to the story inked into his skin.

"If I am Mata, then I am this man. What life have I lived that I would choose to celebrate it with such images?"

He swept his palm over his heart, as if trying to wipe away the tears from the Virgin Mary's cheeks. The ink was a part of him, and though he still did not understand, nor accept what mystery the artwork might represent, no amount of rubbing could erase the deeds he might have been responsible for in the past. The permanence of the tattoos mirrored the weight of the unknown sins that haunted him.

Mata grabbed the shirt from the mattress and put it on. The neckline brushed against the wound on his head, irritating it and causing a dull throb to pulse beneath the cloth wrap. He used both hands to widen the shirt's neckline, allowing for an easy glide past his injury. Before dropping his hands to his side, he straightened his stretched-out collar, then brushed his hands against his face. Stubble prickled his palms, raising yet another question. *How long have I been here?*

Hungry for answers, Mata glanced around the room and found a pair of sandals, then held one to the underside of his foot to gauge the size.

"These must belong to a giant," he muttered, finding that the sandals were three sizes too big.

With no other choice, he slipped into them, stood, and walked to the door. As he reached for the handle, he paused, reflecting on all he had discovered about himself and the little he knew about the old woman who had been caring for him. Should he have reason for concern? How did he get here? Mata tightened his grip on the iron handle, thumbed the latch, and slowly opened the door.

———

MATA STEPPED into the hall and closed the door behind him. Light seeped in from a window at the far end, casting a dim sheen that extended down the hall and spilled into an adjoining room. Across from his room, another door stood, leading to a second chamber. He stepped closer, tilting his head to listen, but heard nothing. He tried the handle, but it was locked.

Still achy and in need of further healing, Mata continued down the short hallway and peered into the open room. It was well cared for, containing modest furniture: a desk, two chairs, a table with a six-arm candelabra at its center, and a small bookshelf placed beneath a large window. Taking a second, more thorough glance around the room, Mata spotted simple yet quaint aesthetic touches of charm.

"The old woman likes her things," he whispered.

Curious about one item in particular, Mata walked to the bookshelf and picked up a book that lay open across the top. Holding it carefully, he flipped to the front without losing the page and smiled, though he was not sure why he felt such a connection to this piece.

"Dante's Inferno," Mata read.

Turning a few more pages, he stopped and read aloud.

"Nel mezzo del cammin di nostra vita,
mi ritrovai per una selva oscura,
ché la diritta via era smarrita."

"In the middle of the journey of our life,
I came to myself, in a dark wood,
for the straight way had been lost."

Mata held the book, cradling it with admiration for the words—how they resonated, how they spoke to him, and for reasons unknown, how they made him feel.

"Canto I: The Dark Wood." Mata set the book down where it had been. "Let your journey begin Dante, as they all do, with a first step."

Mata turned around, taking in the entirety of the room. He saw a painting hung on the far wall. Strokes of watercolor brushed across its rough, textured paper depicted a church courtyard surrounding a single statue of a young girl holding her hand to the sky as if calling a bird to perch on her tiny fingers. Circling the room, Mata noticed an old black-and-white photo lying alone on the desktop, its edges frayed from age. Set within the image, well-worn and smudged by years of fingerprints, was a seated man with a young girl standing next to him. The man had a thick, salt-sprinkled mustache and wore wire-rimmed glasses set upon a creased and pitted face. The young girl's arms were wrapped around the man's neck while leaning into him, her smile beaming with admiration and comfort. Mata admired the photograph a moment longer, then turned and faced an arched entrance to a small kitchen. Next to the entryway, hanging at eye level, was a small, framed painting of San Rafael Arcángel, and on it hung *milagros*—small hearts, a starburst, a pair of hands linked together as if in prayer, a concerned face, and a cross held by fingers—each affixed to chains of varied length. Mata lifted a hand and touched the dangling pieces one by one, wondering how each simple religious artifact found meaning to the old woman. He rubbed the small cross between his thumb and index finger, feeling the cool, smooth design along its silver surface.

"This is a cross worth bearing," he whispered.

A calm warmth fell over him, the present slipping away as his mind wandered back, back to a place that felt like home, where families gathered under the sun, and children's laughter echoed across fields. He could almost smell the familiar scents of cooking fires and hear the quiet hum of contentment. Small, joyful voices called out to each other, as tender, older eyes watched from afar. Running and playing, smiles unfolding, dark eyes pooling, and a group of boys, tangled together in a wrestling match of playful arms and shuffling feet, and from within, a new voice called out. *"Carlos, what are you doing? Come and play."*

"Carlos...Mata." His lips parted, mouthing the names.

A crack like thunder split the air, shattering the dream and jerking Mata back into the present. His eyes snapped open, his heart pounding in his chest. The sound rumbled in his ears, rattling through his bones. He leaned against the wall, steadying himself as the echoes of the past and present collided.

The image was gone, but the thunder crack boomed out again, this time reverberating throughout the house. His body tensed as tremors coursed through him, his muscles taut with the sudden rush of adrenaline. Beneath the shock, there was something else—a sense of recognition, as if the sound, the feeling, had stirred something long-buried inside him.

He ran into the kitchen and looked out a small window. Standing alone a hundred yards down a dusty road, the old woman's figure appeared minuscule against the rising backdrop of jagged rocks and winding hills. She seemed even more insignificant as she faced an old pickup truck, from which several men were hopping out of the bed and cab and walking toward her, but her boldness reached heights where birds had yet to soar. The long, dark barrel of a shotgun angled to the sky exploded a third time, jolting the woman as she pulled the trigger. Mata counted six men, none of whom were dissuaded by her show of force. Like hungry wolves, they continued their advance.

Mata wound his way through the kitchen to a door that led outside and into the dirt-laden yard. His head swirled from a mix of adrenaline and injury, and while the sunlight made it easy to see for miles, its brightness attacked Mata's vision causing him to squint and slow his pace. He heard shouts from the men, each taking their turn to berate the old woman. Laughter followed until the resounding voice of one man bellowed above all the others. His words were demanding, his tone deliberate and threatening. Mata listened, with hands on knees until his eyes adjusted to the intensity of the outdoors.

Below the murmur of the men, the old woman's voice responded without a hint of fear. She scolded them, waving the shotgun in the air, then lowered her weapon and took aim on the man leading the others.

A hush fell over the group, but the old woman raised her voice, continuing her volley until...*crack*!

Smoke swirled from the barrel of a pistol fired from behind the man who had confronted the old woman. She dropped the shotgun and crumpled to the ground, her body swaying with the force of the blast. The men turned to look at the shooter, falling into a raucous growl of salacious victory, while the man who led the charge stepped forward and looked down on the woman.

Mata's muscles felt heavy, making it harder to move. His mind screamed at him to do something. Hide. Run. *Fight*. Don't just stand and stare like a misguided and confused fool. But that was what he was, at that moment.

The roar of the men followed them back into the bed of the pickup. The man standing over the old woman's body turned and spotted Mata. His gaze lingered before he stepped away. Instead of alarming his crew, he raised his hand to his forehead and gave a two-finger salute before smiling and returning to the passenger side of the truck. Upon getting in, he dangled his arm out of the window, casting a lasting stare at Mata as the truck turned around and drove away. Dust rose from the road, swirling in tufts of brown.

Cursing himself a coward, his muscles gave way to his worry for the woman. What started as a jog turned into a sprint, his oversized sandals slipping off as he increased his speed. Seconds stretched into what felt like minutes. The distance between him and the woman seemed to grow with every step, instead of shrinking as it should.

When he came upon the woman, it was the blood that first caught his eye. She lay on her side with her back to Mata but he could see the growing pool of red mixing with the earth. Sliding to a stop and ignoring the screaming pains from his own body, he reached out to the old woman. He placed his palms on her side and rolled her onto her back, cradling her as she had done for him. Trails of blood escaped the corners of her mouth. Her once beautiful olive skin had turned gray, wilting before his eyes. With labored breaths, she forced her eyes upon Mata and found the strength to curl her lips into a smile.

"Do not waste your energy on me," Mata whispered. "Come, let me carry you to the house."

Strangled words bubbled from her throat in rasps of broken English and Spanish.

"No...no. *Voy a casa.* Home...to...God."

"Who did this? Who were those men?"

"No...worry for me. *Su tiempo...llegará.* An angel... will...cast them...into fire."

The old woman's body shuddered. With waning tenderness, she brought her wrinkled hand to Mata, cupping his palm in hers. Mata's vision blurred as the weight of his actions caught up with his broken body. The pain surged through him, like a thousand trumpets blaring in unison, but the relentless throbbing at the back of his head was what finally brought him down. His strength gave out, and he slumped forward. A dark shroud seemed to fall over them, carrying the old woman away, leaving Mata to rest upon her still, lifeless form.

———

A GUST of wind preceding an offshore storm awakened Mata. The sky was dimming into twilight, growing darker still across an angry horizon. Pushing himself into a seated position, he looked around. At first glance, Mata was disoriented. The feeling was quick to pass when he felt the cooling body of the old woman nuzzled up against his leg.

"Who would do such a thing?"

It was a simple question with a simple answer, but to Mata, its complexities were rooted not only in the who and why? Was she killed because of him?

The night was dark and bleak. Mata returned the old woman to the house, transporting her body in a wheelbarrow he found leaning against an outside wall. He had tried to carry her, but his strength had not fully returned. Each time he lifted her, a wave of nausea and dizziness swept over him. It was less than respectable, but the wheelbarrow was his only option.

Once back at the kitchen, he laid her body on a blanket and dragged the blanket through the house to the room in which he had slept. With a final heave, Mata lifted her onto the bed, then sat down next to her until his head and stomach stopped spinning. He felt exhausted, but there was more to do. Arranging her body on the bed and placing the picture of the young girl with the mustachioed man between her resting palms, Mata covered the old woman's body. Atop the sheet, he placed a chain with the hand and cross *milagro*, then pulled a chair next to the bed and sat with her in silence for a time.

Darkness fell and with it came a solitude more uncomfortable than he had ever experienced. Thoughts raced through his mind, searching for answers.

Carlos. Mata. Carlos Mata. Sinister tattoos. Quips of playful childhood memories.

Thunder rumbled, causing Mata to stand and walk to the window. He pulled the *serape* aside and watched the night explode with flashes of web-like strands of lighting. Rolling thunder followed, sometimes blending into one long, tumultuous, skyward groan. As he stood with eyes glued to the storm, the intensity of the flashes increased, the rumble and roar of thunder amplified, and from within him, a faint voice called out.

"The darkness is not just out there; it is within us, too."

Chills rippled along Mata's neck, but a sense of purpose had awakened as well.

"Those words," he said. "I know those words."

Mata turned around and faced the bed. The old woman's form molded the thin sheet draped over her, the image looking like a sarcophagus carved in honor of a powerful deity.

"How I got here remains a mystery," Mata said as he stepped closer to the bed. "And your kindness can never be repaid, old woman. Rest now, for I sense an awakening inside of me. It is one that I cannot yet explain, but more so, something I feel." He paused, his voice lowering in reverence of his next words. "It has been said that the darkest places in hell are reserved for those who maintain their neutrality in times of moral crisis. Let that not be me. When morning comes, I will find the men who did this. *Non ragioniam di lor, ma guarda e passa.*" Mata smiled, adding softly, "It appears we are not so different, you and me. *Let us not speak of them, but look and pass on.*"

———

MORNING CAME, and with it rose a fiery sun whose alpenglow flooded the land, crashing over the faces of the rising rocks and withering crags that stood before the old woman's house. There, in its wash, stood Carlos Mata, his face absorbing the first heat of day. Squinting, he fixed his gaze on the vast cascade of birthing light.

As the night had come and gone, so had the fog that obscured his being. Mata was a man of consequences, his life bearing more scars than tattoos could cover, his soul balanced between the struggles of morality and a deep, sinister ambition in which even the dark was afraid, challenged what deeds the day would bring. Glinting in the early light and swaying beneath his fingers, a silver scorpion dangled at the end of a relic chain.

As Mata made a final pass through the house, it was this *milagro de escorpión* that captured his attention, drawing him to pause before the old woman's shrine. Before, he had overlooked it while admiring the other charms that she had carefully arranged. But this morning it called to him, as though it too had a purpose beyond the walls that entombed her spirit. When he removed it from the wall, warmth surged from his fingertips to his chest. As his eyes traced its small, curling tail and razor-sharp claws, he felt a connection— one that bound him to the woman, to the earth, and to a power he had both revered and feared throughout his life.

Mata slipped the scorpion into his front pocket and turned away from the rising sun. He wore a fresh black t-shirt, but his jeans were on their second day. On his feet were a pair of old boots he found beside the wheelbar-row, worn and cracked, their soles heavy with mud. Like the sandals, they were three sizes too big, but they would have to do for now.

The clothes and the scorpion charm were the only things Mata took from the house. He considered carrying the old woman's shotgun, but as a stranger to more than just himself, he decided it was better to remain that way, avoiding any reason to cause alarm among those he might encounter. He had no money, no identification, but held something more powerful—a purpose, and a pulse of memories churning within, waiting to erupt.

Without looking back, he headed out, walking along the dirt road as morning awakened around him. His mind kept pace with his steps, remaining alert as the house grew further behind him.

The road wound south, rising and falling with the terrain. As he climbed, open water stretched to the west, its smooth surface gleaming like glass in the distance. After witnessing the turbulent storm the night before, he imagined the stark shift from chaos to calm—a theme that seemed to hold more meaning for Mata these days. He glanced to the right from time to time, but each look revealed the same view: rolling rocks, towering cacti spread out like disorganized telephone poles, creosote bushes, and patchy coppices of mesquite and Palo Verde trees. To Mata, it was desolation, a nothingness that stretched for miles.

The heat intensified as the morning wore on. Before

long, Mata's shirt clung to his neck and armpits. Sweat beaded along his brow and in the stubble of his cheeks, but he took no notice. His attention had shifted elsewhere, drawn to something new.

As the road dipped in elevation, a small building came into view. A pair of horses were tied to a corner, shaded for now by the building. Two vehicles were parked out front: an old model baby blue Ford station wagon and a rust-covered VW bus.

Mata covered the distance quickly. The horses caught his scent as he neared, their ears pricking up in alarm. They shuffled their hooves, eyes fixed on him, cautious of the unfamiliar smell and wary of the approaching stranger.

Both cars looked like they could fall apart at any moment. Passing between them, he glanced in each of their windows.

"Filth," he whispered to himself.

Looking away, he spotted a small sign nailed to the wall next to a door: *Chato's Cantina*. His boots rattled the wooden planks as he stepped onto the porch and across to the door. As he reached for the handle, a large cockroach scuttled between his feet, disappearing into a crack in the floorboards.

"Are there more like you inside?" he muttered to the insect. "I imagine so."

Mata pulled the door open, inviting himself in.

———

A DANK, arid smell filled his nose as he stepped into the dimly lit cantina. A small bar made of fifty-gallon barrels standing on end and topped with shoddy plywood served as the focal point of the room. Dusty tables and a mix of rickety chairs stood like day laborers mingling as they waited for the next *camioneta* to swing by and whisk them away.

Mata stepped through the room and approached the bar. Three empty tequila bottles littered the warping countertop. An unopened bottle of whiskey lay on its side at the opposite end. Mata noticed the juxtaposition of each of the bottles.

"A standoff won by the Mexicans, it seems."

A blackened doorway behind the bar led to another room, where a frustrated voice rumbled from the darkness, then called out to Mata.

"Oye, no estamos abiertos."

Footsteps advanced in the darkness until a man appeared in the doorway. His ragged hair, slicked back and receding, hung to his shoulders. His face was etched with age and bad luck, a web of wrinkles and scars crisscrossing his cheeks and the bridge of his nose.

"We are clos't," the man said again, this time in English.

Mata turned and looked at the exit, then swiveled his head and locked eyes with the man.

"You are Chato, I presume?"

"Sí. Who the hell are ju, *cabrón?"*

Ignoring the insult, Mata continued. "I am looking for some men, one man in particular. A man who runs with wolves."

"Wolves?" Chato laughed, turning away. "Ju shoul' no be looking for men like that, I think. These *wolves* will kill you dead, *ese."* He paused, picking up and opening the bottle of whiskey then slugged down a gulp. Wiping his mouth with his arm, he continued. "I shoul' know, but like I say, we are…"

Chato's left eye twitched when his glare met Mata's

once again. He looked closer, then retreated a step, both eyes widening in surprise. He raised a palm to his chin, his face changing to a look of concern.

"*¡Dios mío!* Ju are..." Chato lowered his hand. "Ju are him. *El Despiadado*?"

El Despiadado? Mata pondered, his glare darkening, mirroring Chato's concern.

"Oh, I will tell, *señor*. What ju want to know."

"Where can I find this man?"

"*Sí, señor*." Chato spoke with an unsettling tic. "The man...is Santos Campos. He's...the boss. *El jefe de Los Diablos del Desierto*. They are no far from here, jus' down the road. Ju can no miss the house. There is a red face painted on the side, but you should no go. They are dangerous men, *señor*. *Los Diablos del Desierto* son *muy peligrosos*."

He paused to take a nervous swig from the bottle. Mata watched Chato's arm shake, questioning the barkeep's sudden change of demeanor.

El Despiadado—*"The Merciless." Am I this man to him?*

Chato set the bottle down on the plywood bar top, then crossed his arms over his chest. He looked uncomfortable. "Why ju looking for them?"

Mata leaned on the bar, nodding his head for the man to come closer, as if he had a secret to share. When Chato was close enough, Mata whispered.

"If they wish to call themselves devils, I intend to bring hell to them."

Chato's jaw dropped under the weight of Mata's words. Mata straightened, then took a step away from the counter and looked around the empty cantina once again. Chato uncrossed his arms and walked around the end of the bar.

"There are many, *señor*, and ju are only one."

"You are right, I am the only one, but you know who I am. You said it yourself."

Chato nodded. "*Sí, sí.* El Despiadado."

Mata squinted, his lips curling into a knowing smile. The name had yet to have meaning to him, though the words themselves carried a danger any man could sense. Glancing over his shoulder, he motioned to the door.

"The cars outside...where are the keys?"

Chato cocked his head, at first not seeming to understand the question.

Mata held a palm out, flexing his fingers and his latent, forgotten darkness, commanding the man to help him further. Chato's eyes sank when he realized what was being asked of him. He stepped behind the bar, reaching for something out of sight.

Mata watched until Chato's hands disappeared, then sprang at him with a speed and ferocity that even surprised himself. With one hand, Mata grabbed Chato around the throat and slammed him into the wall behind the bar. Chato gasped. His eyes bulged. He flailed his arms, but did not strike Mata. Instead, he shook his left hand, jingling a keychain in his fingers.

Mata glared at him. Like the sharp clash of flint and steel, sparks surged through Mata, igniting a heat deep inside. His grip tightened around Chato's throat as he watched the man's face flush a deep red.

Lips smacking, gasping for life, Chato struggled to hold on to what little air he had left. And in that moment, Mata discovered something new—*pleasure*. Holding this man's life in his hands felt...good.

Chato wheezed, shaking his hand and jingling the keys in desperation. Mata broke free of the sinful trance and loosened his grip. He plucked the keys from Chato's fingers and stepped back as the barkeep slumped to the floor. Gasping and holding his neck, tears rippling over the wrinkles and scars on his face, Chato curved his lips into a smile as if proud of his contribution. Though, behind that smile, and aware of El Despiadado's reputation, he silently celebrated being left alive.

Mata held the keys up and returned the sentiment before turning around and exiting the cantina. As the door closed behind him, Mata heard Chato's raspy voice call out.

"Do no tell them it was me."

———

DUST ROSE behind the rumbling Ford station wagon as Mata searched for the house Chato had described. The vinyl seats were torn at the seams, the rearview mirror lay discarded in the back seat, and the passenger side door panel was missing, as were the door handle and the window crank, but the car ran well enough to keep him from walking. As an added bonus, he discovered an old Smith & Wesson .38 Special in the glove compartment, its cylinder loaded with four rounds.

Less than two miles from the cantina, Mata spied a house with a faded, red-painted face on the side.

"Just as Chato said."

He pulled to the side of the road, still over two hundred yards away, and watched.

———

THE SUN BEAT down on the station wagon, turning the interior into a simmering oven. Sweat soaked into Mata's clothing. He had tried the air conditioning, but like the rest of the car, it was old and barley operable, blowing only a stiff breeze that felt warmer than the air outside the car. To conserve gas, he shut off the engine while he waited.

It was approaching noon, and Mata had yet to see any activity, so he decided to move in for a closer look. The car sputtered as he turned the key, then choked itself to life as he pumped the gas. Dropping the car into gear, he rolled further down the road toward the house.

As he drove past, he eyed the front of the house. White paint flecked away from its cinderblock body beneath. Its corrugated metal roof showed signs of rust staining the surface from its peak to the eaves. Crinkled aluminum-covered windows. Mata was about to give up on the house and resume his search elsewhere when he spotted a truck parked along the far side. It resembled the one that had driven away with the men after they killed the old woman.

"Yes," Mata muttered through gritted teeth. "This is the lair of *El Diablo*."

The brakes squeaked as he slowed the car to a stop. Shifting into reverse, Mata backed up until the front of the station wagon was even with the entrance to the property. The house stood forty yards from the dirt road. He focused on the front door, keying in on a large iron knocker shaped like a cross.

A fitting symbol to announce me, he thought.

"And for me, as well," a new, deeper voice echoed from inside of him.

Mata froze. Was the voice real? Was he hearing things? Could this be a side-effect of the injury to the back of his head? It had not bothered him to this point today, but was it signaling him to pass by and find a place to rest?

He closed his eyes and inhaled a fresh breath. His lungs stretched, fulfilled. A subtle sting along his ribs reminded him that he was far from recovered, but it also told him he was alive. Behind the blackness of his eyelids, he found a calming moment, but it was the unexpected voice from within that made him thrust his eyes open and shift the car into drive.

"El Despiadado."

The voice, the words, both were as clear as day as if he had whispered them to himself.

He tucked the .38 into his belt, slammed the gas, and drove ahead, the deteriorated Ford's hood ornament locked dead center with the front door in its sights.

The engine revved louder as Mata pressed the accelerator to the floor. Rocks popped beneath his tires. A chicken squawked, narrowly avoiding the speeding car. His heart pounded in his chest, in his head, in the depths of his forgotten, tainted soul.

He sped on, closer with each second, driving faster toward the house. With only moments to spare, the front door flew open, and two men hurried outside, rifles in hand. They were too late to act, but just in time to confirm that Mata—or El Despiadado, whoever was driving— was heading for the right place.

———

THE IMPACT WAS SUDDEN, the effects instantaneous. Mata braced himself as the wide, steel bumper caught both men just below the waist, dragging them with it as the front end of the station wagon barreled into the threshold of the house. Cinderblocks exploded into clouds of choking dust, shooting concrete fragments in all directions, breaking glass and piercing skin. The front door was ripped from its hinges, snagging one man's foot as it was pulled beneath the car. His body followed in a vicious tangling of broken bone, high-pitched screams, and steaming metal. The other man slammed face first onto the hood, both legs snapping above his knees as the car pinned him between the jagged rubble and its steel frame. The engine surged as pistons fired even after the car buried itself in the house.

Surprised shouts echoed beyond the dust cloud in the entryway. Mata forced the driver's door open and got out of the car. He pulled the .38 from his belt as distant chants from inside of him urged him onward.

Pleas for help screeched out from beneath the station wagon in painful bursts of desperate, dying wheezes. A third man rushed out of the house, spraying bullets from a machine pistol into the windshield as he jumped onto the hood of the car. Mata kept low and out of sight until the rapid bursts halted and the man was out of ammunition. With a steady hand, Mata raised up and fired two controlled shots at the man. The first bullet tore through the man's chest, exiting through his back in a red spray of searing flesh and torn cloth. He kept his footing, though looked more like a collapsing marionette trying to balance on the station wagon's hood. Mata's second shot ripped through the man's neck, the bullet clipping his vertebrae. The man's body convulsed, his head lobbing forward, held in place by only skin and spared muscle, before he tumbled to the ground.

Mata crouched behind the rear wheel, taking cover as two rifle barrels broke through the aluminum-covered windows of the house and opened fire. He listened as frantic, angry voices inside the house screamed at one another. He looked at the .38 in his hand.

Two shots left.

The old station wagon *tinged* as bullets penetrated its metal body. Air *swished* as the tires popped under the assault. Beneath the car, he heard gasping and ducked his head to look. When his eyes met those of the man who had been sucked underneath upon impact, he felt two things—sudden remorse for the man and a rumbling in his core, as if Mata had just begun to feed a starving beast.

He gazed at the man as bullets continued to fly overhead. Blood seeped from his tear ducts and nose. His head was misshapen, his skull fractured by the trauma. Mata's eyes trailed from the man to the gun he saw poking out beneath him.

When he spoke, Mata did not recognize the pitch in his own voice, but its delivery felt natural, and to some degree, comforting.

"Poor man, you will not be needing that any longer."

Mata, El Despiadado, reached for the weapon.

The man screamed as the gun was pulled out from under him, each tug jostling his body, firing unimaginable pain into his mortal wounds.

"*¡Héctor!*" a voice from inside the house called out. "*¡Héctor, maldito! ¿Dónde estás?*"

Mata looked at the man, whom he presumed was Hector, and shook his head.

"It is a pity. You picked the wrong people, *mi amigo*. You are paying the price, but your debt will linger with you long after you have expired."

Hector's bloody eyes bulged. His cheeks puffed as if he wanted to reply, but darkness claimed him first.

Mata pulled the gun free. He leaned back against the tire and inspected the weapon.

"Ruger Mini-14, tactical rifle. Quite the piece for such a man." He removed the magazine. "Thirty-round capacity, but you are half spent on me already," Mata said, addressing the weapon.

Another round pinged off the station wagon above Mata's head. He replaced the magazine and shifted into a crouching position.

"It is enough," he told himself, speaking more freely now as if someone else were there.

Keeping low, Mata moved to the front of the car. Even with the house and kneeling on rubble, he saw that the two rifles held their position at the window, their muzzles erupting with a constant volley of gunfire.

"Six men killed the woman, not just the one."

Mata looked out through the gaping hole in the house to where the first of the men responsible for the old woman's death lay broken and still.

"Three more to go, but I have time and patience for more if any choose to get in the way."

Mata nodded, agreeing with himself, then tightened his grip around his newfound weapon. Fear eluded him. With each forward step, he felt an unexplainable comfort, a satisfaction growing as if a void within him was filling with long forgotten meaning.

He crept into the house, following the blasts and chattering voices to the end of a short hallway that opened into a great room. He spied the shooters at the windows. Beyond them, leaning on a kitchen counter, cowering out of the line of fire, were two other men, one of whom Mata recognized immediately.

"I see you," he whispered, El Despiadado's voice taking more control with each word spoken. "You may not have been the one to pull the trigger, but you are the man I seek. I will save you for last."

Lifting the Ruger to his shoulder, Mata felt as if the weapon had become an extension of himself. He took aim, and through the natural ease of his movements, the crosshairs fell into place. Two bursts were all he needed to kill the men at the window, but he had to be quick. He was still unsure if there were others in the house he could not see.

Mata pulled the trigger. The first round exploded

from the chamber with a rattling *bang,* cutting through the air and hitting his target between the shoulder blades. A second, immediate trigger pull saw the top of the same man's head separate from his body like a Frisbee-shaped UFO taking flight.

With fluid movements, Mata adjusted his aim and fired at the second man before the first had even hit the floor. Three quick shots to center mass destroyed his chest cavity, knocking him off his feet and through the already fractured window.

Mata shifted toward the kitchen, searching for the next soul to reap. The men had ducked out of sight, but he could hear their shuffling bodies and frightened grunts as they scrambled along the floor.

The vibrations from firing the rugged weapon sent adrenaline pumping through Mata's body. When the shooting stopped and as the euphoric feeling began to subside, he craved more. Each pull of the trigger was awakening him bit by bit. He felt more control and at the same time, a loss of connection. His thoughts were overrun with harsh, abrasive needs. His actions, while fulfilling, felt like they belonged to somebody else. Everything was wonderful and uncontrolled at once. The rush opened subconscious floodgates, unleashing the full force of the merciless man buried deep within him.

El Despiadado stood wielding the carbine, sweeping the room from the dead men plastered against the windows to the ones hiding in the kitchen. The problem was, killing these men had been too easy. Having only just become self-aware, he found it dissatisfying to glide through a hunt where other, more creative means of killing waited to be explored. He lowered his weapon to his waist and walked to the kitchen. A large cooking island stood in the center of the room, acting as the only barrier between the men and certain death.

"Do come out, my friends. It will be better for you both if we look upon each other like men, and not like the dogs whose lives are meant to be spent on the floor."

"*¡Que te jodan! ¡Vete al carajo antes de que te mate!*"

"No, my friend. You cannot kill that which has already been to hell." El Despiadado entered the kitchen, his oversized boots thudding on the wooden floor. "Come, let me have a look at you."

Profane grumbles sizzled between the cowering men. When neither showed themselves, El Despiadado offered encouragement.

"Suit yourselves, but you may find that I am quite persuasive."

Aiming low, he fired at the corner of the island. Wood exploded as the round tore a hole in the floor. He fired again, blowing away a portion of the island.

"There are rats in the kitchen, it seems," El Despiadado said, hearing the men scrambling along the kitchen floor.

He fired again. The center of the island crackled, sending shards of decorative tile soaring like tiny daggers throughout the kitchen. One man screamed and raised a hand into view. El Despiadado took aim and fired. The bullet severed the man's hand at the wrist. Two fingers catapulted backward, landing on the destroyed island countertop. The rest of his digits and the bony remnants of his hand splattered along the far kitchen wall. A quick glance made El Despiadado grin as he watched the stump of the hand sliding down the wall with its middle finger—the only one left—standing erect in one final defiant gesture.

Screams from both men filled the kitchen.

"*¡Basta, basta, BASTA!*"

El Despiadado lowered his weapon, taking a moment to enjoy the pleading cries.

"Stop! Enough! *Pinche cabrón*, we are coming out!"

————

EL DESPIADADO'S fingertips tingled with anticipation, his eyes squinting, focusing ahead in wait of the men to show themselves. The first man, the leader, the one whose two-fingered salute as he left the old woman's body in the dust was still fresh in El Despiadado's mind, in Mata's mind, rose from behind the island.

"There you are," El Despiadado said. "On the outside, you are not an ugly man. I am sure there is a mother out there who still has some affection for you, but I would wager that she knows not what she loves. You must be Santos Campos."

"You're a dead man."

El Despiadado smirked.

"Take a look around, my friend. It is not I who presently begs for mercy at the gates of hell. You are the only one left standing." El Despiadado aimed the carbine at the man. "Either you are or you are not Santos Campos. Maybe I should just call you *Cholo.*"

Silence between the men offered its own reply.

"Then it is settled. Pick up your man, Cholo. I want to talk with him next."

Cholo bent at the knees and lowered his hands out of El Despiadado's sight.

"Do not make a poor decision, my friend. You are not that fast, and I can tell by the look in your eye that you have already accepted defeat."

Cholo broke eye contact to look down at the man beside him.

"Get up, Chuy."

"*¡No puedo!*"

Chuy's voice carried pain and desperation in it.

"*¡Chinga!* Chuy, now!"

Cholo's body jerked as he grabbed him by the arm and pulled him up. Chuy's face was flushed of color. He held the bloody stump of his arm against his stomach, crossing his other arm over the open wound. Unable to keep his footing, Chuy leaned on the counter for support, then screamed out as he caught the weight of his body with both arms. His red-soaked shirt slopped on the fragmented tile counter, and red pulsed out from beneath him.

"Chuy, Chuy, Chuy." El Despiadado clicked his tongue. "That looks like it really hurts."

Chuy cried out, his sobbing breaths sounding more pitiful with each frantic convulsion. Cholo slammed his fist on the counter.

"*Pendejo!* You invade my house, kill my friends. Who do you think you are?"

El Despiadado paused, reflecting on words he had heard spoken just yesterday between a man and a dying woman. "*An angel...will cast them...into fire.*" Pursing his lips, finding he was content with the memory and his reply, Mata answered, his eyes locked on Cholo's.

"I must be an angel."

"*¿Un ángel? ¡Vete al carajo!* You are more like a demon from hell, *pendejo!*"

Chuy swayed next to Cholo as weakness and blood loss began to overtake him.

"You may be right, but it is you who is a killer."

Cholo laughed, his face contorting with baffled amusement. "And you aren't?"

El Despiadado stepped closer. "No, my friend. I am a deliverer." His jaw tightened, as did his glare. "You killed the old woman. I saw you and your men cut her down and leave her without a second thought. What was she to you?"

Cholo lifted his chin, frowning with pride.

"Nothing." He spoke through clenched teeth.

"Nothing?" El Despiadado echoed.

"She was just another *pinche* bitch that did not know her place. Not even after we killed her husband."

El Despiadado glanced at the boots on his feet, three sizes too big.

Cholo noticed a sliver of vulnerability in El Despiadado.

"Yeah," Cholo continued, seizing what he thought was the high ground. "The man, *El Estúpido*, he tried to stand up to us, too, so we had our fun with him. Not like the old woman. She was lucky. Chuy here saw to that before we had a chance to do anything else."

El Despiadado turned his attention to Chuy. With slow, subtle steps, he rounded the island, passing through the kitchen and past a fully stocked butcher's block.

"It was you, then? You were the one who pulled the trigger."

"Yeah, man. Vicious, no?" Cholo said, celebrating his friend with unfounded, rising confidence.

With one swift motion, El Despiadado grabbed Chuy by the collar and hurled him backward. His arms flailed outward, the bloody stump sprinkling the kitchen with fresh droplets of red. He screamed, his voice hitting pitches high enough to make ears bleed. Cholo stood motionless, stunned by the sudden action, and watched Chuy get slammed onto the surface of the butcher's block.

El Despiadado dropped the carbine on the kitchen floor and reached for a cleaver embedded in the wooden cutting surface. Chuy cried out, horrified delirium replacing his painful screams.

Leaning over Chuy, El Despiadado growled at him, his voice turning feral, his eyes catching fire.

"You should not have done such a thing!"

With ravaging force, he thrust the cleaver down, up and down, again and again, chopping away at Chuy until only a gurgling mess of sliced flesh and carved bone remained where his torso and head had once been.

Cholo yelled out, his voice edging on sheer terror. "¡Estás loco, tú eres el diablo!"

El Despiadado dropped the cleaver and turned to face the terrified Cholo. His clothes were riddled with blood. Lines of red slid down his face, around his eyes, dripping from his chin. His hands were grimy with slaughter spatter.

If Cholo was to have any chance at all, this was it. Standing before him, El Despiadado was unarmed, but he was more than a man. Fueled by an evil even the gang leader was unable to comprehend, it was like he stood face to face with the first gate of hell itself, where hope is lost and an eternity in fire begins.

With a savage, desperate yell, Cholo charged El Despiadado, whose arms had spread wide ready to absorb the last man on his list.

———

STEAM LIFTED off Mata's skin as he stepped out of the small shower. He felt squeaky clean, but more than that, he was refreshed. Wrapping a towel around his waist, he stepped to the sink and used his palm to wipe away the fog that settled over the mirror. Lines of condensation streaked along the surface, distorting Mata's view of himself, but it was enough for him to see. He turned on the faucet, running water over his fingers until it reached his desired temperature. Using a sliver of soap, he lathered his face, then with slow, precise strokes, glided a straight razor over his skin. Flecks of stubble fell into the sink as he passed the razor under the running water between each stroke. When he finished, he leaned over and splashed his cheeks, wiping his chin and nose with his wet hands.

Moving from the bathroom to a bedroom, he dressed in clothes he had found hanging in a closet—a black charro shirt with embroidered red roses over each yoke, blue jeans, a hand-tooled leather belt, clean socks, and a pair of rustic brown Los Altos Snipped Toe Python Cowboy Boots. After slipping into the fresh leather and exotic python, he stood and walked to the dresser, where a stack of one-hundred-dollar bills totaling ten thousand dollars and a Kimber Rose Gold Ultra II 1911 pistol waited. He slid the stack of bills into the rear pocket of his jeans and wedged the pistol between his hip and belt, then turned and walked out of the room.

With careful steps, he walked around the cinderblock rubble and dead bodies near the front door, passed through the great room and two more corpses splayed in awkward, uncomfortable-looking positions, until he reached the kitchen, where hell itself had come calling.

He avoided looking at the butcher's block and instead found himself standing over the body of a man who, at first glance, looked to be asleep on the kitchen floor. His eyes were closed, his body curled into a fetal position, but the purple ligature marks around his neck made it clear— this rest was eternal.

Taking keys from a bowl near the door, Mata stepped outside. Evening was falling. A red and purple haze brushed the wavy wisps of stratocumulus clouds stretching out overhead. A breeze wafted past, its cool- ness caressing his clean-shaven face. Mata savored the fresh air, taking a deep taste of it through his nose, then walked to the pickup parked near the edge of the house, and got in.

The seat squeaked under his weight, the cracked, aged vinyl groaning beneath his legs. He inserted the key, and after coaxing the gas pedal, heard the rumble and clunk of the old engine as it fired up.

Before driving off, he glanced in the rearview mirror. His eyes looked calm. His jaw and cheeks were relaxed. When he smiled, a face he recognized smiled back. It was comforting, a normalcy that had slipped away for a time, but now was back. He reached his hand to adjust the mirror but stopped short. He felt a strange yearning to address the man that looked back at him.

"You. You are Carlos Mata. But it seems as if you are also someone else. Someone whose elegance and malevolence are overpowering. This...*El Despiadado*...he is a creature within you. Although we are one, I cannot look at you and say that when the beast takes control that I feel the same pleasure as he."

Mata paused, thinking to himself, hoping his mind could hide his next thought.

I do feel something, but I fear that my soul cannot afford such things.

Shifting the truck into drive, Mata left the house and the destruction behind him and headed north. Hours seemed to pass in silence, though his thoughts filled the time with introspection and rumination. Darkness fell around him as he pressed on through the night until the truck's headlights illuminated a sign posted along the road. He pulled over, left the truck idling, and stepped out.

"Tijuana...forty-five kilometers. San Diego, United States...seventy-two kilometers."

Mata stretched as he considered his options. His head felt better, but his ribs were stiff from the long drive.

Returning to the truck, he caught his reflection in the mirror.

"Shall we see what California has to offer?"

He nodded to himself and continued his journey north, satisfied with the decision.

As the question lingered, a voice deep inside, too faint for Mata to hear, quietly answered.

"But, of course."

Overland to Hell

A Short Story

By Harlan Hague

Overland to Hell

ABIGAIL WAS NOT AS ENTHUSIASTIC AS HUSBAND RICK ABOUT this plan to move from Kentucky to the distant western prairie. She was content with their little farm, friendly neighbors only a short ride away, or even a pleasant walk, and the little town of Danville nearby where they could buy anything they needed and attend church. Why leave all that?

"Why indeed?" said Rick. He explained again, as he had explained many times, the advantages of the move. They would go to the new town of Dodge City, Kansas, where they would file a claim for 160 acres of public land in the vicinity, free but for a small filing fee. The money they would receive for the sale of their Kentucky farm would carry them until the new Kansas farm began producing and earning an income.

Rick was not just enthusiastic; he was excited. "If we're careful, there might even be enough cash left over from the sale of the farm to *buy* some more acres, hopefully adjacent to our claim. I hear some homesteaders give it up and are anxious to sell their claims. Abby, we're still young and we want to be in the right place to live out our lives." In their midthirties, they were indeed younger than most of their neighbors.

More than once in quiet moments, Abby pondered. *Is that the right place, a Kansas farm? If it could be a place to help me get with child, I would fly there tomorrow. I so want a baby.*

Abby tried unsuccessfully to smile. Would they make it in Kansas, or would they decide after a season or two to give it up? She shook her head. She knew she had no choice. She would not object to Rick's dream.

———

FOLLOWING RICK'S PLAN, they sold the farm in early 1870. They separated their personal possessions into "Keep" and "Dispose." They gave away and sold the latter. They sold all their animals, cows, mules, a few sheep, two goats, and a dozen laying hens. They kept only two riding horses. Sifting advice from everyone who knew they were moving, particularly those who had friends or acquaintances who knew something of trekking west, they bought a suitable wagon and accouterments, such as water barrels, spare wagon parts, gear for cooking over a campfire, a new rifle and pistol and ammunition. They bought five oxen, four for the team and one extra. Friends and acquaintances who knew something about overland travel told them that oxen can survive better on the prairie than horses and mules that are too accustomed to green grass and hay. Also, oxen were less likely to be stolen by Indians.

In early spring, they said goodbye to anxious neighbors and drove away from the Kentucky farm in their new wagon. The spare ox and two riding horses were tied by leads to the back of the wagon. Rick tried, unsuccessfully, to comfort Abby who could not hold back the tears.

At the Mississippi, they were ferried across and joined a party whose captain Rick had corresponded with last fall. William, the captain, had been recommended to him by a Kentucky friend who had heard that William had been over the trail to Dodge City twice before. Now Abby and Rick's wagon and stock were added to the party of fifteen Kansas-bound wagons.

At the evening camp on the first day on the western side of the Mississippi, Rick and Abby sat at a campfire with a couple who had come over from an adjacent camp to say goodbyes to some friends in the Kansas party. The visiting couple's party was bound for Oregon.

Rick and the Oregon-bound man stood and walked toward the wagons, chatting. Abby and the wife huddled at the fire, studying the dancing flames, talking softly about what lay ahead. The enthusiasm of the Oregon emigrant, Marion, she called herself, contrasted sharply with Abby's uneasiness.

Marion sensed Abby's lack of enthusiasm, indeed, her fears. She took Abby's hand. "Why don't you join us?" Marion said. "It's pretty obvious that you're not excited about the move to Kansas. We have a good party, good people. We're joining old friends in Oregon who will help us get settled." She smiled, patting Abby's hand.

Abby winced, looked up at Marion, then turned back to stare into the fire. "Rick has decided."

———

THE PARTY of fifteen Kansas-bound wagons rolled in an undulating line on a lightly traveled trail. The emigrants, all new to overland travel but William, fell into a routine after early days of learning on the trail. Now they moved steadily day after day on the rolling prairie, green from recent rains, the tall grasses rolling in waves across the mostly flat land to the horizon. Scattered wildflowers added color to the prairie. Butterflies flitted about the red blossoms of milkweed. Plains Coreopsis and Black-Eyed Susan added flashes of yellow to the monotonous landscape.

Rick walked beside the lead ox, tapping its back lightly with a switch, more from nervousness than necessity. He had never driven oxen before leaving their home. The ox seemed to ignore him and the tapping. Rick looked back at Abby who walked in the shade of the wagon. She smiled thinly at him, looked aside.

Abby wiped perspiration from her cheek with a sleeve. It was unusually warm for late March. The long sleeves warmed her arms, her bonnet shielding her face from the sun's rays but not the heat. Her long dress dragged on the ground, raising wisps of dust, the hems turning black.

She smiled, recalling the humorous comments directed at a neighbor woman back in Kentucky who strutted in the middle of the main street in Danville, chin raised and smiling broadly, wearing bloomers. *Why didn't I bring bloomers?* She shook her head. She owned no bloomers, embarrassed that she was even thinking of wearing them.

The trail the wagons followed ran parallel to the railroad tracks under construction a hundred yards south. On first sighting the tracks, weeks into the journey, William explained to the overlanders that the railroad was scheduled to reach Dodge City in a year or two. Another sign of progress and prosperity for the region, he said.

William signaled an early stop for nooning this day when the column reached a point as close to the railroad construction site as they ever would be. He and some others planned to walk down to the rail site after lunch. It would be their last chance to have a look at the construction. The wagon train moved faster than the railroad building, and the wagon party would leave the track laying behind tomorrow.

The wagons were lined up for nooning beside the trail in three columns, an arrangement established at the Mississippi camp that would make defense against Indian attacks easier. Most teams were unyoked and put out to graze close by on patches of green grass. A few teams remained yoked, the oxen standing in place, heads hanging. Drivers of these wagons shrugged off the advice of others who urged them to give their animals a chance to rest and graze at noon stop, claiming they wanted to be ready to be back on the trail as soon as William signaled the end of nooning. Bad choice, said the others. You'll regret the choice when your teams begin to fail.

Rick and Abby finished their lunch quickly and walked with others to the railroad construction site. Rails and cross ties lay along the sculpted route. Dozens of workers bent to the task, shoveling stones to form the bed, hoisting and placing ties and rails on the rocky bed. Mule teams pulled wagons transporting ties and rails from the supply cars on the track to the new bed. Rail cars on the tracks immediately behind the construction site provided living quarters and a cookhouse for the crew. Behind the bunkhouse cars, more cars carried construction materials.

Some construction workers had exchanged waves with the overlanders when the wagons stopped nearby for nooning. Now some looked up at the approach of a dozen emigrants, including Rick and Abby. Other workers ignored them. They had seen too many overlanders since leaving the Mississippi to be interested.

One worker raised a hand in greeting, took a step

toward them, pulled a handkerchief from a pocket and wiped his face. "S'pose you folks are headin' for Dodge?"

"Yep. When do you expect the railroad to reach Dodge?" said Rick.

The worker looked westward, back to Rick. "I wouldn't put money on it, but it won't be for some time. Depends on weather, supply of rails and stuff, and the availability of workers. A few months, year maybe."

During the conversation, Abby looked past Rick to see a young worker staring at her. He stood at a pile of stones, leaning on his shovel handle. She looked away, then back to him. *Oh, what a good-looking fella.* They made eye contact. He smiled. She could not suppress a hint of a smile, then looked away quickly, blushing. She slowly looked back, and he watched her still.

At that moment, Rick took her arm, and they walked toward the wagons where the captain was calling all to get yoked up for departure. Abby closed her eyes, determined not to look back. She lagged behind Rick, turned ever so slowly to look back. He still stared. She turned back abruptly and caught up to Rick.

"That's the line that will link us with the towns back East," said Rick, "shipping our produce and bringing us goods and news. People back there think we're to be isolated out here, but we won't. We're just the western edge of the East."

"Nooning's done! Let's get 'em ready to head out!" shouted William. He wheeled his horse and galloped to the front of the three columns. Rick and Abby found their loose oxen, led them to the wagon and yoked them. When wagons were ready, William gave the signal to move out. Following his orders, the three columns pulled into a single line on the road.

Rick gently patted the back of his lead ox, looked toward the north when a soft breeze from that direction cooled his face. A dark line of clouds lay along the northern horizon. The short grasses on the rolling plain flowed in waves, beginning to whip as the breeze quickened.

"Looks like we have some weather coming," Rick said. He went to the back of the wagon, tightened the two horses' reins at the tailgate. He wondered whether he should find their spare ox in the loose stock and tie it to the tailgate but decided it was too late to think about that.

Rick passed Abby as he walked to the front. "Ride inside, if you like," he said. She shook her head. "Remember, if it looks like we're gonna get hit by a storm and the captain calls a halt, we need to get the wheels tied down fast as we can. The stakes and ropes are just inside the tailgate."

She nodded. "I know, I'm ready."

He walked to the lead ox, tapped the ox's back lightly. Abby walked beside the wagon, her skirts trailing in the dry grass, raising a wisp of dust, wondering anew what it would be like to wear bloomers.

The breeze increased, raising swirls of dust on the road. The line of dark clouds at the northern horizon blackened and expanded, then seemed to grow and move southward across the land, toward the wagon train. The breeze increased to a stiff wind, flapping loose canvas on wagons, blowing off hats.

Abby looked ahead at a galloping rider coming their way, swinging a bandanna and shouting. "Buffalo coming! Stampede! Buffalo!" The rider galloped down the column, shouting. "Buffalo!" Drivers frantically began turning oxen toward the stampede, as they had been instructed, increasing spaces between wagons, hoping the rampaging buffalo would pass through the wide intervals.

Too late! The galloping herd was on them. Some stampeding buffalo streamed through the passages, but many crashed into wagons and teams, toppling wagons and crushing oxen. Most walkers who had taken refuge behind wagons escaped injury, but some were caught under toppling wagons or struck by buffalo.

Then it was over. It ended as quickly as it began. The wind died, and it was deathly still and quiet. The buffalo were gone, passing well ahead of the railroad construction site where workers stood silent, watching the stampede pass.

The wagon train was a column of destruction. Half a dozen wagons had been struck and toppled, contents strewn about. Many oxen stood quietly in place, still yoked. Others lay on and around wagons, dead or injured. The herd of loose oxen and horses was nowhere in sight.

Abby stood beside their wagon which miraculously had survived. Dazed, hands on cheeks, she walked to the team. Three oxen had struggled up and now stood, still yoked. The fourth of the team lay nearby, gored and bleeding.

Abby's eyes opened wide. *Rick!* She looked around frantically. She saw dazed men and women wandering about the column, helping each other collect belongings, raise overturned wagons, hugging and consoling those who had lost family members or stock.

She asked those she passed if they had seen her husband. They shook heads, patting her shoulder or squeezing an arm. Then Beth, a woman she had befriended early in the journey, came up behind her, took her hand, and she knew.

Beth led her to a heavy sagebrush off the trail. What was left of Rick lay behind the shrub. He had been gored and trampled. Abby shrieked as she bent down, knelt beside the body, touched his face and sobbed, her hands on her cheeks. Beth put her arms around Abby's shoulders and held her as she rocked back and forth. She helped Abby stand, put an arm around her shoulders and led her away.

———

THE PARTY LAY over three days, repairing wagons, harnesses, and yokes. Most of the loose stock was rounded up, some put in yoke to replace animals that had died in the stampede.

One woman and three men, including Rick, were buried in the middle of the trail. Oxen were driven over the graves to remove any evidence of a burial. William had explained at the beginning of travel that wolves and Indians would raid a visible grave. Most of the family survivors agreed that erecting a marker invited Indians to pillage a grave, but one woman insisted on placing a cross beside the trail. When the woman left the site, a man casually kicked the cross, picked it up and sailed it as far as he could.

Beth's husband, Gary, helped Abby replace the dead ox in her team with the spare ox. At Gary's request, Abby moved her wagon down the line and pulled up beside their wrecked wagon. She slept in her wagon and had meals with them.

Conversation at campfires was heavy with loss and discussion about how to proceed. Abby listened as her head spun. She had never been enthusiastic about the move to Kansas. She simply followed Rick's lead, as she had done all her married life. Now, as she stared into the campfire flames, she thought about returning to Kentucky, but how could she return? She certainly couldn't travel alone, and no others in the caravan talked of returning. Even if a few others considered returning, the trip would be too risky for two or three wagons traveling alone. They would find it difficult to deal with unexpected problems, and they would be easy prey to Indians.

And where would she go? She owned no property in Kentucky, she had no family there, and she would not approach friends to shelter her.

Gary had a suggestion. At an evening campfire, he explained. "Beth and I lost our wagon and most of the team. Abby, you lost your husband. Your wagon is intact, and you still have four good oxen, three from the team and the extra one. What about this, and it's only a suggestion. How about the three of us traveling in your wagon, we share in chores, and we'll see what happens when we reach Dodge City." He leaned back, looked from Beth to Abby. Abby and Beth exchanged sober glances.

Abby stared into the fire. *I don't have a choice. There's no alternative. Besides, maybe, shooting myself.* She shook her head, decided she would continue to Dodge. Maybe she would find something there to tide her over until the train arrived, or she found someone who was traveling to Kentucky by wagon. Then she could return to Kentucky safely. She looked up at Gary. "Thank you, Gary. That's kind of you."

————

WILLIAM RODE THROUGH THE ENCAMPMENT, announcing that the wagons would be on the trail after breakfast tomorrow. A new sense of hope and urgency spurred all to work hard to be ready for the departure.

Abby, Beth and Gary stood over a pile of goods beside the wagon. Since the wagon would now carry the belongings of two families, they had to make the difficult decision what to keep and what to give away or abandon.

Abby looked up from the stack of travel goods and clothing to see half a dozen men coming from the railroad camp. Two of the men waved. With a start, she recognized the handsome young man who had watched her so closely on the visit to the tracks. Now he stared at her again, with a slight smile. She tried to avoid smiling, ducking her head.

"Sorry we didn't offer you folks any help after the storm and buffalo," said one of the workers, "we had a mess to clean up ourselves. I see you have everything under control." Five of the men walked with Gary past the wagon to the cluster of wagons beyond.

The young man stayed. "I heard you lost your husband." She ducked her head, nodded. "So sorry. I wish I could do something for everybody...and you. But I heard you people got everything sorted." She nodded again. "I understand you pull out tomorrow." She nodded. "Where will you go?"

Abby looked at Beth, who smiled, turned and walked to the pile of goods beside the wagon. She bent and picked up a piece of clothing, examined it, glanced back at Abby.

Abby turned to the young man. "Dodge City, I guess," she said.

"Will you stay there?"

She looked aside. "I don't know."

"Let's go, Thomas." The five rail workers walked by.

He ignored them. "What is your name?

"Abigail...Abby."

"Thomas! C'mon!"

He looked at the retreating workers, looked back at her, smiled shyly, and ran after them.

"Goodbye...Thomas," she said softly.

————

THE WAGON TRAIN, now reduced to twelve wagons, moved across the prairie, the grasses flowing in waves toward the horizon. Occasional showers nourished the grasses and scattered patches of pink and purple Phlox and the yellow petals and dark centers of Black-Eyed Susans.

Gary walked beside the lead ox, talking softly to it, resting a hand on its back. Abby and Beth on most days walked in the shade of the wagon, chatting. One or both occasionally rode on the wagon seat.

The women shared in meal preparation and cleaning up at nooning and evening camps. On most nights, Beth slept in the wagon and Gary under the wagon. Abby slept on blankets beside the fire circle. On nights when rain fell or threatened, Gary pitched a small tent for Abby.

Abby tried to focus on the day's chores. When her mind wandered and she thought about tomorrow, she was quietly terrified. While in this mood, she welcomed any diversion, even on this day, the warning from William that a dozen Indians were in the middle of the trail ahead.

The captain called a halt, early nooning, he said. He sent four men out to the herd of loose stock to assist the two herders, in case the Indians proved to be trouble. He didn't expect a problem, he said, since there were two women in the party. The presence of women usually signified peaceful intent, he added. Nevertheless, he ordered drivers to move the wagons up into three closely aligned columns of four wagons each.

The move proved unnecessary. William and two others rode out to the Indians. They chatted with the leader who spoke passable English. All rode off the trail, dismounted and sat in a circle. Andy offered the leader of the group a tobacco pouch and package of cigarette papers. The leader nodded and took the proffered pouch and papers. He took a paper, tapped tobacco on the paper and rolled it expertly. He handed the pouch to a man beside him. An overlander sitting beside William offered a pouch to the Indian sitting behind the leader. He nodded, took the pouch and rolled a cigarette and passed the pouch to the man beside him. William struck a match and lit the cigarettes of the two men. They in turn lit the cigarettes of the men behind them. The Indians inhaled, eyes closed, raised chins and exhaled puffs of smoke.

The Indians stood, nodded their thanks to William. He responded by giving the leader another tobacco pouch. The leader took the pouch, nodded sharply, almost smiled. All stood, the Indians made to leave, then stopped abruptly, frowning at Abby.

She had walked behind William to stand before the two Indian women. She offered a string necklace with a silver cross pendant to one of the women. The woman slowly took the pendant, turned it over and over, looked up at Abby, her look a question. To the other woman, Abby offered a silver-colored brooch pin. The woman took it hesitantly, looked aside at her companion.

The two women chattered a moment, looking at their gifts, then at Abby. The first woman reached behind her head, untied a bead necklace and held it out to Abby. Before Abby could respond, the woman put a hand on Abby's shoulders and turned her around. She placed the necklace around her neck and tied it at the back. Turning Abby back to face her, she smiled, patted the necklace. Abby started to hug the woman.

"Abby! Better not," said William, "could be misinterpreted."

Abby touched the necklace, smiled. The two women smiled, reached for Abby and hugged her.

William laughed. "So much for being misinterpreted. Must have had some friendly contact with whites."

The Indians went to their horses, mounted and rode away at a gallop. The two women looked back and waved.

William turned toward the cluster of people nearby who had watched the whole affair. "Entertainment's over. Noon stop's done. Let's finish and be on our way."

Abby had not moved, still relishing this bright spot in her dismal days.

———

WILLIAM POINTED. "There it is, folks. Dodge City." The entire party stood beside the lead wagon, looking across the flat prairie at their destination. The town was a gray outline against the distant horizon at sundown. The overlanders had some notion what to expect since William had described the town he had visited twice. They were relieved to see the end of the journey. They knew the town was only a few years old, still in the process of birth and early years, but the disappointment was still apparent in their frowns and grumbling.

William laughed. "Okay, it ain't New York City, but it's a new town with a real future. The railroad will be here soon, tying the town with the East, and Texas cowboys will soon be bringing herds of longhorns up to ship to the East. The railroad will bring any goods you need, and it will carry your produce to eastern buyers. You gotta look on the bright side. No baby was ever born full-grown."

Abby stood apart from the others, staring at the dim outline on the flat horizon that was Dodge City. *What will I do in this town till the train arrives to take me home? Home? Where is home? Is home a place, or is home a house? Sure don't have a house, anywhere. We sold it all. Maybe by the time the train arrives, I'll have it all worked out.*

She was startled by the captain's loud voice. "Last night, folks. Tomorrow morning, anyone interested can ride in with me, and I'll show you the real estate office where you can talk with people about homesteadin' or buyin', whatever you have in in mind. I think you know, at least, some of you know, that I filed on a homestead last time I was in Dodge. My pard, who has a claim adjoining mine, is keeping an eye on my place while I'm away. I put in a dugout after I filed. Now I'm about to build a board house!" He smiled, obviously proud of himself. "Anyway, anybody interested, ride in with me in the morning. I'll also point out the post office, in case some letters for you reached Dodge before you did. Then we'll ride back and break camp for the last time."

———

ABBY, Gary, and Beth sat at their campfire in the gloaming, slowly eating this final supper of beans, potatoes, and chunks of bread. They had poured coffee before the meal and now the empty cups lay at their feet. They stared into the dying fire, low flames waving, sending up scattered golden sparks. No one spoke, fearful of beginning the conversation that must probe and define the future.

Gary slowly set his plate on the ground at his feet, cleared his throat. "It was a good decision we all made back there. I think it worked out for all of us." He looked aside at Abby who stared into the fire pit. "What do you have in mind now, Abby?"

She stared at the low flames, shook her head. "I don't know. I want to go home, but...I don't know where home is."

Gary looked at Beth, paused a long moment, then back to Abby. "We have a suggestion, Beth and me. We're going to file a homestead claim. We'll need a place to live in until we can build a soddy or a house. Abby, what would you think about selling the wagon and animals to us? If you have no plans for them, that is."

He waited. Abby stared at him blankly, then spoke to the fire. "I have no plans, no plans at all. I don't know what I'm going to do. I couldn't..." She looked at Beth who quickly turned away to look into the darkness. She turned to Gary. "I couldn't...I couldn't...stay with you?"

Gary replied immediately, sharply, as if he had been expecting this from Abby. "No, no, it's not possible. I'm sorry, Abby, but we must get on with our separate lives." Abby recoiled as if struck. She looked at Beth whose head was turned away, a hand at her cheek.

"The money we pay for the wagon and oxen could tide you over until you decide what you're going to do," said Gary.

Abby leaned forward, sobbing, her face in her hands.

"Oh, for god's sake!" said Gary. He stood abruptly and strode into the darkness, kicking the sod in anger.

Beth put an arm around Abby's shoulder, embraced her. "I'm so sorry, honey, I had no part in this. He is so... so...sometimes I can't talk with him. He won't listen to me."

Abby stood and stumbled to the wagon, knelt, and collapsed on her blankets.

————

ABBY STOOD in front of the Pleasant View Hotel, the only hotel in Dodge City. It was the most substantial structure in the sole street of small shops that included a grocery, a haberdashery, the land office and a few others. The Last

Hope Saloon, across the street from the hotel, was almost the same size as the hotel and considerably busier. A livery and blacksmith shop behind the hotel completed the town's enterprises. Tents at each end of the street suggested coming commercial establishments. Everything in the new town appeared to anticipate boom times with the arrival of the railroad and Texas longhorn herds.

Abby looked around, quietly terrified. Gary had pulled up in front of the hotel, and he and Beth had helped Abby unload her things and carry them inside. Abby untied her riding horse's reins from the wagon tailgate and tied them to the hotel hitching rail. Beth hugged her, Abby's arms hanging at her sides. Gary avoided her, taking pains to avoid looking at her.

Then Gary and Beth climbed aboard the wagon and pulled away. Abby kept watching until they rounded the last shop and disappeared. Abby closed her eyes, wiped her tears. She walked slowly to the hotel, went inside, registered and paid from the purse that held Gary's payment for the wagon and team.

What to do? She knew Gary's payment would not last long in this town with high hopes of growth. She would have to find work until the train arrived and rescued her. The thought of sitting in a train coach and watching Dodge City disappear behind her gave her a slight boost, and she almost smiled.

Her despair returned too soon. She took a deep breath and went to the grocery. The clerk-owner had no positions available. "Come back when you see the first Texas cowboys ride into town," he said, smiling. She received the same reception from the haberdashery and a boarding house beyond the town limits. She even tried the livery. The liveryman replied as the others had replied. All owners expected to need hands before long, but not now in this economic climate, this waiting for the growth of town and business activity.

A young worker at the livery, leaning against the corral poles and chewing on a strand of hay, looked her up and down, listening to Abby's conversation with the owner. "Have you tried The Last Hope?" the worker said.

She turned to him, her face blank. "The saloon?"

"Yep. They got a couple of girls workin' there, but not as pretty as you." He smiled.

She looked down. "I...I hadn't thought about working at a saloon."

"I should thank it'd be a good job for a pretty girl. Saloon's the busiest place in town. It'll be even busier, lots busier, when the Texas cowboys ride into town." He smiled again. "I'll walk you over if you want to have a look."

She looked aside at nothing, frowning. "Okay. Thank you."

The worker looked at the liveryman. "Boss?"

The boss nodded.

"Ready?" the man said to Abby.

"Now?" Her eyes opened wide.

"Ready if you're ready." He took a step toward the street, stopped. She went up beside him, and they walked side by side to the street, then across the street to the saloon. She stopped there, looked aside at him. He took her arm and guided her up on the boardwalk and through the saloon door.

She recoiled. The pungent smells of alcohol and tobacco smoke struck her like a blow to the face. She rubbed her nose and eyes. She looked around and cringed when she realized that every eye in the place was on her. Men sat at three of the four tables. Two men leaned against the bar. The bartender, a tray of drinks in hand, stopped in mid-stride near a table. Two women stood behind the table. The younger of the two glared, the middle-aged woman smiled.

The young man leaned toward Abby, looking at the table. "You've been noticed, pretty lady," he said softly. "I wager you've got a job, if you want it."

The bartender set the drinks on the table, walked to Abby and her companion. "Can I help? If you want drinks, find somewhere to sit or lean."

"This here pretty lady wants to talk about a job," the young man said. She looked abruptly at him.

The bartender looked at her. "That true?"

She hesitated a moment. "Well, I would like to ask... uh, to see what kind of job you might have open."

"You never worked in a saloon? What sort of work have you done?"

"I never had a job. I've always been a farm wife."

"Hmm, well, you're a purty little piece, I'll give yuh that. I might could hire yuh. What's your name?"

"Abby. Can you tell me what I would be doing?"

The bartender looked at the liveryman who pulled a face. The bartender looked toward the two women, still standing behind the table, watching the interview. "Betsy, would you come over here?" he called.

The middle-aged woman walked around the table and stopped beside the bartender. She smiled at Abby.

"Would you talk with this young woman, sweetheart? She wants to ask about the job I'm about to offer her."

Abby recoiled, frowned at him.

Betsy smiled again at Abby. "Oh, she does, does she?" She turned to the men. "You two get lost. We're gonna talk."

The bartender headed for the bar. "See you later, Abby," said the liveryman. "I'm Hank." He strutted toward the door, chin raised.

Betsy smiled. "You want to know what we do here, do

you?" Abby nodded. Betsy took her arm and guided her to the empty table in the corner. Betsy pulled out two chairs, and they sat. She glared at the three men at the adjacent table until they looked back at the cards they held.

She turned back to Abby. "All right. You get dressed up in pretty clothes, like these." She ran a hand over her gaudy, colorful dress with frilly lacy hems that ended at her knees. "And put up your hair real pretty. Like this." She patted her thick locks that swirled atop her head. "When you come down to work—you'll have a room upstairs—Bennie, the bartender we just spoke to, may ask you to take drinks to customers. You'll sometimes dance with customers. We got a piano over there that produces something that substitutes for music. You do dance?"

Abby shook her head.

"Doesn't matter really. When one of the boys wants to dance, he's usually so drunk, he stomps and circles around in something that he thinks is a dance, and he'll pull you along."

She paused, smiling, looking at Abby. Waiting.

"That's it? That's the job?"

"We-e-e-ell, there is this other thing. Some patrons who have had a good time drinkin' and dancin' want to finish off the evenin' with a little romp upstairs."

Abby frowned. "Do you mean sex?"

"Yep. You got it."

"It's not possible to work here just to serve drinks and dance with the men?"

"Not if you're female, hon." She paused. "You have another job waitin' for you?"

Abby looked down. "No. I looked all over town."

"It ain't the best job for a woman, but it's a job. You meet some nice fellas, and you meet some not so nice.

You learn to live with it."

"How…how do you avoid gettin' with child?"

Betsy leaned back, sighed heavily. "Yeah, there's that. Mostly you don't think about it. It's a risk that comes with the job. But there are some things you can do. There's different ways to have sex other than the usual way, and these other ways don't get you with child. I'll talk about them some more if you take the job. There's some few things you can do even when havin' sex in the usual way. A halved, emptied lemon skin put inside at the right place can help. I'm told that a sponge soaked in vinegar can help. Never tried it.

"There are different kinds of little sacks that can be pulled over a man's unit if you can persuade him to wear it. Good luck with that. Most men got one thing in mind when they get to your room upstairs and don't want any delay. But some will listen to reason." She waited. "Got any questions for me?"

"No. I'll think about it. If I come back tomorrow, I'm taking it. Not because I want it."

"I understand. Only too well, hon." Betsy leaned over and kissed Abby's cheek. "I won't say I hope to see you tomorrow. You do what you must, hear?"

Abby nodded, stood and walked to the door.

Abby stumbled from the saloon in a daze. She walked toward the hotel, her mind racing. Inside, she slowly climbed the stair to her room on the second floor. Slumping in a chair at the sole window, she stared at the street below, her mind blank.

What to do? Maybe she'll buy a packhorse, load her things and head for the nearest town of any size where she might find work. Or maybe she could locate a home-steader family locally who has decided to call it quits on a claim and is preparing to head east, and she could go with them. She could pay. But what would she be going back to? She has no home there, no family, and she would not ask any friends to take her in.

She stood and went to the bed where she had dumped her things on arriving this morning. Untying the bundle, the pistol fell out. She slowly picked it up, turned it over and over, stared at it. *Maybe I'll shoot myself and be done with it.* She pondered, staring at the pistol, then shook her head vigorously and laid the pistol on the bed.

———

ABBY HAD breakfast the next morning in the hotel dining room. The two eggs, biscuit and gravy, potatoes and beans, hot coffee, on any other day might have been tasty, satisfying, especially since she had no supper yesterday, but this morning she pushed the plate away after two bites.

She spent the rest of the morning and half of the afternoon visiting the same establishments she had visited on her arrival day, searching for employment. She promised proprietors she would work long hours for little pay, she appealed to their good nature, and she said she was desperate. Their response was the same. They felt for her, but they could not afford to pay for a worker they did not need.

She went to the saloon, stepped inside and looked around. The bartender saw her, said something to Betsy who was sitting on a stool at the far end of the bar. He motioned with a nod of his head toward Abby. She walked slowly to Abby.

"I was only half-hoping you wouldn't show today, hon, but here you are." She half-smiled. "If you're sure about this, come to my room, and I'll get you suited up. She put an arm around Abby's shoulders and walked toward the stair. Half a dozen men sitting at two tables watched them.

"Ooooh, Betsy, who's your friend? We gonna meet her?" said a grizzled old-timer.

"Mind your manners, Eustis. She's new in town. Be a good boy, and you might be able to buy her a drink." Eustis and others at the tables laughed, thumped the table and said they were ready to buy.

Climbing the stairs, Abby looked down at the tables. The men watched them, grinning and commenting to each other softly.

Betsy held Abby's arm as they climbed. "The bunch that come in during the afternoon, like these boys, are usually a pretty good bunch, here for cards and conversation mostly. The fellas who come late are more unpredictable. Don't worry about the fellas who drink heavy and have trouble keeping their eyes open. We try to guide them to a chair in the corner where they can snooze safely. Even if they follow you upstairs, they'll probably go to sleep before they get their pants off.

"On the other hand, some fellas who drink heavy don't go to sleep easy; they're wide awake, and the more they drink, the more you need to stay away from 'em. If one of these wild 'uns wants to go upstairs, I'll do my best to take care of him. Early on, at least. We'll see." Abby shivered. Betsy put an arm around her shoulders and hugged her.

Inside Betsy's room, while she looked through the dresses hanging in the closet, Abby looked around. The room appeared like a bedroom in any house. A double bed nicely laid with quilts and spread, a dresser with mirror, holding combs, a collection of costume jewelry, a small stack of letters, a chair beside the dresser and another at the single window. The clean lacy white curtain at the open window waved gently.

While Betsy stood at the closet door, searching in the array of dresses, Abby glanced at the letters. The top envelope showed a return address in Tennessee. *She still has contact with somebody back home, or somewhere. Why doesn't she go there?*

"Okay, how 'bout this?" said Betsy. "I think this will look good on you." Abby frowned, looking at the frilly dress Betsy held up for her inspection. "If you give me the okay, I'll take it in a bit in the waist." She held it up, waiting.

"Yes, that will be fine. Thank you."

"Have a seat over there," she said, pointing at the chair at the window. "This shouldn't take long." She took needle and thread from the dresser drawer and sat on the bed.

Abby sat down in the chair at the window, looked down at the street, her mind blank. She thought again of the pistol.

After but fifteen minutes, Betsy stood. She held up the dress for Abby's inspection. "This will do until we get you something of your own. Now, let's get your room ready." She laid the dress on the bed. "I would have got it ready if I knew you were coming back, but..." She motioned, and they went out the door, down the hall to the room at the end.

Betsy opened the door, and Abby gasped. "Yeah, it looks like a tornado hit it. Girl who had it lived in this mess, never did keep it straight."

"What happened to her?" said Abby.

Betsy paused in the doorway, her face blank. "Good question. She didn't come down one morning, and I went up to check on her. She was gone. She had mentioned a couple of times that she had a friend in Wyoming. I hope that's where she went. I hope that's what happened to her. Never did really settle in here. She was here only a month or so. There was a fella who said more than once that he was gonna steal her from us. He always laughed. She didn't. She was afraid of him. I..."

Betsy shook her head, went inside, and Abby followed. "We'll wash all this mess tomorrow and clean the place up. I've got some clean sheets and blankets you can use tonight. Let's get the bed made. Then we'll go to the hotel, get your things and have a bite in the hotel dining room. Then we hustle back and get dressed. The boys are anxious to meet you."

BETSY HOOKED an arm on Abby's arm, and they walked from Abby's room. "Ready?" said Betsy.

"Ready as I'll ever be, I s'pose," Abby said, smoothing the frilly dress. She looked down. "You can see my knees."

Betsy smiled. "Yes, you can. I'll not be the last person to tell you that you have nice legs. C'mon. Let's give the boys a treat." They walked down the hall to the stairs.

All four tables were occupied, and half a dozen men stood at the bar. The room was suddenly quiet. All watched the two women descend the stair. At the bottom, four men rushed to the women, making their case to be the first to dance with the new pretty girl.

"Back off, fellas. She's promised Eustis the first dance."

Abby looked at her sharply.

Betsy leaned over, spoke softly. "It's okay, honey, Eustice can't dance either, so you'll just be walkin' around the floor, talking. Eustice don't drink much, and he's a nice old fella. Everybody respects him."

Betsy looked across the floor and saw Hank, drink in hand, leaning on the bar, grinning, looking at them. Abby followed her gaze. "Most everybody. Hank is gonna make a play before the evening's out. Be careful." Abby shivered. She was so tense she thought she must break into a thousand splinters. Betsy took her hand gently.

As predicted, Eustis was no dancer. While the piano player began pounding on the keyboard, Betsy went to Eustis's table, told him Abby was ready for him. He stood and went to her, smiled, took her hand, put the other hand behind her waist, all in the normal dance position, then walked around the floor, leading Abby, with no attempt or semblance to dancing as the piano player plunked a tune, displaying that he had never had a piano lesson.

Eustis had consumed a couple of whiskeys, smiled, asked her how she liked Dodge, told her how much he had been looking forward to this dance, and opined that she shouldn't be in a place like this.

Abby relaxed. She almost smiled. "I don't know what to think of Dodge. I didn't expect to work in a saloon." She wondered what reception she would get if she told him about her circumstances but decided against it. "How did you end up in a place like this, Eustis?"

Eustis frowned as he led her in a walk that almost resembled dancing. "Well...I've always worked around cows. It's all I know. Back in Fort Worth, I heard about Dodge City bein' the place to be if you wanted to handle cattle without working on a ranch. So I rode up with a couple of fellas who planned to homestead. They did, and I did. And here I am, waitin' for the Texas cowboys to bring up the longhorns so I can work cattle without workin' on a ranch."

"Are you happy?"

"Nope."

She frowned. "Why not?"

He looked over her shoulder. "I miss Texas. Now, don't ask me why I miss Texas. I cain't explain. I just do."

The music ended at that moment, ending conversation. Eustis bowed low, his hand at his back, to the raucous laughter from his pards at his table. He stepped away and Abby turned to see Hank, wearing a smug smile, standing behind her.

"My turn," Hank said.

Eustis frowned, went to his table to back slapping and chuckles from his friends.

Hank grinned, weaved slightly, his eyes glazed. He put an arm around her shoulders and reached for her hand, brushing against a breast. "Uh oh, s'cuse me." He pulled a face. He looked toward the piano, shouted, "How 'bout some dance music, Jason?" He looked back at Abby, grinned, weaved, lightly touched a breast through the dress.

Abby winced, pulled back, but he tightened his hold.

"Abby, Bennie wants to talk to us." Betsy had walked up behind Abby. She took Abby's arm. "Sorry, Hank, the boss calls."

Hank weaved. "Th' hell he does."

She ignored him and guided Abby toward the bar, leaving Hank glaring.

They leaned on the bar. Bennie stopped drying the glass he held. "It won't do, Betsy. Abby accepted this job. She knows what we do here. You can watch out for her, but you can't interfere doing the job she was hired for. Understand? Both of you?"

Betsy nodded. Abby looked at Hank who still stared at her.

"Abby?" said Bennie. "Okay?"

"Okay."

———

NEXT EVENING, Abby stood at the bar, talking with Freddie, a quiet young man who had watched Abby with interest. She sipped the sarsaparilla he bought and talked softly with him. He had said nothing about going upstairs, but if it were inevitable, she thought he might be an acceptable first timer.

Then she saw Hank come in the front door. He looked around, saw her and strode toward the bar. He obviously had been drinking elsewhere. He leaned on the bar beside her. "I wanna see your room, sweetie."

Freddie stepped away from the bar. "We're talking, Hank."

Hank turned slowly, stepped toward Freddie. "You just finished talking, sumbitch."

"You can't talk to me like that, you"

Hank punched Freddie hard in the jaw, and he stumbled backward.

"That'll do, fellows!" Bennie ran around the end of the bar and stepped between the two antagonists, holding out his arms toward each. Freddie rubbed his jaw, shook his fist at Hank and walked toward the door. H

ank watched him go, nodded to Bennie.

"Thanks, Bennie," Hank said. "That man don't know how to act in a saloon." He turned to Abby, smiling.

Bennie went behind the bar and resumed washing glasses. Hank leaned against the bar beside Abby. "Now I'm anxious, hon. I want to go upstairs. How 'bout it?"

Abby looked around, hoping to see Betsy. She was nowhere in sight.

"If you're lookin' for Betsy, she's upstairs, pleasurin' a lucky fella. That's where I want to go, upstairs for a little pleasurin'. Let's go." He took her arm, smiling.

She was terrified. She looked around the room. Looking for what? She turned to Bennie. He motioned with a nod toward the stair. A grinning Hank took her arm, and they walked up the stair.

An hour later, Hank stumbled down the stair, ignored those who watched him, went to the front door and outside. Another hour later, Abby came down, a hand to her bruised cheek, the skin around her eye already beginning to darken.

————

THE DAYS PASSED, and Abby surprised herself that she found the means to adjust to her new life. She learned to dance and socialize in this new environment, drinking sarsaparilla when it was available. She became proficient in fending off suitors without overly antagonizing them. And when she could not fend them off, she became proficient in sexual techniques that would avoid or lessen the likelihood of pregnancy. Betsy was a good teacher and confidant, a friend.

Most of the upstairs encounters were completed peacefully enough. Most of the men were drunk or almost drunk and performed routinely. Some were so inexperienced, even embarrassed, that she had to offer some instruction. She surprised herself that *she* could and was willing to offer instruction. She surprised herself that she could pity some customers.

Abby also was surprised that most of the suitors were considerate, some even kind. Some few however were rough, treating her like an object for their pleasure rather than as a partner. She was left on occasion with a facial bruise or black eye. If the perpetrator was still in the saloon when Abby came down in that condition, the regular patrons often roughed up and threatened the man who had hurt her. The regulars were becoming especially impatient with Hank who often abused her.

She surprised herself that she was able to tolerate this new life without giving up a desire to live. Oh, there were occasions when she was so down that she pondered shooting the man who had abused her. Or shooting herself. Those were the worst days. For the most part, she lived each day, not thinking about tomorrow. She had forgotten how to smile. She had forgotten how to hope. She simply passed the days, one after the other after the other.

Then on what began as an ordinary evening, it all changed. She was reluctantly dancing with Hank. He had spent enough time with Abby on enough days and nights to consider himself her regular. She did not welcome the attention, but she could not refuse it. Tonight, he had consumed enough alcohol to be stumbling happy and was insistent on heading for the stair.

Then it happened. While dancing with Hank, Abby looked over his shoulder toward the outside door and saw Thomas standing there, staring at her. She stopped dancing, dropped her arm from Hank's shoulder and took a step back, her eyes wide and mouth open.

"Hey, what's 'is. You cain't stop dancin' right in the middle of th' dance!" Hank scowled, angry. He grabbed her arm and pulled her roughly to him.

Thomas strode to Hank, put a hand lightly on his arm, spoke softly. "Take your hands off her."

Hank turned abruptly to him, frowning. "Who the' hell are you? We're dancin'. Wait your turn."

Thomas tightened his grip on Hank's arm. "Let her go. Now," softly.

Hank let her go, stepped toward Thomas with a fist coiled. Thomas punched him hard in the belly, then punched him with a hard blow to the jaw. Hank collapsed to the floor, out cold.

"That'll do it." The bartender stood behind Thomas, holding a shotgun across his chest.

Thomas turned to him. "Back off, old man. Don't lift that scattergun, or you're a dead man." He rested a hand on his pistol grip. Bennie hesitated only a moment then lowered the gun.

Thomas turned to Abby. "Will you go with me?"

She blinked. "Yes, I will. Yes."

"Let's get your things. We're going."

"Now?"

"Unless you have other plans."

"Come with me, upstairs." She took his sleeve and pulled him.

Everyone in the saloon, all standing now, had watched the confrontation, tense. Now they relaxed, some smiling, as Abby and Thomas walked to the stair.

"You go, girl." It was Betsy. She hugged Abby and patted her cheek, smiling at Thomas.

"Go on, Abby," said a smiling cowboy, standing at his table. "Good man," said another, slapping Thomas on the back. Others cheered, laughing, clapping. One danced a jig, shouting drunken nonsense.

Two men helped Hank to a chair in the corner where he shook his head and watched Abby and Thomas walking up the stair. "Be damned," he said, shaking his head.

———

THOMAS AND ABBY rode on a dusty lane, leaving Dodge City behind. He held the lead of a loaded packhorse.

"Where are we going?" she said.

He smiled. "Away. I thought maybe California. What do you think?"

"California will do." She leaned over, grabbed a handful of sleeve, pulled him toward her and kissed him.

"Wahoo!" she cried and kicked her horse to a gallop.

The West

A Yellow Hair Series Prequel

By Ron Briggs

Foreword

This is a work of fiction. The characters, events, and places are contrived by the author. An honest attempt has been made to describe real cultures and interactions as they may have taken place late in the tenth century and early in the eleventh century.

The story forwards a possible factor for Norse west-ward expansion beyond Iceland. The reason presented here is pure speculation by the author but is entirely possible and plausible, though no documentation has been found to date that supports the fictional character's thought process.

The cultures depicted as interacting in this story are the Norwegian Norse, Greenlandic Norse, Icelandic Norse, and Beothuk of Newfoundland, known as Vinland by the Norse in the late tenth and early eleventh century AD.

This prequel to the *Yellow Hair Series* highlights some reasons how and why the Norse explored lands west of Iceland. While the Greenland colony lasted about four hundred years, it may have been doomed from the start. The distances involved, lack of reliable communication, events that distracted the Norse in Europe, a shortage of new settlers, a hostile indigenous population with more manpower, lack of a commitment to communicate with those they encountered, changing climate, and other factors all combined to end the westward expansion of the Norwegian and Icelandic Norse deeper into North America in the eleventh century.

But no one can deny that the Norse had the pioneer spirit that drove them to seek out new horizons. Their intrepid attitude and innovative ship building opened the door for Europeans to find, explore, and eventually dominate the Western Hemisphere. The Viking Era provided the first "cowboys" that rode clinker-built ships across the vast "plains" of the North Atlantic Ocean to western lands that few dreamed even existed.

In the Yellow Hair series, we will meet a few Norsemen who found a way to communicate with Indigenous North Americans and learned that humans were humans, no matter where they were found. With more people like Rolfcarl, Thorkell, Erik, and Tor, the rest of Europeans may have learned a different way to deal with those they encountered in the New World.

A Duck

Rolfcarl Carlsson stood at the steerboard watching his crew as the knorr rose and fell with the swells while they sailed toward the new colony of Greenland. The sky was not stormy, but a stiff westerly wind was driving gray clouds from horizon to horizon. The seas were gray with waves taller than a man, and whitecaps were plentiful. The dominant sounds were the edges of the sail flapping, wind whistling through the rigging, and ropes straining against tie blocks. Occasionally the crew would break out in a sailors' ditty that spoke of the sea, heroism, home, a beautiful lass, or a mother.

It was the third day after the fleet left Reykjavik and Iceland behind. Many ships had been recruited by the charismatic Erik Thorvaldsson, known as Erik the Red, upon his triumphant return to Iceland. The air was cool, blowing off the cold water of the North Atlantic. All the men wore heavy wool or hide tunics. A handful of wives and some children were crowded in cramped quarters on the mid-deck of Rolfcarl's big knorr. They were determined to build a new life in Greenland.

_____

ERIK THE RED had been exiled from Iceland for three years on a charge that he had murdered two friends. Rumor had it that he had fled to Iceland with his father, who'd had to deal with his own murder charge in Norway several years prior. After finding and exploring Greenland for nearly three years, Erik had returned to Iceland to clear his name once his sentence of exile had been completed. Upon his arrival, he had expounded on large green pastures empty of people and free for the taking. The Icelandic colony of Greenland was established with Erik the Red Thorvaldsson the head of the Greenland *Godar*.

_____

"I AM DETERMINED to fulfill a dream I have harbored since Father brought me to Iceland, thirty years past. Father had brought me along on a voyage to trade sheep to Snorri Niflheimrsson, a gothi, who had a seat on the Godar, of Iceland. It was common knowledge that many of the gothi also kept and hunted with gyrfalcons. Father desperately wanted his own gyrfalcon, but in Norway, his rank among the jarls did not qualify him to buy one on the open market. The only way he could possess one of the prized birds was to obtain it elsewhere and bring it back home," Rolfcarl had explained to his four sons before they set sail for Iceland.

I should curse myself for waiting thirty years to make this voyage, Rolfcarl scolded himself. *When Father brought me to Iceland those many years past, we went hunting with Storri Niflheimrsson's falconer. Mjolnir, the great gyrfalcon, killed four ducks that day. Three were common types found in Iceland and often in Norway. But one of them was of a breed no one*

*could recognize. And, I am told, none of that type has been seen
in Iceland since. I knew, somehow, the bird had made its way to
Iceland from somewhere in the west, but Father insisted it was
just an unusual specimen of some local type of duck. "A freak
of nature," he called it; "There are no lands west of Iceland," he
often said. Too many things got in my way, and I was not able
to make an undertaking of this magnitude until now. As it
turns out, that scoundrel, Erik the Red, gets credit for finding
the lands that I should be famous for!*

Shaking off the missed opportunity, Rolfcarl looked
proudly at his two strapping sons sitting on their sea
chests in their rowing positions. He was skillfully using
the steerboard and ordering sail trimming to speed them
through the swells. The rowers could rest for the time
being. His two older sons: Harald, twenty-six winters,
married with a young wife and son back in Ulfrstadt, and
Thorkell, twenty-two winters, still unmarried, had
decided to continue the voyage from Iceland. Both
Haakon, twenty winters, also married with a young wife
and son left in Ulfrstadt, and Sigurd, eighteen winters,
still unmarried, had decided to stay in Iceland. While in
Borg, they had been recruited to participate in a raid on a
village in Irland. The shipmaster leading the raid was a
friend of Rolfcarl's and he let the boys go with his
blessing.

Little did Rolfcarl know, his youngest son, with his
fiery orange hair, had caught the eye of a young house
thrall who had coaxed him into her bed. Nor was he
aware that Thorkell had met and fallen for the daughter
of the master of the same farm. Thorkell had plans to find
a suitable place to establish his own farm in Greenland
and was determined to marry that maiden.

It had been nine months from the day they arrived in
Borg, Iceland, until the second fleet of settlers departed
for Greenland. In that time, Thorkell and Sigurd found

work on a local farm. Thorkell's future father-in-law was a local gothi and was counted among the those that had a seat on the godar at the Althing.

Rolfcarl let his mind wander again. *Harald is a solid one. He will make a fitting jarl. He will take my place in that capacity when I am no longer able. Alas, he is no warrior — hard work and producing are his way to wealth, not raiding and taking from others. He is on this voyage to learn what he can about ships. His plans to enlarge the shipworks to take advantage of Ulfrland's forests and high quality bog iron from the numerous bogs along the fjord prove his mettle and eye on the future. Thorkell seems to love Iceland. I will not be surprised if he stays when we return to Ulfrstadt. I cannot say that I blame him — he knows Harald will one day become jarl and Thorkell would always be in his brother's shadow. In Iceland, he can be his own man.*

Haakon has the heart of a warrior — he will make a name for himself. His shieldmaiden wife will do little to discourage his warrior ways. In the old days, I would say he would make a petty king. As things now stand, I think he will lead men to glorious victory, in many wars — in the name of the one king of all Norway. He will want no part in politics. Now, Sigurd is another matter. His temper is as fiery as the hair on his head. He will be a lady's man, though not the kind to marry. If he lives long enough, he will have many tales to tell his grandchildren. With that hot temper, his future may not be that long. But no one can dispute his skill with weapons. Yes, the wife and I have four young men to be proud of.

Rolfcarl's reverie was cut short when someone shouted that the other ships had begun to lower sails and prepare for a night at sea. The next day, the coast of Greenland would come into view. He ordered the sail lowered to half and steered the ship straight into the oncoming waves, just as the masters of the other ships in the fleet.

When the sun was at its peak in the sky the next day, snow-topped mountains loomed to the west and north. The much anticipated Greenland coast was coming into view. But the fleet, led by Erik the Red, kept a steady southwest course, staying a good distance offshore. Many of the settlers were complaining about not going into any of the fjords along the coast. The grumbling continued, but Erik ignored the naysayers as the ships approached the southernmost point along the jagged east coast of the island. Late in the afternoon when they, at last, rounded the point of Cape Farewell and started northwest along the west coast. Fog obscured much of what lay ahead of the fleet. In the gathering darkness, Erik guided his ship up a fjord with exposed beach enough for each of the ships to find a place to settle into relative safety for the night. Fuzzy yellow lights marked where halls and farms were occupied.

While the settlers were welcomed into camps already established, they erected tents along the beach. Several of the shipmasters, including Rolfcarl, made their way to Erik's hall to discuss what came next. The night brought only dimmed light as the sun barely sank out of sight northwest of their location. Though the daytime temperature was warm enough that thin wool or linen shirts and dresses were comfortable, when the sun began to lose its strength, the air rapidly cooled down and heavy shawls for the women and wool tunics for the men were quickly thrown on. Piles of driftwood were collected, and raging campfires were soon seen up and down the beach.

"Go easy on the driftwood," Erik warned the shipmasters. "Although it seems like an endless supply is present, those of us who have wintered here know the driftwood is our only source of wood for fuel, and it has limits. Hastily using the wood for fires will spell disaster for your camp. No trees grow in these lands. Use what you find sparingly until we find the source!" Erik admonished each of the shipmasters who had gathered in his hall.

"There must be trees growing someplace close with this wood piled like it is along the beaches," one of the shipmasters said, looking at his counterparts for support.

"Some place, surely, but we have yet to find it," Erik repeated.

"We have more work here than we can accomplish before winter. I warned everyone before we left that the first few years would be hard. Only the strong-willed and strong-backed should make the voyage. Tomorrow we will arrive at the camps that are available for claiming. There is room for several farms in this region—enough for all in this group. Farther up the coast there are countless farm sites available. I suggest we get an early start." Erik's words ended the meeting.

Over the next few days, farms were claimed and building sites marked along several of the many fjords along the coast. Erik's crew assisted the newcomers in selecting the best places and marking the plots. Teams of settlers went to work building halls, barns, and outbuildings.

Thorkell told Rolfcarl he had seen many places he liked, but none suited him completely. Erik suggested he look farther up the coast—there were still many desirable farm sites. They continued north along the coast. After two days sailing, they came to a place where the land flattened into a wide, low valley with green pastures that seemed boundless. The fjords were narrow, and the snow-covered hills seemed to recede farther from the coast. "This is my new home," Thorkell stated.

A shocked Rolfcarl asked, "Are you sure? It seems you will be isolated from the rest of the colony, and this will be so much work for just one man!"

"I will not be alone, Father. My wife has three brothers who are eager to move to Greenland and start farms of their own. This valley is the perfect place," Thorkell replied enthusiastically.

"What wife?" Rolfcarl implored.

"I wanted to wait until I had a place picked out before I told you. As you know, I have worked for Hjolfr Laugaudair these past months on his farm north of Borg. The gothi and his wife have a daughter, Hildr, whom I have fallen in love with. As a wedding present, he has offered to send a crew to build our hall, barns, pens, and whatever else we need to get started. Even a starter flock of sheep. My bride price is to find suitable farm sites for us and two of her brothers in Greenland. But for preparing for Althing, they would have come on this voyage."

"I am speechless," Rolfcarl said quietly. Then added, "Your mother will want to meet your bride and her new in-laws."

"Yes, well, I figure two years to get these farms up and running. We will settle on a date before you leave for Norway."

"It looks as if only Harald and I will be returning to Norway. Haakon and Sigurd are gone raiding with Lardar Armannsson. We will make it all work. It is odd. My father arranged my marriage to your mother, and I arranged Harald's marriage. .Haakon found his shield-maiden wife in battle. I had not even thought about you ever marrying, and here you go and arrange your own marriage, to a gothi's daughter no less. I could not be prouder."

"Life works in mysterious ways. I never considered myself ready for marrying, either. I came on the voyage because I was curious. I had no idea I would find a woman, let alone a huge farm in a new land," Thorkell confessed.

"And I came on this voyage because of a duck." Rolfcarl chuckled as his son looked at him with questioning eyes. "I think I told you about how Father came to be owner of a gyrfalcon. Well..." Rolfcarl related to Thorkell about the duck in Iceland thirty years past and his yearning to find where that duck had come from.

"It seems you have a new, or old, mystery to solve now. All that wood piled up along the shore came from somewhere not too far to the west. Many of those bigger logs were not waterlogged. That means they were not in the water long before they washed ashore," Thorkell added.

Rolfcarl nodded his acknowledgment. "Yes, and some of those logs look as if they have axe marks. So, there must be people. That means trade, and more profits!" Rolfcarl said enthusiastically.

The New Colony Grows

WHEN ROLFCARL AND HIS FAMILY RETURNED TO ICELAND two years later, they found the big news was that new lands had been spotted west of Greenland. Excitement was growing for westward expansion. Every available farm site in Iceland had been occupied for many years and people were willing to keep searching for new lands. At the same time, Erik the Red was still promoting the benefits of Greenland. The Western Settlements were open now and choice farm sites were available.

From Hjolfr Laugaudair, Rolfcarl learned that Thorkell's holding was the largest farm in the Western Settlements. The gothi was very interested in buying some sheep and a couple of horses from Rolfcarl's stock.

"I look forward to a long and prosperous relationship with my daughter's father-in-law," Hjolfr told Rolfcarl.

"I trust Thorkell has been living up to your standards these two years," Rolfcarl replied.

"Yes, her mother and I could not be prouder of the man our daughter is bringing into the family. In two years, my sons and yours have raised three halls, three barns, several livestock pens, and harvested tons of hay.

They have expanded their sheep herds, killed dozens of caribou, wolves, foxes, a handful of walrus, seals, and even three ice bears. I would say he is fitting in very well, indeed."

"What is all this talk of new lands?" Rolfcarl asked, no longer able to contain his curiosity.

"It has come to light that recently, a shipmaster named Herjolfsson was blown far to the west and south of Iceland and spotted some lands west of Greenland. He did not know where he was and had cargo destined for Greenland, so he never put in along the coast over there, eventually finding his way to his intended port. Now, it seems everyone is interested, but Erik's son, Leif, is organizing a voyage of discovery soon. Erik is telling everyone else to wait until Leif gets back with fresh information. I would say then is when the real exploring will begin."

"I will be there with a ship and crew!" Rolfcarl responded enthusiastically.

The wedding was a major affair with nearly all of Borg and half of Reykjavik in attendance. Rolfcarl and his wife, Gudr, were not surprised that both pagan and Christian rites were part of the ceremony, and no one in attendance seemed to care. The main topic of discussion in all the social gatherings surrounding the wedding were the possibilities for new lands and new colonies. Many could see Iceland expanding to become a major trading force in the world. Rolfcarl cautioned that some of those new lands could be occupied by people not willing to be colonized. He emphasized his argument by noting some of the driftwood he had seen on the Greenland coast had tool marks that could have been left by axes. The counterargument was that in Christianity, there were no people except those chronicled by the prophets. Anything else would not be real people and would be of no concern. The pagans argued that any peoples that objected to Norse rule would soon be conquered.

I wonder if it is wise to consider ourselves superior in warfare. We have yet to meet any people in those lands. We have no notion about how many there are, and what weapons they may use, let alone what language they may speak, if they speak at all. These are things we must learn before we blunder into a hornet's nest.

Vinland

How different this voyage is than the first time we set sail for Greenland. We had all four of my sons on board for that sail and had no idea we would get to Iceland to find out Erik Thorvaldsson had found Greenland. I had to see it for myself. Little did I know that Thorkell would stay there. In just two years he has become a respectable master of a prosperous farm in the Western Settlements. His young wife lost her first child just days past. Thorkell, understandably, had to stay with her. Harald is still only interested in improving knorr design and raising livestock. He surprised me by even leaving Ulfrstadt on this voyage. Still, he stayed in Greenland, rather than adventuring to Vinland. Haakon is on a raid to Irland and hoping to avenge the death of Sigurd. I told him revenge killings usually come to naught, but he insisted.

With all that, I am still eager to see Vinland with my own eyes. If all Leif has to say about it is true, we will come away with some treasures. I wish we had gotten to Greenland two years past so that I could have accompanied Leif on his voyage of discovery. Now, with Erik the Red having just died, Leif has too many responsibilities to sail for the new lands. But Thor-

vald Eriksson, Leif's brother, is the leader on this voyage, and I finally have a chance to see what lands lay to the west.

Rolfcarl's ship held most of his crew from Norway and several Icelanders who volunteered to come. When Thorvald damaged his keel on a rock along the coast of what he called Vinland, and sailed north for Leifsbudr, Rolfcarl's ship accompanied those that Thorvald sent west along the coast.

The wonders of this land are indescribable. The trees, grass, and animal life are beyond my dreams. Waterfowl is so abundant, the birds darken almost every body of water. I wonder if I will see a duck like the one I saw in Iceland all those years past? Despite his advancing age, Rolfcarl was beside himself with wonder and giddy with excitement. *I should have eschewed my family and gone exploring thirty years past! I would be the head man in Greenland and maybe this new Vinland. Ah, jealousy will get me nowhere!* Rolfcarl scolded himself for his childish attitude.

They put ashore as the sun approached the horizon, which was obscured by distant hills. *There are more lands to the south and west—that is why the sun is setting over land, even though we cannot see it clearly.* Rolfcarl was awed by the trees. Many were of similar types in Norway, but none of the biggest specimens had been marred by axes. They found a few smaller trees that had been cut down by men, but beavers had done most of the harvesting in the area.

Curious about local inhabitants, they explored with caution and stayed in groups. On the third morning, the man Thorvald made leader, Logi Munarvagrsson, became concerned about Thorvald, and determined to follow the coast back to try to find Thorvald and rest of their party. They found them at Leifsbudr and learned that Thorvald had been killed by an arrow from one of the strange men they had encountered. After Thorvald's death, they had moved up to Leif Eriksson's encampment and were preparing to winter where they had some protection. The winter proved to be long, cold, and snowy but all managed to get through it, without further losses.

When the weather broke and the long winter appeared over, the exploration party prepared to return to Greenland to report to Leif Eriksson. While on a foraging hunt the day before they departed for Greenland, Rolfcarl's party ran across a group of men the Norsemen were now calling Skraeling.

The strange men approached with some carrying bundles of tanned furs, others carrying strung bows with arrows nocked. The apparent leader stepped forward and held his hands out in front of his chest, palms up, a sign of peace.

"I am Logi Munarvagrsson, Chief of this band of hunters. Who are you?" Logi said with arrogance.

All the Norse except Rolfcarl had spears or loaded bows at the ready. He was fascinated and just wanted to talk to these men.

The strange man, dressed in a tan skin draped over one shoulder and hund near his knees with a fringe of rawhide strings hanging down to mid-calf. A rawhide belt tied around his waist held two small leather pouches and a stone-headed club. Some kind of rawhide shoes were on his feet, held on with rawhide strings. A single carved-bone pendant hung around his neck on a dark string. His exposed skin was a dark red color, and his face was oval. His hair was shaved on one side with a thick braid down to his mid-back on the other side. Two osprey wing feathers dangled from the braid. He had several lines of blue and black tattoos in spirals and odd designs around his upper arms, shoulder, and face. He looked to be about forty winters old. His eyes were dark brown, and his face was deeply wrinkled.

The man looked at Logi and shrugged his shoulders. He then made a string of unintelligible sounds and pointed to the Norse spears and then to the bundles of animal skins his followers held up.

Logi shook his head and pulled a swatch of red wool cloth from his belt and pointed to the animal skins. The man put one finger up, then pointed to the red cloth and to a single skin. Logi offered the cloth to the man. The man told the one holding the furs to bring one skin to him. The man brought a caribou skin in prime condition. The leader gave the man a look of derision but accepted it and turned to Logi. Logi accepted the skin and nodded his head. The leader smiled for the first time.

Logi turned to his men and told them to pull out any spare wool cloth they might have. Only three pieces suitable for trade were found. Those pieces were soon exchanged for a deer, a wolverine, and an otter skin. The Norse were satisfied and Logi waved his arms indicating the trading was over. The strange, red-colored men argued among themselves a short time before the leader turned to Logi and pointed to the Norse spears and made a gesture for exchange.

Logi emphatically shook his head and slammed his right hand into his left palm, indicating the trade was finished. All the red men started shouting and making threatening movements.

Without word from Logi, six Norsemen fired arrows into the group of red men. Three dropped with arrows through their hearts. Three others had minor wounds. Silently, the red men faded into the trees and were out of sight.

Logi ordered his men to take up defensive positions

and prepare for attack. After a full hour, no attack had come. The forest was silent.

"All is was quiet, now," Rolfcarl said. "We should gather our kills and move back to the bay and the ships," Rolfcarl suggested to Logi.

"Keep a vigilant eye all around. Just bring two of the deer. Let the Skraeling have the rest and maybe they will leave us alone," Logi commanded.

Just as the two ships came into view, a "thud" sounded. Rolfcarl felt a fist pound into his back just below his ribs. He reached around in surprise to find an arrow protruding from his back. Trembling, he dropped to his knees. Dizziness overcame him as he leaned onto his side. *Where...? How...?* His thoughts clouded. Pain became overwhelming just before he passed out.

An arrow had come out of nowhere and struck Rolfcarl in the back. No one saw any of the red men, who had seemed to have disappeared. Two men quickly carried Rolfcarl back to his ship. The entire party was soon underway back to Leifsbudr, leaving four of the six deer they had killed in the forest where Rolfcarl had been wounded.

As soon as practical, the four ships sailed for Greenland. It took three days to reach Brattahlid on Eiriksfjord. By then, Rolfcarl's wound had become invaded with evil spirits. His survival was in doubt.

Harald Rolfcarlsson was beside himself. In a rare moment when Rolfcarl was lucid, Harald berated him "for coming on such a fool's errand to this Godforsaken place."

"If God had wanted real people to inhabit this foul, worthless corner of the world, He would have put us here! What were you thinking, bringing us so far across the sea? To find some nameless duck you *think* you found thirty-odd years past? In God's name, it does not matter

—-Our Lord does not want us dying in this remote place! This whole westward expansion thing is pure folly!" Harald was spitting his words as he paced rapidly around the room where Rolfcarl lay wounded and dying.

In a weak voice, Rolfcarl responded, "Our people have always expanded our horizons. It is in our blood to find and explore new places. Mark my words, the future is in the west. In days to come, the west will be the place where prosperity will know no bounds. You will not be able to resist change all your life, Harald. You will see..." Fever sapped his strength as his body gave out and he fell into a restless sleep.

Harald looked at his hapless father, diminished in his weakened state, and tears came to his eyes. "I-I am sorry I yelled at you, Father. Forgive me for my outburst. The Christ tells us not to act rash. I have sinned."

Harald leaned down to kiss his father's forehead and was overwhelmed by the smell of his wound. Rolfcarl's shipmates had cut the arrow shaft off below the skin and plugged the hole with a wooden dowel. A poultice was applied with little effect on the infection from the deep wound. No one dared try to remove the arrow before they returned to Brattahlid. Adding to the foul air, Rolfcarl had soiled himself.

There was not a healer in all of Greenland skilled enough to treat Rolfcarl's wound. They did manage to get the ailing man to swallow a strong-smelling drink. When the odor of the drink emanated from his wound, they determined Rolfcarl's situation was hopeless. He never had another lucid moment after his short argument with Harald. His life ended after three days in agonizing pain from his stomach wound. After he died, they dug the arrow out to determine it was made of stone and possibly tainted before it was shot into his gut.

In accordance with Leif's orders, Harald arranged a

Christian burial for Rolfcarl Carlsson in Greenland. He was laid to rest not far from Erik "Erik the Red" Thorvaldsson, in a cemetery near the small church Thjodhild, wife of Erik Thorvaldsson had built shortly after the colony was established. Her grave was next to Erik's. Both Erik and Thjodhild died of a sickness in 1003. Rolfcarl's dream of exploring the west died with him.

After Rolfcarl was buried, Harald and his father's crew sailed back to Ulfrstadt, Norway, where Harald assumed his father's duties as Jarl of Ulfrland. "I will never set sail to these lands again!" Harald declared.

Stick to Your Guns

A Short Story

By Nicholas Osborn

1

August 1882

It can be bewildering to question why spiteful, violent men do the things they do. Some are destined to never live by the same rules as the rest, nor to yearn for the lifestyle most desperately work their whole lives for. If one guess is as good as any, it's helpful to consider that even the best among us live the way they do for the same reasons—nature simply intended for it to be.

Thinking about why people are the way they are just ain't quite as important when trying not to suffocate from enough dust kicked into the air to fill a pair of lungs. Such a gut-wrenching place was exactly where Katy Holliday found herself. The sun was beating down on her, lumps of dirt caked her lips and caused her eyes to burn, but it was the jarring, rhythmic bouncing of the horse that hurt her the most. Her chest was pounding onto the edge of a stiff leather saddle, up and down, over and over.

Katy had been thrown haphazardly over the back of the worn-out mare a few miles back. She'd been taken from her home, from everything she'd ever known. At first, she screamed and kicked worse than a pissed-off mule. She behaved just like her papa had always told her to do in such a situation.

"Put me down, ya son of a—"

She was determined to cuss the man who'd done this to her. It was all she wanted to do. The steel pearl-wrapped handle of a Colt six-shooter slamming down onto her forehead put a stop to all that real quick, though. Blood spurted from the indent it left, breaking the skin and causing a splitting headache to flare up in a split second.

Katy remained conscious through it all. She was a fighter, always had been. Her papa used to say there wasn't anything good in the world that wasn't worth fighting for, and she figured well enough her own life was worth putting up a fight for.

"How'd ya like the taste of steel, ya little hussy?"

"You can't even fight a woman fair," said Katy, holding nothing back in her tone.

"I ain't fightin' you..." her kidnapper's voice answered before trailing off into the pounding of hooves on the ground. "I'm fightin' them."

Just as the man who'd taken it upon himself to steal Katy away finished speaking, a thunderous roar of horses, men, and blasting six guns seemed to come to life all around them. Katy knew it meant her salvation, but only if she didn't catch a stray bullet in the process.

She could barely make out the wave of cowboy hats riding toward her against a backdrop of sweeping pines silhouetted in the sunlight. A muggy heat enveloped her, causing sweat to pour in her eyes as she bounced upside down on the rear end of the horse. It was difficult to see much of anything worthwhile, but she knew help was coming.

"You ain't gettin' outta this alive! See those men?

They're comin' for you, and they're gonna fill your ass full of lead just like you deserve," Katy tore into him.

"They're gonna have to shoot through your yappin' mouth first dammit," the grizzled man clad in a black dusty jacket and worn, stained pants shot back.

"You wouldn't—"

Bam.

A bullet whizzed by the rider's head, piercing the felt brim of his awkwardly shaped black cowboy hat. Katy could see daylight shining through the perfectly round hole. For a fleeting moment, she thought her kidnapper might actually be right about what was going to happen to her.

The man's calloused hand reached back suddenly, and Katy just knew it was coming to finally knock her unconscious. She squinted her eyes, braced for impact, and waited for the worst. It never came, though. When she opened her eyes, she saw the man holding a small, round golden coin pinched between his thumb and index fingers. That's when everything that had just happened to Katy over the last hour made a lot more sense.

A dozen or more horses were gaining on them. If she could have, Katy would've kept fighting to bring this nightmare she'd found herself suffering through to an end, but the rope was tied too tight around her ankles and wrists. She knew what the coin meant. For the criminal with an odor that only happens after a month without a bath, it meant that even for just a few seconds of his worthless life, he was rich. For Katy, it meant she was downright disposable.

"Name's Pete Ringo," the rider shouted down to Katy. "You help me get out of this. There's a hell of a lot more where that came from."

Although she didn't care much to know about the

man who was about to get her killed, she couldn't deny that even just a few pieces of those gold coins could set her up for the rest of her life. It was more than her whole family would make in a few years living off the land. He must've known that about her, else he wouldn't have even tried.

"Even if I wanted to, it ain't like I could do all that much from here."

"Just don't cause no problems. When we get outta here, we'll talk. That's how you help, ya hear?"

The lawmen were approaching closer against the rapidly disappearing tree line in the distance. This time, Katy could see a plume of ominous black smoke rising behind them. She knew those chasing her weren't too happy about what that fire had taken hold of. In south Shelby County, not even forty years after the county had found itself an official seat at the table, the city of Center had found itself engulfed in flames. Known for its relatively simple namesake of being located in the center of the county, for Pete and his hostage, it meant they had an equal distance to outrun local authorities no matter what direction the horse ran.

Time was short, and the law was on their trail. A blazing sun overhead left no room to hide, and the hollering from the six-shooter-toting lawmen only grew closer and closer. Katy considered Pete's offer silently, willing to think about anything other than the saddle slamming into her chest to the rhythm of the horse's hooves. She wanted a life that was better than what her parents could've ever given her. That's why she moved to town, but not if it meant a life on the run. Her brief taste of what could be was pure hell, and she wanted no part of it.

Pete Ringo rode harder, pushing the mare to the brink, gritting his teeth harder with every step forward. The lawmen started firing more rounds in his direction, but none came close enough to give him second thoughts about what he was doing. He reached into the leather sack tied to his saddle and dropped the gold coin in with the rest. Pete knew there was $5,000 of gold bouncing around in the sack, and he'd be damned if anyone would get even a single coin out of his hands.

Katy knew this better than anyone. Her brief time with the thief told her everything she needed to know about that man. As she watched him reach into the cracked leather bag he coveted so much, she had an idea. It was the kind of idea that could get her killed, but it was the only one she had. Pete had kindly tied her hands up in front of her, and it was the only advantage she needed for what had to be done.

With the lawmen riding close enough to rope them both, Pete reached next for the last resort. It was a .30-30 Winchester lever action rifle, worn smooth from bouncing in the saddle. Although it didn't look like much, he'd trusted that rifle to get him out of more than a few sticky situations, including one just a couple of days ago before coming into town. Just as his fingers gripped the familiar wood stock, his heart sank.

He'd forgotten to reload the damn gun.

Just then, Katy made the decision to save her own life.

Everything happened in just a few seconds. She took a hard swipe at the leather bag tied to the saddle and knocked it up into the air, then turned with everything she had and hurled herself from the back end of the horse.

Time had already run out for Pete Ringo's daring escape from Center, Texas. With the reins in his teeth, he was caught red-handed shoving a single bullet into his rifle when Katy made her move. What mattered most wasn't even in question. He had to act. As the gold he'd risked it all for was thrown into the air, the .30-30 bullet fell from his hands on one side and the rifle on the other.

Katy Holliday was already rolling into the dirt in a mess of frayed fabric and hair, so Pete had only one chance left. He reached his hand out, grasping for the promise of a lifetime of riches. What he found instead was the last thing he'd ever seen in his life—a bullet. A .45 Colt round ripped through the leather sack, spilling the gold coins to the ground, before piercing Pete Ringo's neck, puncturing his jugular and bringing the high-speed chase to a gruesome close.

Katy stood up, brushed her dress down and wiped the sweat from her brow with her forearm. She watched as the man who took her met his own demise, slouched over, and collapsed from the back of the horse. Before those who had chased her down could come any closer, she gently kicked a pile of dirt over the glinting brass and gold stuck into the ground, burying it right where it fell.

One of the lawmen broke from the pack and made his way up to her with only a tip of his hat to greet her. She glanced in his direction before squinting her eyes and overlooking the bare land extending out in every direction, broken only by patches of pine trees reaching into the sky. At first, she couldn't hear what the strange man still holding a lever action rifle of his own tossed over his shoulder was saying to her, she was lost in a future that could still be. A future where everything she'd laid eyes on could be hers.

"Gonna need a ride back to town, ma'am?"

"Huh?" She finally snapped back to reality.

"It ain't safe out here. We can take ya with us, even have an extra horse."

"Won't need it."

"Ma'am?"

"That man y'all killed back there was Pete Ringo," she

said without making eye contact. "He thought he could take whatever he wanted. I'm livin' proof of that. There's a big difference between him and me, though."

"What you mean by that?"

"I *know* I can take what I want."

2

July 2024

"Did you know what Katy Holliday did with that land she tumbled onto from the ass end of a horse? If ya need a hint, just take a look around."

Nathaniel and Nellie both couldn't be bothered long enough to lift their eyes away from the phones cradled delicately in their fingers. A soft glow reflected in their dazed eyes, distracting them from the intricately detailed retelling of their own family history by one of the last living Holliday matriarchs.

"More than one thousand of God's greenest acres stretch out further than either of y'all could see in any direction, a place we call home because of that woman," said Nathaniel and Nellie's meandering grandmother Mary Burroughs-Holliday. "She built this place from the very ground she picked herself up from after being kidnapped. Holliday Ranch is what it is today because of that woman, and before you ask, our family has been hunting that buried gold for decades. I'm *sure* it's still out there…"

Nathaniel and Nellie pretended to listen with a half-hearted nod of their heads. Luckily for Mary, both of their parents had just walked back through the front screen door, bringing with them a wave of humidity rushing in and an outpouring of annoyed cries from the kids.

"You aren't telling that old tall tale to the kids, are you, Mom? You know we already talked about that," said Angeline McKey, daughter and sole heir apparent of the Holliday Ranch.

"I told it to you just the same growing up. You didn't have no problems with it then," Mary shot back. "These kids need to know something about themselves they didn't find on that dang phone."

"She's right about that one." Angeline's husband, Virgil McKey, pushed the screen door open again with his shoulder gripping a handful of grocery bags as he spoke. "Kids, screen time is up. Go grab a bag from the truck and help your mom."

"Oh, come on," Nellie groaned.

"You mean help *you*," Nathaniel cut in. "You always make us do your chores."

"I got a few more years of help before both of you move off to college. When you do, I'll carry every bag your mom can muster up, but until then, you're on grocery duty too. Get to it."

With slouched shoulders and a pair of phones being turned off for what was probably the first time in hours, both the kids shuffled off through the screen door to find a grocery bag to carry inside. Virgil shook his head with a smile as he listened to their arguing flare up just outside only seconds later. If the two weren't scrolling their lives away, they were bound to be at each other's throats. It'd been like that for a couple years now.

Virgil and his wife, Angeline, dropped the bags of groceries on the already crammed full countertops. It was one tin foil-wrapped casserole dish after another, broken only by the occasional pot of half-wilted flowers scattered about. Despite the raucous that followed the McKeys everywhere they went, the Holliday Ranch home held a somber atmosphere inside.

"I can't believe you went and got more food," said Mary. "Especially after our neighbors made sure we wouldn't go hungry for the next month."

"Already told you, Mom, that food won't last for two weeks," Angeline answered after trying to hide a sigh under her breath. "From the smell of this kitchen, some of this stuff is already going bad."

"I can't believe we're gonna be here for two whole ass weeks," Virgil whispered under his breath.

Angeline cut her eyes over and sent daggers through Virgil in a matter of seconds. He shrunk away and did his best not to laugh it off and get himself into more trouble. In the awkward silence that followed, he caught word of the television that had been playing nonstop in the background. The reporter reading monotonously from a teleprompter may have sounded boring and harmless, but what he was explaining couldn't have been further from that.

"The recently escaped convict pleaded not guilty to a string of more than a dozen attacks across the state of Texas, including three counts of first-degree murder. He was found with just a pocketknife and two dollars when he was brought in, but even prosecutors said what he left behind was simply too deranged to discuss during his trial. He was later found guilty and sentenced to life in prison without—"

"You have got to be kidding me," said Virgil as he stumbled to the television resting on the floor in the corner of the living room. "You really sit around and listen to this depressing crap all day?"

"Sometimes I even watch it," Mary told him.

"—was the name the media gave him. Bill Ringo was last seen passing a convenience store south of Pinehill, Texas. Residents near the area are encouraged to call local authorities and not to engage, as he is considered to be armed and dangerous," the reporter droned on.

"Come on, you two," Angeline interrupted the television to put a stop to their bickering. "I'm still trying to come to terms with the fact that Dad isn't here anymore. I can't deal with both of you arguing every chance you get. Besides, we're supposed to be helping you, Mom."

Angeline turned her attention to her husband turning down the volume on the news channel. What he saw when he looked at her was all the convincing he'd ever need to go along with what she wanted. He nodded quietly at first but spoke up once he watched her gesture for more.

"That's right, Mrs. Burroughs-Holliday," Virgil started.

"Oh please, call me Mary."

"My wife is right, as always, we're here to help you get along after losing your husband. Family means the world to us; we just want to be able to lend a hand. You name it and we'll get it done, as long as it isn't more food. I won't even comment on the news. Cross my heart."

It had been only a few days since Mary's husband John Burroughs Jr. succumbed to a lifelong battle with the bottle. The doctors called it cirrhosis of the liver, but Mary and Angeline knew it really meant he'd finally drank himself to death. The response from the community was overwhelming. Everyone seemed to find something to love about that man. Their fondness for casseroles left just a little to be desired on Virgil's part, though.

"There's just so much to do around here." Mary sank

back down and pushed her face into her hands, a position she'd become far too familiar with since John's passing. There were no more tears to give, but if there were, they damn sure would've been falling. "We were gettin' ready for calving season, setting up the feeders and prepping the next pasture to move everyone over. Last I heard before everything happened, one of the fences went down. Who knows what else is wrong out there."

"In that case." Virgil stood up and stretched his arms out halfheartedly, trying not to give away the fact that Mary's vague request was the perfect chance to get away from the tension hanging over every second. "Looks like it's time for me to learn how to patch a fence."

"Is that right?" Angeline would never come clean and admit that she found the willingness to help her family coming out in her husband to be attractive, and the self-imposed sense of confidence sure didn't hurt either. She took a step closer and spoke softly, so her mother couldn't hear.

"Does this mean you will consider what we talked about now?"

"No, Angel," he told her with a stark tone finding its way into his voice. "I already told you. We just can't. It doesn't make sense for us."

"You mean for you."

"I'm right there, so close to an ownership role. I just need a little longer."

"That way you can be away from us even more?"

Virgil's entire career had been devoted to an oil and pipeline company. He started rolling pipe more than a decade ago and had worked his way up through the years. This meant trips to west Texas, being on call damn near every night, and the simple fact of always showing up. His work ethic had taken him far, few could dispute that. After a few spontaneous golf trips a few years back with the owners, his climb up the corporate ladder at the company had shifted into another gear.

Trendlining Pipeline Partners had an open seat at the table for Virgil McKey and he couldn't bring himself to jeopardize it. He'd been trapped in a no-win situation, though. He needed to work even harder to build his career, to take care of his family, all while his family suffered due to what that career required of him. Angeline may not have wanted to put him in an ultimatum position, but it had befallen him regardless.

"Stick to your guns, son." The voice of his own dad echoed through his mind, words that had come to shape him as a father, a husband, and a man. They didn't always make sense, though.

Getting away from the house to be on his own for a bit would help to clear his mind. Even though he wasn't sure if he should be leaving Angeline behind to take care of her mom and the kids, he knew sticking around would only give him the opportunity to dig his grave a little deeper. When he reached down to pull a pair of old work boots on, he caught Mary whispering to Nathaniel and Nellie something about a bunch of lost gold while pointing at the front door. Angeline's soft, welcoming giggle gave him pause. In those few fleeting seconds, Virgil's entire reason for existing was made crystal clear once again. His wife was always right. If he missed too many of those moments, everything he'd done would be worthless anyway.

Virgil was at the age where he couldn't stay bent over like that for too long, though. The blood was rushing to his head, and it forced him to stand. Before he could speak, Nathaniel and Nellie both hauled ass beside him, almost knocking him to the ground, arguing about who was going to make it outside first. It was something he'd never seen before.

"What the—"

"We're going treasure hunting," Angeline called out to him. "You just help with the fence."

Before long, he had pushed the screen door open to make his way out. With one steel-toed boot out the door, he heard Mary call out to him.

"Don't forget the ol' saddle gun. Never know what'll greet ya out there!"

"Yes, ma'am," he called back to her, trying his hardest not to roll his eyes. He didn't need a gun to fix a fence— even he knew that.

With the old patinated .30-30 Winchester wood stock lever action in his hands, Virgil made his way out onto the porch nestled in the middle of Holliday Ranch. The heat and humidity brought sweat to his brow within seconds, but he welcomed the breath of fresh air none-theless. As he made his way to the side x side ATV parked beneath a tin shed next to the barn that had never had the key removed since it was purchased, he couldn't help but notice the miracle unfolding in the dirt driveway.

His kids were actually playing together, not fighting or staring at a phone. They were even laughing. They'd found shovels and garden tools and had started digging what amounted to potholes all down the driveway. Virgil may not have known why they were digging around in the dirt, but he wasn't about to interrupt it. Virgil drove around the kids on the side x side to not distract them any longer before flooring the gas pedal to pick up some speed.

The East Texas tree line of towering pines—utterly failing to block out the glaring sun—stretched out as far as he could see. Grasshoppers bailed out of the way of the ATV and overgrown grass threatened any viable line of sight as Virgil pushed further through the first pasture.

Natural forces dominated everything around, making him feel small, forcing him to relinquish any idea of control he had in his head. It was a place made for self-reflection by a hand that was not man's.

As much as he hated to admit it, the Holliday Ranch held an inexplicable sense of serenity.

3

THE 695CC 4-VALVE LIQUID-COOLED MOTOR OF THE SIDE X side came to life through patches of woods and into every new pasture, carrying Virgil from the modern conveniences of the historic home of the Holliday Ranch deeper into the hundreds of acres that still remained part of the homestead. A humid breeze filled his lungs, taking his troubled thoughts with it as the wind blasted his face.

If not for a few strands of barbed wire crossing the pastures with surprising precision, it would be easily assumed that the ranch was a place yet to be claimed. Virgil followed one fence line after another, tracing his way through overgrown pens that haven't seen the touch of a tractor since the passing of Mrs. Holliday-Burroughs's late husband.

Against a sweltering sun overhead, far in the distance, Virgil could just barely make out the problem that brought him out. A handful of calves had crossed over into the next pen, leaving behind a batch of bellering cows looking for their babies to no avail.

"Well, that sure ain't good," said Virgil to no one but himself.

The Holliday Ranch was known for running Angus-cross cattle before it was a popularized logo slapped on any piece of red meat by those looking for a quick buck. These were generations in the making and the twenty or so head that had found themselves to be part of the problem of a broken fence line were a mere fraction of what the entire herd had to offer.

It only took a few minutes to reach the commotion and even less for Virgil to see that he had his work cut out for him. The once sturdy five-strand barbed wire fence had lost the bottom two rows between only two wooden posts driven deep into the ground, but it was more than enough for the clever calves almost ready to be winged to slip right through.

As he slowed his approach, Virgil saw that the calves were moving up and down the fence line, following the calls of their mommas with no luck of returning. He stopped the ATV and took the liberty of helping them out by climbing through the snapped barbed wire and walking the calves further along the fence line to find their way back home. Thanks to years of generational breeding, docility was something that came innately to these calves, even at a young age, and it wasn't long before they were barreling right back through where they came from.

He followed the calves back through the fence and shuffled through a rusted toolbox strapped to the back rack of the ATV with worn-out bungie cords. It didn't have what he would've wanted to take on such a job, but there was enough to make it work regardless. With a handful of vice grips in one hand and pliers in the other he went to work.

The sweat in his eyes and the cuts on his fingers made the task uncomfortable. His mind wasn't on any of that, though. His thoughts dwelled on the fragile balance of survival in such a place. It was a fine line where life or death could depend on only a few strands of wire. There was no one nearby to help and no cell phone signal to call for either. There was only Virgil, and the work to be done.

With such a delicate tug-of-war always at play, Virgil couldn't help but think about what his wife was asking of him. Their lives had suffered because he couldn't find the balance they needed, and she was trying to tell him. Hell, she'd been trying to tell him for quite some time, he just didn't want to listen. His focus on climbing a corporate ladder for a company who most likely wouldn't think twice about replacing him if they had to more often than not created tension, and strife, to what he knew mattered most—his family.

He yanked on the loose fourth strand, clamped down and twisted it tight. He knew a permanent fix was still needed, but he could at least keep the calves on the right side until then. When he moved to the bottom run of barbed wire, the blood from his fingers he left on the fence made him second guess just about everything he had worked for through the years.

Virgil thought about what Angeline had told him before he left the ranch home. Their lives did revolve around him and his own blind ambitions. What he couldn't figure out was why he should expect them to care about him making it as a partner? He'd have nothing to show for it other than some numbers in a bank account and regret for the memories he'd missed out on with his family.

"Damnit," he yelped as he stuck himself with the barbed wire again.

He knew what an intervention looked like, even if he was all alone in the overgrown pasture. The fence was so much more than a barrier between two pastures or a man-made attempt at controlling nature, it was a symbol of what it would really take for him to see what had escaped him for too long. His blood, sweat, and even tears could be the difference in one company's bottom line or the difference between his family's dreams and their reality. There was a decision to be made, not an ultimatum, but one that would define how he knew himself and how his family would remember him.

Just as the final barbed wire strand was secured, a sharp, frantic scream pierced the night air and sent Virgil's hair standing up on the back of his neck. It was terrifying, panic-stricken, and carried through the trees and across the pasture.

He could recognize that fearful shriek from anywhere —it was his wife.

4

"ANGELINE!" VIRGIL SCREECHED AT THE TOP OF HIS LUNGS, knowing he was still too far for anyone to hear. "ANGEL! I'm coming!"

His voice was cutting out, already going hoarse from the panic coasting through parts of him he didn't even know existed. She wasn't someone who scared easily. Even worse, he'd only heard that specific scream once in their life of over two decades together. It was too unspeakable of an experience for each of them, remaining dormant as but a memory between them. He could've gone his whole life without ever hearing that scream again.

"AHHHH!"

It happened again. Three times too many now in one lifetime, he'd heard that scream. Echoing through twisting limbs in patches of trees, tearing Virgil in two every second it lingered on. Desperation dripped into the back of his throat. Thoughts of his wife and kids sent trembles to his fingers turning bone white from gripping the steering wheel. Something deep inside him, an inexplicable primordial instinct swelled in his chest. His left hand fell to the passenger seat where the beat up .30-30 Winchester sat waiting.

Just in case.

The ATV had nothing left to give. Virgil was racing against time itself to make sure his family was safe, but it wasn't fast enough. It took minutes—ticking by like the last few hours of a 700-mile haul across Texas—to finally get sight of the Holliday Ranch farmhouse where his family was supposed to be staying.

He told himself every lie he could think of as he closed the distance. Maybe it was as simple as one of the kids coming across an unwelcome snake. Maybe it was even a hilarious misunderstanding they could all share a laugh at later. He hoped with everything he had that was the case. As the Holliday Ranch farmhouse got closer and closer, all of those notions disappeared. When he saw his family wasn't alone in the front yard anymore, his white-knuckle grip on the steering wheel gave way and his clutch on the Winchester grew that much tighter.

There was a stranger standing in front of his wife and kids, with Mary frozen in place on the porch. He couldn't make out what they were saying, but he could damn sure see the strange man's outstretched arm and what he held in his hand, pointed right at his family.

"That son of a—" Virgil cussed under his breath as his thoughts scrambled. Without thinking of what could happen, he screamed for his wife once again, this time drawing the attention of everyone out in the front yard. "ANGEL! RUN!"

Just as he told them, both Angeline and his kids, Nathaniel and Nellie, bolted without hesitation. Virgil watched them scatter for a few seconds before he took matters into his own hands. The stranger had turned his attention to the ATV racing in his direction and pointed his polymer pistol at Virgil.

"He's got a gun!" Angeline called out to her husband.

"Just run!" Virgil's voice came back.

That was all the time they had before the first bullet was fired by the stranger standing out in the front yard. It missed Virgil wildly, giving him enough time to close the distance and turn the side x side for better cover.

Bam. Bam. Bam.

Three shots from the intruder and not a single one came any closer to Virgil. If he wasn't shaking from the surge of adrenaline, he might've even cracked a smile. There wasn't any time for that, though. He shoved his cheek down onto the worn-out stock of the saddle rifle and eyed his target.

The stranger wore a blue jumpsuit, stained and torn as if it was the only thing he'd ever worn. His hair was a matted mess and even from sixty yards out, Virgil could make out a crazed look in his eye that told him everything he needed to know about the man. There was little doubt in his mind that this was connected to the manhunt going on by the authorities.

Boom.

The Winchester rang out with a timeless blast that knew just what to do against intruders. It had been facing them down for more than a hundred and twenty years, and this man was no different.

Virgil was actually taken back when he saw his target fling himself backward onto the ground and grab frantically at his right shoulder. He knew he'd drawn the first blood, but it wasn't enough to put an end to the threat yet. The stranger picked his pistol back up, scrambling to his feet and doing his best to get back to firing at Virgil.

The lever action kept the fight going, doing all the work itself and leaving Virgil feeling like he was only along for the ride. He rocked the lever down, chambered a new round and let it loose at the man terrorizing his family. Without so much as a pause, he fired two more rounds into the dirt near his feet, sending the stranger running for cover and blindly firing off rounds behind him.

The East Texas sun had become relentless, and with no shade to be found outside the home from trees or clouds, Virgil could only hope the sweat pouring into his eyes wasn't enough to distract him when it mattered most. It was odd to listen to the calls of cardinals as he moved away from the safety of cover; they typically put him at ease, but today they only served to set him on edge. Mosquitoes hovered around him without fail and the dried-out grass crunched beneath his boots before it was overtaken by only dirt and dust.

There was a small lean-to shed on the other side of the yard, the only source of cover for the intruder. Virgil went over every scenario in his head as he walked slow and steady toward the shed. It was difficult to focus the surge of adrenaline in his veins, but Virgil knew there was no other choice. He moved forward toward the stranger who had set out to harm him and his family without thinking twice.

He'd reached the driveway his kids were just digging holes in no more than a few hours ago searching for lost treasure. Potholes deep enough to twist an ankle scattered the dirt driveway, leaving Virgil no other option but to weave his way through them with the Winchester aimed straight ahead.

He was locked on the shed, waiting for even the slightest movement urging him to squeeze the trigger. He didn't have to wait long. Before Virgil could make it through the driveway, the stranger popped his head around the wrong side of the tin building and lifted his pistol. Virgil acted as quick as his body would allow, but two gunshots immediately blasted out, one right after the other.

Bam. Boom.

The intruder was still standing, but this time, Virgil went down hard. He'd caught a bullet of his own. His calf was soaked with blood and the dirt next to him was quick to follow. As luck would have it, he'd fallen into one of the holes dug by the hand of his kids. The only thing he had to be thankful for was the simple fact that the stranger trying to kill him didn't know how to compensate for the drop of a bullet.

Before anything else, Virgil went to work on the lever action still in his hands. He tugged on the lever, but this time, there was no brass shell staring back at him eager to be chambered. His heart sank.

Virgin had run out of bullets.

Desperation set in, and his fingers began to shake. He couldn't get up. He could barely even move with the searing pain coming from his calf. It was the first time he'd been shot, and he was already hoping it would be the last. Half buried in a hole in the driveway dug by his own kids, he watched anxiously for the stranger to make himself known.

"I know you seen my face on the news," he called out in the distance with the voice of a decades-long smoker. "I ain't stupid, I just got nowhere to go."

"You can't come here, you piece of—"

"I ain't goin' back there! You hear me? I ain't goin' back to that place!"

The man was right. Virgil knew it was the escaped convict Bill Ringo, and he knew it wasn't going to end well. He shoved one hand into the dirt while he still could, hoping to give himself enough leverage to push himself to his feet if he had to. There just weren't many options left for him. His fingers fumbled for stability in the pothole he was bleeding into.

"They say it was my great, great granddaddy who came through these parts," said Bill. "I always wondered why we were cursed to suffer in this damned place. Now, I guess I just don't care."

"Doesn't have to be this way." Virgil gave it a shot, knowing it wouldn't get him far.

"Should've thought about that before you tried to blow my face off, you asshole."

Virgil couldn't deny that much. He scratched in the dirt nervously, trying to find an answer to keep himself alive. There were no answers to be found, though.

With every step closer the escaped prisoner got to Virgil, his hand clawed at the ground even harder. His options were limited. The pain of his fingernail bending backward against the dirt sent his mind into a flurry of confusing, racing thoughts.

Virgil watched as the man was almost close enough to see the whites in his eyes before he felt a cool, slick object brush against his bleeding fingers buried deeper into the pothole he'd fallen in. It felt familiar, like a godsend from a stranger looking out for him. Without thinking twice, he gambled with his life and yanked at whatever he'd found lost in the dirt.

It was the right size, the right fit, and it chambered into the rifle like it was made to be right there. Virgil's gut told him he'd struck gold in the dirt—or better yet, brass —but there was only one way to be sure. He jerked the lever action up to jam whatever he'd shoved into the rifle where it needed to be and watched as the man threatening to take his life scrambled for his pistol.

Bam.

Virgil couldn't believe it. He was alive. Somehow, he'd found the perfect caliber bullet hidden away in the dirt. As a red streak of blood made its way down the forehead of the escaped prisoner Bill Ringo, who immediately collapsed lifeless to the ground, he knew he'd found his own rightful path in life.

The Holliday Ranch provided him with everything he'd needed when he had no other choice but to depend on it. Now it was his turn to use his second chance at life to do the same for those who depended on him.

5

"You're lucky to be alive, my love."

"Hell, I'm lucky to have you. What happened back there, that wasn't luck."

"What do you mean?"

Virgil stared at his beautiful wife, tracing the lines of her face with his eyes and doing his best to memorize every single one of them in the fleeting moments between sentences. He'd almost lost his life on the Holliday Ranch, and as the law enforcement, first responders, and even a local journalist filed into the property, he couldn't bring himself to care about anything other than what he'd nearly just left behind.

"You were right, Angel. About everything, as usual. If Mary'll still have us, I think we oughta call the Holliday Ranch home."

"After what you just went through, almost getting shot to death by a madman out in the front yard, you want to *stay*?"

Virgil didn't hesitate. "Yes, ma'am."

"I'll be honest, I've given up hope for much of anything else besides you chasing a promotion with those pipe liners. It's all you've talked about for years." Angeline leaned in closer to her husband, trying to hide the smile on her face. She wrapped her arms around his waist and put her head on his chest. "What changed?"

They both stared out beyond the police cars and the ambulance, ignoring the pictures being taken of them just a few feet away, and watched patiently as the sun crept closer to disappearing behind the tree line in the distance. There was a sense of purpose to be found in the sunset. It was calling to Virgil, the same way it called to the Holliday family for generations.

Finally, Virgil understood the answer to Angeline's question. "We changed," he said. "This place changed us for the better the second we stepped foot on the ranch. It gave each of us what we needed, exactly *when* we needed it, like it was looking out for us."

"Since when did you get all soft on me? I'm starting to like this version of you."

"Think about it, Angel," he continued, saving her compliments to reflect on for later. "It brought the kids together. They were actually playing outside without fighting, and they didn't even try to look at their phones. When was the last time that happened?"

His wife laughed and nodded, choosing not to say anything else while she listened to her husband prove yet again why she'd married him.

"It gave you the chance to reconnect with your family," he continued. "With my parents dead and gone, Mary is all we've got left. The Holliday Ranch welcomed us in with enough room to stretch our legs and enough love to make even me feel wanted here. It stood ready to take care of us."

"That's because you *are* wanted, Virgil," she commented.

"But it also took care of Mary. She could've been here

alone when that son of a bitch turned up. He could've killed her. It's like the Holliday Ranch beckoned to us, urging us to be here exactly when we should've been."

"Well, when you put it like that…"

"Something I haven't told you," Virgil admitted. "I ran out of ammo in the rifle. The man had me dead to rights while I was bleeding out into the dirt. Those holes the kids dug up, though, there was a single bullet laying there, like it was waiting for me to come along for all those years."

"A bullet?"

"Same caliber as the rifle too, a .30-30 Winchester, probably as old as the damn gun. There's something about this place," said Virgil, refusing to take his eyes off the sunset. "It's special."

The two stood in silence, allowing what was left of the sunset hiding behind the piney woods to grace their presence, the gentle breeze coming off the north pasture to remind them of how to be thankful, and the anticipation of what was to come for their family whisk them into the future, far from what they'd just endured. It was a serene moment they'd not soon forget, punctuated by the only thing that could make it all better.

"Mom! Mom!" Nellie shouted.

"Dad!" Nathaniel was quick to follow. "We found it! We found all of it!"

"We found the lost gold!"

Canyon on the Plains

A Short Story

By John D. Nesbitt

Canyon on the Plains

THE BLUFFS THAT HAD BEEN VISIBLE FOR THE LAST SEVERAL miles came into full view, facing west with blue sky behind them. The land in the foreground sloped up from the trail that Brand and the others had been following, and the drying grass of late summer ended at the base of the bluffs. The first layer or level of the earthen wall, reaching over halfway up, was a light-colored clay with brush and stunted cedars growing on the steep slopes. The upper layer, almost vertical, was of a darker, brownish grey with no plant growth. The walls were not faced like cliffs, as they had formations jutting out like armrests. Between two of these large protrusions, a box canyon reached back in. A weathered building at the entrance caught the afternoon sunlight.

Brand rode with his group more than half a mile up the slope, the horses breathing and snuffling. Brand tipped his head up to see the ridgeline of the bluffs. On the right, a cloud bank of white and dark grey was moving eastward.

A man came out of the building as the group came to a stop. Watkins had said that he knew the man.

"What do you need?" The man had his hands at his waist, holding back the tails of his jacket. A six-gun and holster hung on his hip.

Brand kept his hands on the saddlehorn.

Watkins said, "Wonderin' if you've got a cabin for a few days."

The man looked up and down. "You've been here before."

"Once. Name is Watkins."

"You can have a place. Second one on the right. Five dollars now. Pay five days ahead each time."

"Sure." Watkins reined his horse around and handed the man a five-dollar gold piece.

"No trouble," said the man, in the tone of a command.

"We don't have any."

Watkins and Bill Jones rode first, with Brand and Dowden behind them. The camp consisted of two rows of shacks, or cabins, with an acre in back fenced off for horses. The whole canyon was less than five acres, with the walls rising up to hem it in. Across the way, a couple of men sat on a doorstep; farther down, a man leaned against a doorjamb. Half a dozen horses watched from the enclosure at the end.

As the four men moved their gear into the cabin, Brand said to Watkins, "This looks like a kind of robbers' roost."

The boss's face had a tired, heavy look, with a bushy mustache that was beginning to grey. "It isn't. It's just a camp. Like Huller said, no one causes trouble here."

"He seems to guard the place to control who comes and goes."

"He doesn't worry about who leaves. Just who comes in."

"You say it's a camp."

"That's right. Spill Canyon Camp."

"What's the Spill for?"

"I don't know."

They finished moving in their belongings, then stripped the horses and put the gear inside as well. The men at the other cabins were still hanging around as Brand and Bill Jones took the horses to the paddock, an area of bare ground torn up by horse hooves. As they walked back with the bridles, the man standing in the doorway went inside. The two men at the other cabin were not in sight. Brand saw the camp as a kind of colony such as he had known of, where men in small groups, or alone, found a place to stay with others of their kind.

Brand wondered, as he did from time to time, how much longer he wanted to be living like this. He had about sixty dollars in his pocket from the last job, the equivalent of two months' basic wages for a cowpuncher. He had made it in three days, delivering a group of steers and heifers to a ditch-building camp, but there was always unpaid time between jobs. At one time, he thought he would change when he turned thirty, but he was well past that now, looking at thirty-seven. One day seemed like the next, but when he found himself in a place like this, he thought of his age and what it would take to get out.

The four men sat in chairs around a table made of plain lumber. Watkins had already sampled from the whiskey, and his face was relaxed. He handed the bottle to Bill Jones, who took a pull and passed it on to Dowden.

Watkins spoke. "We're here for five days, to begin with. We've got a job comin' up, and more work after that. No one leaves the group."

Bill Jones nodded. Dowden gave no expression as he lowered the bottle and handed it to Brand.

Watkins went on. "In a day or two, we'll ride out and

take a look at our next job. In the meanwhile, we mind our own business. Like Huller says, no trouble. Bill, you and Brand can take the horses out to graze in the morning."

Bill Jones nodded. Dowden, whose nickname was Bucky because of his front teeth, had his upper lip drawn down tight.

———

ON THE WAY TO fetch the horses in the morning, Brand saw three horses in front of the cabin across the way. The two men he had seen before were tying duffel bags onto the backs of the saddles. A plain-looking woman in jeans and a work shirt came out of the shack. She had dull blonde hair tied back, and she pressed a dust-colored hat onto her head before she climbed up into the saddle. She was not an attractive woman, as she had a hard face and a sagging build, but she caught Brand's attention.

As they walked on toward the fenced area, Brand said, "That's something you don't see much in a place like this."

Bill Jones spoke in his low voice. "So much the better. They don't fit in well. Not in this life."

"They're not so bad in other settings."

"That's up to the individual. They've never done me any good. All they want is for a man to owe 'em something."

"Owe 'em?"

"Yeah. They care for him, or show feelin's, and they want somethin' in return. I don't want someone to care about me. And they're no good in this way of life. Men don't think right when there's one around."

———

OUT ON THE GRASSLAND, each man wandered with two haltered horses and let them graze. The lead ropes dragged on the ground as the horse hooves shifted. Most of the time, Brand moved backward to keep an eye on the hooves and the ropes.

The sun was bright, and the sky was clear. With nothing more complicated than keeping the lead ropes clear of the hooves, Brand allowed himself to think of a time and a place that he had kept blocked off for most of the last fifteen years. Josephine, with straw-colored hair and blue eyes, came to him in an image of a sad smile and a tense face. It was the last time he saw her, a day that it pained him to look back on, the day that she told him she was not going to see him anymore. She had waited for him to find a steady, respectable job, and he had clung to what he saw as his freedom, or independence. With time, he saw that he had been unwilling to commit himself to responsibility and, he now admitted, to doing things right.

It had all passed him by. Here he was now, on the way to what some people considered to be the downhill slope after forty. There was no point in wishing he could go back, and looking ahead brought a frown to his face. He couldn't go on like this forever, one day at a time, with no plan. When these horses had grazed enough, he would have to go back to the camp, a place he knew he wanted to leave. Moreover, he recognized to himself that this whole way of life was something he would like to be free of.

———

As BRAND and Bill Jones led the horses between the rows of cabins toward the fenced area, two strangers came walking their way, each carrying two bridles. Brand nodded to the men, and they returned the gesture. At the paddock, Brand counted the horses out of habit and saw four that had not been there earlier.

At the cabin, Bill Jones said, in his slow, deep voice, "Looks like another outfit came in."

"That's right," said Dowden. "There's five of 'em, all together in the next cabin."

"Five?" said Bill, drawing out the word. "I counted only four horses."

"Well, there's five of them. There's the two that put the horses away, and two other men, and a woman."

"A woman?" said Bill. "I thought we just got rid of one."

Watkins said, "Well, there's another one, but it's no concern of ours. We have our own stuff to tend to."

———

FOR AS MUCH AS Dowden seemed to keep his opinions to himself, Brand noticed that he was something of a busy-body and liked to be the one who knew things. Toward evening, he came in with the news that one of the men in the new group of five had died.

"Name of Muldoon. Seems he was shot up when they came in, and he kept to his bed, but he didn't make it. They lost a horse out of the deal, too." Dowden's teeth showed in contrast with the light brown stubble on his face. "I thought five was a lot for a cabin, and I don't know if it got any better. The one who died was the one who had the woman."

"They'll have to bury him," said Watkins.

"Oh, yeah. They had to tell Huller, and he said anything that dies, whether it's a man or an animal, has to be buried outside. He can't be losin' ground to a bunch of graves."

Watkins frowned. "That's up to them to do. You don't need to be gettin' too close."

———

BRAND AND BILL JONES grazed the horses through the long middle part of the next day. The boss said he wanted the horses well fed because they were all going to ride out the following day to look around. Brand thought that his time did not seem to have much value, at least in the boss's eyes. Watkins himself was short with words, and Brand guessed that he was stewing about what they were going to do next.

Shadows were lengthening when Brand and Bill Jones finished with the horses and put the halters away. Brand went out back and tried the door of the outhouse but found it locked. With only one outhouse for each pair of cabins, he figured he was just as well off to wait for this one.

A click sounded as someone lifted the hook from the eye inside, and the door opened. A woman stepped out and did not seem surprised to see someone waiting, which Brand supposed was normal, as he had tried to open the door, but he felt flustered at seeing her seeing him. She kept her composure as she stepped forward.

He took off his hat and said, "Sorry."

"No need for it."

He had recovered enough of his senses to see that she was a little younger than he was, maybe in her early thirties, with a medium build that was not accentuated by her plain riding clothes. She had dark-brown hair, grey eyes, and a complexion that had seen some weather.

Words came to him. "What I mean to say is, I'm sorry to hear of your sadness."

"There's no helping it," she said. "It's done. But thanks."

"I don't know what else to say."

"Maybe you've said enough." Her eyes met his. "I'm sorry. That may have sounded too cross."

He found a breath. "It's all right. I'm sure things are not easy for you."

Her eyes lowered and came back up. "Thank you. They're not. I think they're going to be harder than before. But there's no reason to..."

"If there's anything..."

"I don't know what it would be."

Silence hung in the air in the fading daylight. He felt a desire to move forward and take her hand, and he thought she might have felt something similar. But he held back.

She made a preliminary motion to leave, not quite taking a step as she put her hands together. "Very well. Thank you for your...thoughts."

He held his hat with both hands. "And my best wishes to you."

———

BRAND PLAYED the scene over in his mind as he rode out with the others the next day. They left some of their belongings in the cabin but brought enough to stay out one night. Watkins took them to a broad, rolling plains country, not unlike the area to the north where they had worked a week earlier.

They camped on the east side of a bluff. Watkins said most of the storms came out of the west and it was not uncommon to have a hailstorm in the night, and the bluff would give them some shelter. He said they didn't want to have a fire after dark, and each of them would take a two-hour shift on guard.

They sat around the fire as it burned down. Watkins said he didn't like this part of the country very well. The windmills were too close together. There were too many small spreads, with fences. And then there were the wheat farmers.

As on other occasions, Bill Jones nodded in agreement, while Dowden gazed straight ahead with his brown eyes showing no expression. He had his mouth closed over his teeth, and his stubbled face reminded Brand of a gopher.

They drew straws, and Brand felt lucky to have the first shift. The night was dark when the others turned in. Time dragged on, and he walked one way and another to stay awake. At last he finished his time and nudged Bill Jones to take his turn.

Bill pulled on his boots and beckoned for Brand to go with him beyond the edge of the camp. When they stopped, Bill's lean features showed in the moonlight. He spoke in his deep voice and kept it close to a whisper.

"I didn't get a chance to tell you this before, but I need to say it. I'm not tellin' anyone else, but I seen you talkin' to that woman. No good will come of that. It's only trouble. You make yourself vuln'able."

"I understand. Thanks for telling me and for keeping it to yourself." Brand's eyes were heavy, but now he had something to keep him awake. He mulled it over as he turned from one side to another beneath the blankets, trying to find a soft spot on the ground. The camp was silent. He drifted in and out of sleep, and then he did not think about much.

HE AWOKE to the boss's harsh voice.

"Damn it all."

Grey light was beginning to show. A horse snuffled. Another, or the same, stamped its foot. A spur clinked, and Brand looked up to see the boss's face, puffy as it peered down at him.

"Get up and put your boots on."

"Is something wrong?"

"Son of a bitch pulled out on us."

"Who?"

"Dowden. He had fourth shift."

Brand sat up and let the blankets fall away.

Watkins said, "I'd guess he's over in Nebraska by now."

"What do you want to do?"

"I don't care what we do. I'm not gonna waste time runnin' after him. And I don't like the looks of this job I was thinkin' of. I don't like anything right now."

Bill Jones spoke in his low, measured voice. "Might as well build a fire and make some coffee. No law against that."

———

AFTER A LONG, sulky ride back to Spill Canyon, they unsaddled the three horses. Watkins took a seat at the table with a bottle of whiskey in front of him. When Brand and Bill Jones returned with the bridles, Watkins said, "It's stuffy in here. Let's sit outside."

They took three chairs out the back door and sat in the shade on the east side of the cabin. Before long, one of the men from the next cabin stepped into view at the corner of the building.

"You've got the right idea," he said. "What would you think if we joined you?"

Watkins smoothed his mustache and said, "I guess it would be all right." When the man left, Watkins passed the bottle to Bill Jones and said, "Let's all take a good drink before they empty it on us."

Within a few minutes, three men appeared, carrying chairs. Brand recognized the other two as the men who had put the horses in the paddock. The three men set their chairs facing Watkins's group and sat down.

The one who seemed to be the leader sat back and crossed his arms. He had straight, light brown hair, rounded features, liquid brown eyes, and a light mustache. "My name's Snell. This is Curtis, and this is Kirby." He tipped his head to his left, where the other two sat. After a moment, he said, "I thought there was four in your bunch."

Watkins sniffed. "One of 'em left."

"One of ours did, too. Maybe you heard."

"We did," said Watkins. He lifted the whiskey bottle and held it forward. "Feel free to pass this around."

"Thanks," said Snell. "We've got some, too. One of us'll go get it in a little while." He pulled the plug from the bottle, took a drink, and winced. "That's the stuff." He handed the bottle to the man on his left and turned his attention to Watkins again. "What kind of work are you in?"

"Do a little work with cattle."

"That's good."

"And you?"

"We do different kinds of work. Sometimes we're like the fella in the song, workin' on the railroad."

"More than one of those songs."

"Oh, I know." Snell took the bottle from the third man and handed it back to Watkins. "It's hard to get by."

"Never easy. And then your help walks out on you."

"We're down to three, just like you. With some kinds of work, you need more than that."

Watkins took a drink and held up the bottle to see how much the level had gone down.

"Don't worry," said Snell. "We've got more. Kirby, go get that bottle that we started. Go there and come straight back."

The man at the end got up and walked toward the other cabin in a forward-leaning stride.

"Been out west of here?" Snell asked.

"Some." Watkins handed the bottle to Bill Jones.

"There's a couple of places where the train goes so slow you could get out and walk faster."

"I've known of places like that."

"And others, so far out in the middle of nowhere that it takes a day or two for someone to pick up a trail."

"I thought all those trains had an armed guard these days."

"They do, and they've got a safe you've got to blow up. So not just any yokel can do it."

Brand took the bottle that Bill Jones handed him, and without drinking from it, he handed it across to Snell.

"Thanks." Snell spoke to Watkins again. "The thing is, if you do it well, there's money in it."

"You could say the same thing about manufacturing bicycles."

Brand frowned, trying to follow the meaning. He knew that a bicycle was a slang term for a wheel, the lowest possible hand in poker.

Snell said, "You could say it about a lot of things." He squeaked the cork open, took a drink, pushed his lips out, and dipped his head as he swallowed. He handed the bottle to his left and said, "Where's Kirby?"

"Here he is," said the other man.

Kirby handed Snell a bottle wrapped in newspaper.

Snell peeled the paper down to inspect the level of the whiskey. "My old man used to tip the bottle upside-down and mark it, to see if anyone had been stealin' a nip."

"I didn't," said Kirby. He sat in his chair and tipped his hat to one side.

Snell took a long, sniffling snort through his nose, cleared his throat, and spit on the ground. He wiped his mouth with his cuff and took a drink from his own bottle, then set the bottle by the leg of his chair. "We'll pass this around when the other one's done. Easier to keep track of that way." He cocked his eye at Kirby. "You should have told her to bring us some sardines and crackers."

"You didn't say anything. Do you want me to go tell her?"

"Curtis can tell her."

"I'll go."

"Don't take so long."

Kirby got up, straightened his hat, and went into the cabin. He was back in a few minutes.

Snell said, "A man told me the best way to make money was to have a business where you sell something that no one else has. He made sandwiches and sold them, right there in Denver. Made a shit-pot full of money."

"What did you think of that?" Watkins asked.

"It was good for him. But I couldn't have made anything at it. Somebody else was already doing it."

"You could have gone somewhere else with it."

"Where? To some cow town?"

The woman came out of the cabin carrying a tray that consisted of a piece of pasteboard and a couple of sheets of newspaper for a clean surface. Three open cans of sardines and four rows of soda crackers lay on the newspaper.

Snell looked up at her and put on a broad smile. "Thanks, Earl."

She handed him the tray and turned around and left. Snell's mouth hung open as he watched her walk away. He turned his attention to the food and said, "Let's dig in."

Brand found it easy to resist. His stomach had been burning with all the coffee and bacon grease of the last few days, and one drink of whiskey had been enough. He could tell the difference in those around him, who had each had two drinks or more. Snell, with all his self-assurance, had had at least three slugs, and perhaps more earlier. His hands were unsteady as he worked a sardine onto a cracker. Brand thought that with a little more self-control, Snell would not have stared after the woman the way he did.

The afternoon light was fading when the sardines and crackers were gone. So was the bottle that Watkins had offered. The other party's bottle was now in circulation, and its newspaper wrapping lay on the ground.

Snell's eyes rolled up into his head after he passed the bottle on to Curtis. He took out the makings, and with some effort, he rolled a cigarette and lit it.

"Here's what I think," he said. His voice sounded thicker now. "We're each short one man. We should think about throwin' in together. There's some jobs that need four to six men."

Watkins raised his eyebrows, but his eyelids remained heavy.

"Seems like you don't like the idea." Snell blew a double stream of smoke out of his nostrils.

Watkins said, "We can talk about it again tomorrow."

"Sure," said Snell. "We've got time. Haven't we, boys?"

The other two men, who also had drooping features, muttered agreement.

Snell fixed an eye on Bill Jones. "How about you?"

Bill's voice was slower than usual. "I do what the boss says."

Snell turned to Brand, who was outside his line of vision for much of the time. "I won't ask you."

"Why not?" said Watkins.

Snell took another drag from his cigarette. "He doesn't act like he wants to be one of us. He hasn't had a drink with us all evenin'."

"He had one to begin with."

"That was before I got here."

"It doesn't matter. He's all right. He's one of my men."

"Why doesn't he say anything?"

"We can all talk again tomorrow."

"Sure we can. We can talk till the cows come home."

————

BRAND'S STOMACH was queasy as he walked outside in the early morning. He was glad he had not drunk any more whiskey or eaten any sardines. As far as he knew, no one had eaten an evening meal. He had gone to bed after Snell brought out another full bottle, and he had heard the talk drone on as he tried to sleep. Now he stood a few yards in back of the cabin and took in the calm of the morning.

The scuff of a door came from the next cabin, and the woman walked outside, taking light steps. She was wearing the same drab clothes as before. Her glance met his, and he waited. He thought she might have been on the lookout for him, but he did not know if it was just his wishful thinking.

As she drew close, she spoke in a low voice. "They're all sleeping it off."

He nodded. "Not a good place to be stuck in, is it?"

"No, and that's what I am. Stuck here. I wish I could get out, but I can't just take a stage or a train. Not out here."

"I know what you mean."

"On the other hand, I'm not going to leave with just any old guy."

He had heard the word "guy" before, and he did not think it was favorable. He did not think she would be so blunt as to use it to refer to him. "What's your name?" he asked.

"Earleen," she said. "Earleen Talbot."

"You were with the one who died."

"That's right. His name was Pat Muldoon. As in 'Pat Works for the Railroad.' He had inside knowledge, and that was what he got for it."

Brand imagined she must have heard the whole conversation the evening before. "I don't blame you for wanting out. Sometimes I think about it myself."

She looked around. "It's not just here. I want out of this whole way of life. Where you never have anything of your own, and you're always looking for the next job, the bigger and better job, and you can catch a bullet at any time."

He felt as if she had it all worked out and was waiting for someone to say it to. "I know," he said. "It's a dead end." He looked around at the canyon walls, which did not look so oppressive in the freshness of the morning. "If I get an idea, I'll tell you."

She studied him. "What's your name?"

"Sorry. I should have said it. Wilson Brand. I go by Will when I'm on a first-name basis with people." He held his hands forward, palms up, and she put her hands on his.

Her grey eyes met his. "I'd better go back. I don't

need any more trouble. If you get an idea, I'll be ready to hear it."

"Sure." He felt her closeness, but he knew this was no time for saying more. He let go of her hands. "Be careful," he said.

"You, too."

He waited for her to go into the cabin, and he went into his. He recognized Watkins's snoring in the next room, and he thought Bill Jones was still asleep as well, but he couldn't be sure. He sat at the table to let the time pass.

———

BRAND AND BILL JONES took the horses out for another long period of grazing. Brand's stomach was uneasy again from the coffee and fried potatoes, but he had avoided the bacon and thought it was a good decision.

Bill Jones, or the man who went by that name, did not say anything of a personal nature the whole time. Brand wondered if his brief meeting with the woman had been observed by anyone.

———

WHEN THEY RETURNED to the canyon with the horses in the latter part of the afternoon, Watkins was sitting outside with Snell, Curtis, Kirby, and two other men. The whiskey bottle was making the rounds.

Brand and Bill Jones put the horses away, brought out two chairs, and joined the group. The two outsiders were sitting on the ground. They both wore new denim trousers and had a clean shave. One of them sat up taller than the other. Brand recognized him as the man who had been standing in a doorway the first day. He had a prominent waxy nose, blue eyes, light-colored hair, and ears that stuck out. He had a leer on his face and an air of self-confidence about him. He took out a pack of tailor-made cigarettes, offered one to his pal, took one for himself, rapped it on his thumbnail, and lit it.

"What-all's in the wind?" he asked.

Snell said, "Not much."

"Not quite the time of year for everyone to be sittin' around. You'd think someone would be doin' somethin'."

"You would," said Snell. He seemed to flex his arms as he rolled a cigarette. He stuck it in the side of his mouth, popped a match, and lit it. He shook out the match and flipped it away.

The newcomer held his tailor-made out to regard it. "I kinda had the impression that you-all were re-groupin'."

Watkins said, "When you say 'you-all,' who do you mean?"

"Just them," said the man, tossing his head toward Snell.

"How do you mean?" Snell asked.

"Heard you lost a man."

"Maybe we did."

"Don't know if that leaves the woman like an odd one out."

Brand's pulse jumped at the man being so brash.

Snell's eyes narrowed. "What do you mean by that?"

The man shrugged and tipped his cigarette up as he took a puff. "Extra wheel. Don't seem like she's with any one of you."

Snell spit out a fleck of tobacco. "You ought to mind your own damn business, fella. Bad enough if you're spyin' on us, but to butt into our—"

"Aw, don't get a bug in your ass. I'm just sayin' what anyone could see. A woman in a place like this is like a mare in a corral."

"And you think you're the stud?"

"Just wonderin' if anything—"

Snell dropped his cigarette and stepped on it as he stood up. "Just watch your mouth."

The man in the new trousers stood up and squared his shoulders. He was an inch taller than Snell, and he had a six-gun on his hip. He held his cigarette in his left hand and said, "You act like you think she's yours, but I'd bet she's not."

Snell had his right hand near his own .45, and his eyes held on the other man. "Just get the hell out before I do somethin'."

The other man glowered. "Don't threaten me, or they'll take you out of here like they took the other one. The one who got somewhere with her." He waved with his right hand and lowered it toward his gun.

Snell's eyes tightened as he drew his pistol and fired. The gunshot made a wallop in the air, and the stranger doubled over. Snell shot him again, and he crumpled.

Snell turned his gaze on the man's friend, who was wide-eyed as he pushed himself to his feet. "Get him out of here. He came lookin' for trouble, and this is what he got." Snell spoke to his own men. "Help him drag this body over to their cabin. And just so everyone knows, I don't take talk like that. And I'm not goin' to let someone draw down on me."

———

Brand and Watkins were sitting at the table inside half an hour later when Bill Jones came in. He said the dead man's partner had packed up everything including the body and had ridden out.

Watkins had not said anything about the incident. Now he said, "Snell seems a little touchy, but that other fella had no place saying the things he did. Just asking for trouble. And then that motion with his hand."

Brand thought that Watkins could say what he wanted about the place not being a robbers' roost, but the law didn't bother to come to such places, and Watkins knew it. So did Snell.

The boss's chest went up and down, and he breathed out through his nose. "I'll say what I said before. We've got to stick together. No one leaves, and no one sticks his nose in someone else's business."

Brand exchanged a glance with Bill Jones. He wondered again whether Bill had seen him talking to the woman, and now he wondered whether Bill had passed a comment to the boss. Maybe Watkins was just trying to keep order. For all Brand knew, Watkins was planning something else with the other boss.

———

BRAND WAS USED to Watkins not saying much ahead of time, so he was not surprised the next morning when the boss said that he and Bill Jones were going to ride out with Snell and Curtis.

"He's leaving Kirby to keep an eye on the woman. For God's sake, don't do anything stupid like go over there and talk to her."

Brand nodded. He assumed that Watkins and Snell were going out to look at or talk over a job that they all might do together.

On one hand, he thought it might be the perfect time to bust out of there and take the woman with him, but he hadn't seen her since the shooting, and he had no idea whether she still had the determination she had expressed or whether she had her doubts. He had known women to lose their will when a man made a show of force. He decided he would have to know her state of mind before he tried anything drastic, and he was going to have to wait to see her.

And so he sat through the day, in the near-empty cabin, thinking about the woman being held in the cabin next door.

————

BRAND WAS OBSERVING the canyon walls in the light of late afternoon when the party of four returned. They had an air of good humor about them, as they had brought back meat, potatoes, whiskey, and a dozen bottles of beer. Snell said they would let the beer settle for a day before anyone opened one.

Watkins told Brand to take their three horses out to graze because they were going to ride out again the next day.

"All of us?" Brand asked.

"I didn't say that. They take care of their horses, and we take care of ours. Snell bought some grain for theirs."

Brand fetched the third horse and took all three out. The sun went down, and a quarter-moon showed. Brand listened to the sound of the horses as they shifted their hooves and tore grass with their teeth.

Back at camp, he found the other five men seated around a fire pit of coals and low flames. Bill Jones laid a steak in the iron skillet and set it on three rocks that rose from the coals.

"Be a few minutes," he said.

Brand went inside, found a plate and a fork, and took them outside with a chair.

The other men talked in a casual tone, their voices

relaxed and at times slurry. Snell and Curtis were reviewing the landmarks they had passed by, in a kind of rehearsal to fix the details for anyone present.

Snell poked at the ground with a stick. "They call this Flat Top. You can see it for miles around. That's why we don't meet there. We meet here, three miles to the east, where there's an old chimney standin' by itself."

Curtis said, "It's a whole fireplace, made of rocks."

"They call it the chimney," said Snell.

Brand waited for his steak and ate it. The others were drinking whiskey from tin cups. He did not have a cup, and no one offered him one. He did not want any whiskey, anyway. When he finished eating, he folded his knife and put the plate and fork with the others.

"I'm going to turn in," he said.

Watkins raised his head. His eyes drooped, and creases showed in his face. "We all should. We won't be long."

Brand had not seen the woman all evening, and he thought it was just as well.

———

BRAND AWOKE, and his mind was clear. He figured it was well past midnight. The camp was quiet. Watkins and Bill Jones were both snoring in the next room.

He had an image of where he was, in a camp with canyon walls around and an open sky above. He could feel the presence of the woman in the next cabin. He was confident in his feeling that she wanted to talk to him. It was as if their two spirits had risen above the confines of the two cabins and had communicated without speaking.

He made himself think it through. He had to keep in mind what his purpose was. He wanted to get out of this life he had grown into. He could not make that course of action dependent on whether the woman wanted to go, and he could not make a fool of himself and try to be a hero and rescue someone if she didn't want to be rescued.

A woman could say she wanted a change and then, when it came to the crunch, she could weaken. So could a man, for that matter, but what concerned him was what a woman could do. He had the example of Ellie, not that different in appearance from this woman. She said she wanted to leave, but the man she was with put pressure on her. He told her he wouldn't let her. Brand said, "Let's just go settle it right now." She panicked and said, "No, not right now. Let's wait a little longer." And that was all he had done—wait. So he had to be sure this time.

He turned the blankets away and sat up in his bed on the floor. He listened for a change in sounds, and when none came, he reached for his boots. He stood up and carried them to the back door, eased out, and sat on the steps. He kept an ear tuned to the cabin as he pulled his boots on.

He took deep breaths to steady himself. The quarter-moon had moved toward the west. It had to be well after midnight, maybe as late as two in the morning.

A scuff sounded, then the rub of a footstep. Movement showed in the dimness.

He rose and walked to the open area near the burned-out fire. "Here," he whispered.

In a moment she was near him, and they walked away from the buildings toward an area where the ground was rougher and began to slope up. The base of the canyon wall was not fifty feet away, and he knew that clay boulders lay around.

"Be careful," he said. "We don't want to trip on anything."

"I was waiting," she said. "I was hoping you would come out."

"I thought you were."

Their hands found each other.

"I don't know how much longer I can stand it. Lee makes me sick."

"Is that Snell?"

"Yes."

"You don't sound like you have much doubt about what you want to do."

"I don't. I've had way more than enough of all of it. And now they're planning another job."

"I thought they were, though no one said it straight out to me."

"Well, they are. Then we'll all be on the run again, stuck together." She heaved a breath. "I just want to get out of this place and this whole rotten way of life."

"I'm with you," he said. "I just had to make sure. I didn't want to get into a situation of one shoe on and one shoe off."

"There's no danger of that with me."

"I'm glad to hear you say it. Because if you start something, you have to follow through. Even more so with something like this. If you don't, things will be worse than before, and they could be...fatal. Well, they could be anyway. That's a chance I take. I don't think it was just a show he put on."

"With that other guy? He was pretty stupid."

"You could say so. He blundered. I thought he was too sure of himself. But we need to think of our own case, and here it is." He had not prepared a speech, but the words came. "We don't know each other very well. We both want the same thing, or at least we've said so. We want to get out, and we want to go straight. We've got to stick with both parts of that. None of this, one more job and then we'll go straight. As I see it, I'm a fella who's done some wrong things that in some ways make me what I am, and I can't deny it, but I want to make the best of what's left. Unless I miss my bet, you're like that in some ways."

"I'm not perfect, that's for sure. I've done some things. But I told you I'm fed up."

"We've got to be determined not to fall back into the same old ways, once things get easier."

"That's the way I would have said it."

He took a full breath. "We seem to be of the same mind, then, and I think we can go through with it. If we get out of this all right, I don't care if I have to wash dishes or muck out stables."

"I've already told you. I'm done with all of this."

He had felt both of their hands tremble as they spoke, and now he gave way. He took her in his arms and kissed her, not once but again and again, holding her close, feeling her breasts and lower body press against him.

They released and drew apart, but not so far that they had to speak loud.

"We'd better not do any more," she said. "Someone might come out."

"I know." He had his hand on her hip, and he wanted more. At the same time, he heard the warning voice within, the voice he had not always listened to.

"I should go back in," she said. "Before I do, let me ask. How are we going to do this?"

He settled as he exhaled. "I'll have to find the right moment. When I do, you'll know. And I'll trust you to follow through."

"I will." She stood back half a step with her hands at her sides.

"Before you go, I need to ask you a question."

"Go ahead."

"Are you his woman, or have you been?"

"Lee? No. He makes me sick."

"I had to ask. Because if he had any power over you, it could come out."

"He doesn't. Not that he hasn't tried. And as you can see, he's crazy jealous of anyone else."

"Then you can look him in the eye and walk out, when the time comes."

"It might make his pot boil, but, yes." She took his hand. "I just can't do it by myself."

They kissed again, and she went back to the cabin with slow, quiet steps.

———

BILL JONES DID NOT SPEAK MUCH as he and Brand saddled the horses in the morning. At last, Brand asked him outright.

"What does the boss have in mind for today?"

Bill kept his voice down. "He found out yesterday where Dowden is holed up. Over on a place called Crow Creek."

"Does he want to make an example of him?"

"I can't read his mind, but I think he wants to show him that someone doesn't do things like that without answerin' for it."

"He wants to punish him for it."

"In some small way. Nothin' big."

———

THE BOSS'S face was florid, and he coughed as he heaved himself up into the saddle.

The three of them struck out across a high grassland and rode at a fast walk for a couple of hours. They stopped at a windmill to water the horses, and Watkins took off his hat and splashed his face.

Water was not flowing out of the pipe, and Brand did not like to drink out of the tank itself. He peered over the edge and into the water, where he saw a couple of white bird skeletons in the silt in the bottom.

Watkins sniffed and rubbed his sleeve across the bottom of his nose. "Not far now," he said. "A couple more miles."

Brand said, "We're quite a ways south of Horse Creek, aren't we?"

"Oh, yeah," said the boss. "Quite a bit."

They continued across country until a thin line of cottonwoods ran along a curve where the grassland sloped down. They hit the creek and followed it west to a wide spot where two tents were pitched. Three horses were staked out, and one of them was the sorrel that Dowden rode. Brand's stomach tensed.

A rangy bay horse neighed at the approach of strangers, and a heavyset man appeared at the opening of the tent on the right. He had thinning hair and a short dark beard. He put a flat-crowned hat on his head and stepped into the full light.

"What do you need?" he asked.

Watkins said, "I came to talk to Dowden."

"I don't know anyone by that name."

"That's his horse. Send him out."

Watkins dismounted, and Brand did likewise. Bill Jones stepped down and took the boss's reins.

Dowden came out of the tent, followed by the heavyset man and a slender fellow with a scraggly blond beard and a faded military cap.

Brand had thought that the boss had brought him along in order to make an example of Dowden in front of him. Now he estimated that as much as anything else, Watkins did not want to be outnumbered.

The boss drew his gun and said, "Step forward. I'm not goin' to shoot you unless you do somethin'."

Dowden's eyes shifted. "Then what did you come for?"

"To tell you that someone who works for me just doesn't turn his back on me and run. Do you understand that?"

Dowden glanced at the gun and said, "Yes."

"When people run, they talk."

"I'm not going to tell anyone anything. I don't know anything to tell."

"Of course you don't. But I'm going to impress that on you."

Dowden's eyes flickered.

"Step up closer. So I don't have to talk so loud."

"I can hear you."

"Come closer." Watkins made a motion with the pistol.

Dowden's face fell, but he moved forward.

Watkins shifted the gun to his left hand. "Now do like this." He opened his mouth and stuck his right finger in through the side. "Your pointer finger. Yep."

Dowden had his mouth open, with his large front teeth showing, and his right index finger stuck in from the side.

Watkins continued but without his finger in his mouth. "Now press down on your tongue, and repeat what I say. My mother…"

"My mutha…"

"My mother has…"

"My mutha hath…"

"My mother has a big red…"

"My mutha hath a big red…"

Watkins came up with his right fist from waist level and slammed Dowden in the jaw.

The man let out a howl as if he had been shot, and he left a streak of blood on his lip as he pulled his hand away. He shook the finger and grabbed it with his left hand. "Ow, ow, ow," he cried. "You broke it."

Watkins said, "I could have hit it with a hammer or shot it off, but I didn't. Now if you think you ever want to get even, just think about pullin' the trigger with that finger. It would be better for you if I never saw you again."

"You won't."

"Go back to Iowa where you come from. You're not cut out for this country."

Dowden looked off to the side and said, "I need a handkerchief or something. This thing's bleeding."

The slender man went into the tent.

"That's all for today," said Watkins. "Don't let me see or hear of you again."

Dowden turned to the side to take the white cloth his friend handed him.

Watkins put his gun in his holster, took his reins from Bill Jones, and said, "Let's go."

Up on the grassland again, Brand rode behind the other two and fell into his own thoughts. He could not say that he ever knew the boss very well, but this was a new side of him. Cruel and humiliating, not just bossy. They had never done any work at gunpoint. It was always on the sly and out of view. Watkins must have been like this along. Maybe Snell's example had helped bring it out.

———

FROM A DISTANCE, the entrance to the canyon, with the lower level jutting out farther than the upper, looked like a giant throne on a hill, with the way station at the entrance lower than a footstool. As the horses picked up their pace to climb the slope, Brand felt a nervousness in his stomach. He had a dusky image of the woman and a sense that he was not in this situation on his own. He was not just looking out for his own interests, as he was conditioned to doing. He was committed to something bigger. The notion was elusive, but it was bigger than two times one. They had made more than a deal; it was a pledge. They had a shared hope, and they had a right to try for it. He knew that she could still cave in at the last moment, but he could not. He thought it was possible that Watkins would side with Snell to bully or humiliate the woman and do worse to him. He had to be ready.

The afternoon sun was casting shadows on the irregular surfaces of the canyon walls. Brand and Bill Jones left the saddles and blankets in the cabin as usual and took the horses to the enclosure.

When they returned, Watkins and the three men from the next cabin were sitting in chairs outside, each with a bottle of beer. Brand felt that something was shaping up.

They stopped a few feet from the group of four. In his low, slow voice, Bill Jones said, "Guess we could get a coupla chairs."

"I've got something to say." Snell stood up, holding the beer bottle at his side. He took a couple of steps toward Brand. "To you."

Brand stood his ground. He tried to keep an eye on both of Snell's hands without looking away from meeting Snell's gaze. He saw that Snell was wearing a gun belt. He had left his own inside with his saddle at the end of the day's work.

"I know you've been sneakin' around," said Snell. "Where you shouldn't."

Brand did not answer. He had a full sense of what Snell had done before, in almost the same spot.

Snell hollered over his shoulder. "Earleen! Get out here!"

Brand kept his eye on Snell and on the cabin beyond. The door opened, and Earleen stepped outside. Her eyes met Brand's. She appeared sullen but not whipped.

"Closer," said Snell.

Curtis and Kirby moved aside, and Earleen took a couple of steps forward but did not come up even with them.

Snell said, "Tell him it's over. Tell him that anything you thought you had between you is over."

"I'm not going to tell him that."

"Maybe I will." Snell took a step closer and glared at Brand. His face had a sheen of light sweat, and small, broken blood vessels were visible across his upper face. The whites of his eyes showed the first stages of turning yellow. "Big boy." Specks of saliva flew. "Big brave boy. In the dark. How brave are you in the daylight, in front of everyone? Ah?" He settled a little. "It's what I thought. She put it all on you, and you can't do a thing. What made you think you could? Did she spread her legs for you, too?"

Brand flinched. Time seemed suspended. If there had been a moment to take the first punch, it was past.

"Just a little puke!" Snell pronounced the last word with such force that a spray of saliva came out, and when Brand flinched again, Snell brought up his right hand, wrapped around the beer bottle, and drove his knuckles into Brand's cheek and jaw.

Brand's hat fell off as he stumbled back. He kept an

eye on Snell's hand as the man drew back and made ready to club him again.

The hand came around, and Brand grabbed the wrist with both his hands. He twisted, and the bottle fell away.

Snell's left hand came up, grabbed Brand by the hair, and pulled him off balance. Snell pulled again, raised his knee, and tried to bash Brand's face, but he did not quite make it.

Brand lowered his shoulder and drove toward his opponent. He thought that if he could knock him down, he might be able to control him. But he went off course.

Snell pushed down on his head, grabbed the neck of his shirt, and flung him face forward. Snell whirled and rode him to the ground.

Brand fell flat on his stomach, and the breath went out of him. He felt fingers in his hair again, pulling his head up and back. The man's other hand was clawing his face, pulling the cheek down, digging in.

Brand knew what kind of a fighter he was up against. It was whatever it took to win—no quaint notions of a fair fight. Brand pushed himself up, jabbed with his left elbow, and thrashed. The other hand held onto his hair, but the clawing fell away. Brand put both hands on the ground, pushed up, got a knee under him, and bucked.

They rolled aside. Snell still had hold of his hair and now clamped a forearm against his throat. The force was immediate. Brand flailed and elbowed, kicked back, threw his hips to one side, and ended up on top of Snell, front to front, like a lopsided X.

Snell pulled his hair again, and Brand pressed his forearm against the side of the man's head, trying to push him away and break his grasp. Snell moved his head back and forth, opened his mouth, and bit Brand's forearm to the bone.

They rolled again and came to a rest with Snell, the

heavier of the two, sitting on Brand's chest, his knees against his arms, one hand on his throat with the wrist pushing up against his chin, and the other hand working, claw-like, up his cheek.

Brand felt his breath being cut off. He opened his mouth and tried to breathe in, but the clamp on his throat made him gag.

The clawing hand worked up to his eye, and he felt a thumb pressing into his socket.

Everything exploded. He lost a sense of who he was and what he was doing. He had a surge of force he had never felt before, something in the animal core of him that burst and took him outside of himself. He saw and felt himself driving his fists into his enemy's face and taking hold of him. He made a rag doll of the man with straight, dirty-looking hair, a sparse mustache, staring, off-colored eyes, and an open mouth as he choked and sputtered. Brand had both hands on the man's throat and was slamming his head on the ground over and over again.

Voices above him were shouting. "That's enough! That's enough! You're going to kill him! Get off! Let him go!"

Brand came back into himself. He could feel the breath in his own throat, a throbbing in his head, a swelling in his eyes. He let go, climbed off, and sat in a crouch.

He felt his left eye. It was still there. He looked at his hand. It was wet but not red. He closed his right eye. His vision was blurry, but he could see.

Snell's men were kneeling next to their boss. "Lee! Lee!" they said. "Can you breathe?"

Watkins was looking down with his heavy face flushed. "Is he any good?"

Kirby said, "I think he's done for." He stood up and

laid a hand on the butt of his pistol. "You've got somethin' to answer for, mister."

Brand stood up, rubbed his left eye, and blinked. "What the hell do you mean? He would have done the same to me. I don't even have a gun on me."

Kirby lowered his hand. "What do you think you're goin' to do?"

Brand found Earleen and saw her nod. He said, "What I already had in mind to do."

Watkins seemed to be recovering his breath. "Don't do anything you'll regret, Brand."

It was as if he was next to himself, hearing himself talk. "I'm going to pull out of here. And not by myself."

The other four men looked at the woman.

"He's right," she said. "I'm going, too."

Bill Jones gave a narrow look at Brand as if to say he didn't want to have anything to do with it.

Brand felt he had everything together again. He directed his attention to Kirby. "She should have one horse coming out of your bunch. You'll still have more than enough. I'm going to get mine ready, and one of you can bring hers."

Watkins cleared his throat. "You know, once you do something like this, no one will have anything to do with you."

"That's all right with me."

———

WHEN BRAND HAD his horse saddled and his gear tied onto the back, Earleen lugged a saddle out of the cabin. It was evident that no one would help her.

"This is the one I was using," she said. "I'll get the blanket for it. And I've got a bag to go, as well."

The sun was slipping toward the distant mountains

when they rode to the front opening of the canyon. Huller stepped out of the station and stood in the shade of the overhang. He wore a pistol as before, and his narrow eyes held on Brand as the two horses stopped.

"Don't come back," he said.

"We won't." Brand glanced at Earleen. Her grey eyes were steady, and her face had a clear, open expression as she nodded. The two of them rode forward out onto the spreading grassland.

You May Also Enjoy:
Ridin' with the Pack Volume One

Step into the saddle and embark on a journey through the untamed landscapes of the American West in *Ridin' with the Pack*, a captivating anthology that pays homage to the enduring magic of Western fiction.

From the enigmatic reflections of a down-and-out fella questioning the choices he's made to an action-packed expedition in the wild expanses of the Old West, each story paints a vivid portrait of the American frontier's enduring heart.

Readers will navigate the steamy bayou as a determined young man faces unimaginable challenges to rescue a kidnapped friend, experience the seafaring odyssey of a man shanghaied on the eve of his wedding, encounter the convergence of past and present as a young bounty hunter meets his match, traverse a California hitchhiker's fateful choices as they lead him to a dark and unpredictable highway, and join a Wyoming family in the aftermath of a banking system collapse as they fight for their land and heritage amid a new dimension of uncertainty.

No matter the story, the spirit of the West is ever-present, each tale unfolding like a chapter in the grand narrative of the untamed frontier—where freedom, resilience, and the relentless pursuit of justice echo like the haunting melodies of a cowboy ballad.

Penned by a cadre of masterful storytellers, both seasoned legends and promising newcomers, *Ridin' with the Pack* is a testament to the timelessness of the Western narrative.

Ridin' with the Pack: Volume One **features Western short stories by:**

New York Times Best-Selling Author W. Michael Gear

Best-Selling Author Peter Brandvold

Best-Selling Author B.N. Rundell
Best-Selling Author L.J. Martin
Best-Selling Author Ken Pratt
Award-Winning Author John D. Nesbitt
Award-Winning Author Chris Mullen

AVAILABLE NOW

About B.N. Rundell

Born and raised in Colorado into a family of ranchers and cowboys, B.N. Rundell is the youngest of seven sons. Juggling bull riding, skiing, and high school, graduation was a launching pad for a hitch in the Army Paratroopers. After the army, he finished his college education in Springfield, MO, and together with his wife and growing family, entered the ministry as a Baptist preacher.

With many years as a successful pastor and educator, he retired from the ministry and followed in the footsteps of his entrepreneurial father and started a successful insurance agency, which is now in the hands of his trusted nephew. Having finally realized his life-long dream, B.N. has turned his efforts to writing a variety of books, from children's picture books and young adult adventure books, to the historical fiction and Western genres, which are his first loves.

About Ken Pratt

Ken Pratt and his wife, Cathy, have been married for 22 years and are blessed with five children and six grand-children. They live on the Oregon Coast where they are currently raising the youngest of their children.

Ken grew up in the small farming community of Dayton, Oregon, where he worked to make a living. But his true passion always lay with writing.

Having a busy family, the only "free" time Ken has to write is late at night—getting no more than five hours of sleep every day. He has penned several novels that are being published, along with several children's stories.

www.kenprattbooks.com

About C.K. Crigger

2019 Spur Award winner for *The Woman Who Built a Bridge* and 2020 Spur Award winner for *The Yeggman's Apprentice*, C.K. Crigger lives in Spokane Valley, Washington, where she crafts stories set in the Inland Northwest.

She is supervised by a feisty little dog with a Napoleon complex and ignored—except when he wants to lay on the keyboard—by a reclusive cat. Not satisfied to write only of the historical west, she also writes contemporary mysteries and dabbles in the speculative genre.

A member of Western Writers of America, she reviews books and writes occasional articles for *Roundup* magazine. *Buried Under Books* also features her book reviews.

www.ckcrigger.com

About John D. Nesbitt

John D. Nesbitt is the author of more than forty books, including traditional Westerns, crossover Western mysteries, contemporary Western fiction, retro/noir fiction, nonfiction, and poetry. He has won the Western Writers of America Spur Award four times—twice for paperback novel, once for short story, and once for poem. He has won the Western Fictioneers Peacemaker Award twice—once for novel and once for short story. He has been a finalist for the Spur Award twice, the Peacemaker seven times, and the Will Rogers Medallion Award eight times. He has also received two creative writing fellowships with the Wyoming Arts Council—once for fiction, once for nonfiction—and he has won the fiction award four times with the Wyoming State Historical Society.

www.johndnesbitt.com

About Chris Mullen

Chris Mullen is an accomplished and award-winning author, recognized for his captivating storytelling and literary talent. Hailing from Richmond, Texas, he is a proud graduate of Texas A&M University.

With a career spanning twenty-three years in education, Chris has been a dedicated teacher in both Kindergarten and PreK, cultivating his passion for storytelling and nurturing young minds. In 2019, he received the prestigious Connie Wootton Excellence in Teaching Award—a testament to his commitment to education and his profound impact on students' lives, bestowed upon him by the Southwest Association of Episcopal Schools (SAES). It was during this time that the idea for his young adult western adventure series, Rowdy, was born.

When he's not weaving stories, you can find Chris honing his craft in local coffee shops, pizza places, or even the neighborhood grocery store.

www.chrismullenwrites.com

About Harlan Hague

Harlan Hague, PhD, is a native Texan who has lived in Japan and England. His travels have taken him to about eighty countries and dependencies and a circumnavigation of the globe, thereby proving the earth is round.

Harlan is a prize-winning historian and biographer and award-winning novelist. His history specialties are exploration and trails, California's Mexican era, American Indians, and the environment. Early on, while a professor of history, he wrote articles published in scholarly journals. His novels are mostly historical Westerns with romance themes. One Western includes a time travel twist. Two novels are set largely in Japan, with a novella in Belize. Some titles have been translated into Spanish, Italian, Portuguese and German. In addition to history, biography, and fiction, he once wrote travel articles, as well as a bit of fantasy. His screenplays are making the rounds.

For more information about what Harlan has done—and is currently doing—visit his website at harlanhague.us.

About Ron Briggs

Ron Briggs is a veteran, having served four years in the USAF. His education includes a Bachelor of Science in Range and Wildlife Ecology at Oklahoma State University and a Master of Science in Range and Wildlife Management at Texas A&I University.

He is retired from the USDA-Natural Resources Conservation Service, and his career encompassed twenty-five years as District Conservationist in Linn County, Kansas. Prior to college, he worked seven years in the building trades.

Having developed a deep interest in history, especially in the pre-colonial period of North America, Ron's interests prompted him to begin researching a pre-history story about the Tallgrass Prairie Region of the Great Plains. That research evolved into his current multi-volume work, the Yellow Hair series, which includes scenes from northern Europe to the mountains of western North America.

Ron and his wife, Debbie, currently live in Mound City, Kansas, and have two grown children and seven grandchildren. His interests include spending time with family, writing, hunting, fishing, traveling, and woodworking.

www.authorronbriggs.com

About Nicholas Osborn

Nicholas Osborn is a second-generation ranch owner and storyteller from the heart of deep East Texas. With a career encompassing everything from entertainment marketing to news journalism over the last decade, he has studied the craft of authentic storytelling and honed his writing throughout the years.

Nicholas's debut series aims to mythologize the pineywoods he grew up in and welcome readers to a new chapter of modern Westerns, born of the tall tales that helped shape the genre. His writing is inspired by the history of the Lone Star State, the greater United States, and the larger-than-life heroes, gunslingers, and "black hats" that gave us the myth of the west we know and love today.

Nicholas is an owner at his family's limousin cattle ranch and first-time father with his wife of over ten years. As one of multiple generations of his family working on the Red Rock Limousin Ranch, Nicholas has put his experience into words as an author with a passion to keep timeless Western culture alive and thriving for today's readers.